CW00376903

THE MAN ACROSS THE STREET

MARCIE STEELE

CHAPTER 1

*H*annah Lockley had lost count of how often she wished she could travel back in time to when she'd been eighteen. Maybe then she could have stopped the accident that had ruined her life.

She was forever daydreaming about starting again. Now though, she was coming up to a big birthday, and wondering what on earth she was going to do next.

'It's been another chilly day, Mum,' she said. 'You remember how it was a couple of weeks ago? Well, it's much worse than that. We have clear blue skies but it's *so* cold. I can't wait for a bit of sun, to sit out in the square under the oak tree. It will be different this year of course.' Hannah paused. 'Actually, I'm not quite sure I'm ready to sit there, not this summer anyway. Maybe next year. I'll still let you know how things are going in Hope Street. I know how much you didn't want to leave us all.'

She bent down to change the flowers in the pot. 'Bev and Steve have been arguing again. Why they don't call it a day, I'll never know. I'm sure they'd be better off without each other. Bev threw Steve's clothes out onto the pavement

1

yesterday… *again*. Funny thing was, she didn't pop them in a black bag this time, so everyone saw his undercrackers. He wasn't too pleased when he got home.' She giggled. 'At least they keep me entertained – and half the street too. Oh, and Harry tried to get in last week. I had the fright of my life when he started banging on the door.'

Hannah was the only one there, the cold weather no doubt keeping people away, but she preferred to come early before anyone else was around. She didn't want someone to see her talking to the dead, no matter how comforting it was to her.

It was so peaceful sitting there in Somerley Cemetery but after a few more minutes, she pressed her fingers to her lips and then touched the top of the headstone. 'See you next week, Mum.'

Half an hour later, she was back on the high street. At Somerley Stores, she shopped for a few essentials and a copy of the *Somerley News*. Then she turned the corner, posting the newspaper into the first door as she passed.

Hope Street was two rows of houses facing each other over a cobblestone road. At the far end it was blocked off by a ten-metre-high wall that held up a grassed area, leading to a railway line that was out of use now. Hannah's house was number thirty-four.

Outside number seven, Emily Milton was wrestling with a screaming child, trying to strap him into his car seat.

Hannah stopped. 'Someone isn't happy this morning, I see.'

'Neither of us are. He's kept me up for half of the night.' Emily rolled her eyes at Hannah as she dodged an errant tiny fist. 'Teething.'

'Poor lamb.' Hannah leaned into the car and pulled a funny face at Marco. He was normally a cheery baby but today he wouldn't raise a smile for either of them, no matter how much Hannah gurned at him. 'You and Sean should get out for the night,' she added. 'Call me if you need a sitter.'

'I will, thanks.'

Hannah crossed the road in between cars belonging to number eleven and thirteen. At number twenty-four, Alma Whitby was standing on her doorstep, arms folded. She and her husband had created quite a stir when the front of their property had been coated with pebble-dash some twenty years ago. It was the only one not to show the old brickwork, standing out like the proverbial sore thumb. Hannah much preferred the red to the cream, although she'd never dare say.

'You haven't seen my Harry on your travels, have you? He said he'd be ten minutes fetching a loaf of bread and that was over an hour ago.'

'No, sorry.' Hannah gave her a half-smile in sympathy, omitting she'd had a visit from him the other night. 'But it's a beautiful day. I bet he's gone for a stroll.'

'If I find out he went no further than the bookies, I'll swing for him.'

Hannah knew Alma would do nothing of the sort. Mr and Mrs Whitby had been married longer than she'd been alive. Harry liked to put a bet on the horses, but it was never any more than a pound each way. Luckily, he enjoyed the cama-raderie at the betting shop more than the winning, and 'getting away from Alma for a breather every now and then'.

As she drew level with her home, Hannah took her keys out from her handbag. The door to number thirty-two was open wide. She looked inside, able to see through to the back room of the property, where a lady was sitting on a settee.

'Hi, Thelma,' she shouted through, choosing to stay in the doorway rather than go inside. 'How are you today?'

'Never better. More to the point, how are you?'

'Getting through, getting by, getting there.' Hannah

clicked her smile back into place before Thelma could notice it had slipped, even though it seemed so alien right now.

Thelma nodded. 'That's understandable.'

'Do you need anything?'

'No, I'm fine, thank you.'

Hannah let herself into her house, removed her scarf and coat. After putting them away, she went through to the kitchen to make herself a warm drink. As her mum used to say, she was chilled to the bone.

Only now would she allow the tears to roll down her cheeks, the emptiness not going away. Since her mum died last month, she'd tried to fill her days as best she could, and her part-time job at the hairdressers kept her busy enough. It was a blessing in more ways than one, though. Money would become tighter now her carer's allowance had gone. What little savings she had put aside were dwindling.

She had lived in Hope Street all her life, yet things felt so different for her now. She was alone, even though surrounded by friends. For the first time in her life, she was lost. She had no career prospects and it was frightening at her age to start again even *if* she was able to afford college fees. Mum had always said she'd make a good nurse, but she didn't want to look after anyone else.

So there was worry and uncertainty. All those years she'd trundled along because she hadn't been able to think about anything but Mum's care. What on earth was her purpose in life going to be now?

CHAPTER 2

*D*oug Peterson sat at his desk, going over the same spreadsheet he'd been looking at for the past half hour. Their current building project was coming in just over budget. He needed to trim a bit of money from somewhere, robbing Peter to pay Paul, or else cut someone a bit of slack and tell them to go for it, hoping to recoup the loss from the sale of the properties.

His office, situated in newly-built premises in Salford Business Quarter, had floor-to-ceiling windows across the length of the wall to his left. His desk overlooked a park and he would often catch a flash of colour as a runner, or someone throwing a ball to a dog, caught the corner of his eye. The room itself had a view he would never tire of, starting from greenery, rising to large oak trees with only a few high-rise flats popping up in the distance. Further behind was where he lived, a few miles from the city centre.

He and his brother Alex had only recently moved the company into the building after they'd expanded the business. Doug loved the open feel to the floor they were renting, the friendliness they'd instilled in the staff who joined their company. The sense of pride to come to work every day, not just the feel of a nine-to-five-get-it-done-and-get-away-home job.

He picked up another spreadsheet from the mountain of papers on his desk. They were coming to the end of a two-year project, a block of apartments by the side of the canal. It had been one of their most ambitious builds yet, demolishing a derelict factory and gaining planning permission to build sixteen flats, four to a floor. It had been touch and go at first, involving many rounds of new plans but finally it had been approved. Doug couldn't wait to get it finished now, start moving people into them. PR and press were going to bring in huge potential this year because of them, and they were already thinking of their next project due to finish next year. As well, Alex was scanning the area for more pockets of land or buildings to renovate or demolish.

The reason for going over budget on the waterfront apartments was to create a luxurious internal feel. The area had grown tenfold since they'd started the project so even though it took a bite out of their overall profit, it would work out better in the long run.

He walked over to the water cooler and downed a glass of cold water. It was mid-February; chilly outside yet weather forecasters were already predicting a hot summer. He hoped so as he didn't have time for a holiday.

A knock on the door brought him back to the present.

'Hey, bro,' Alex greeted Doug as if they were still in their teens when actually they were both late forties. 'Are you done with that information yet? Only we have a meeting in twenty minutes, and I need to—'

'It's all here.' Doug returned to his desk and handed the spreadsheet to him.

'We can manage it?' Alex took it from him and sat down.

'Yes, I think so. Plus, it will make the remaining properties sell better.'

'How many are left?'

'Five – but I have two viewings lined up this week.'

'They'll go once these are finished, if not before.' Alex nodded confidently. 'Everyone wants a waterfront home.'

Doug smiled, always in awe of his brother's sense of optimism. Alex had been born of the opinion his glass was half full. Doug was a glass half empty man. Something that had cost him his marriage and his family as he'd become a workaholic worrying about providing for everyone in the long term.

He watched as his brother studied the sheet. Like Doug, Alex was tall with fair hair and a penchant to have a beer belly one month and to lose it the next. They both had strong features, deep-set brown eyes, and broad smiles.

Doug was the eldest by two years but often it seemed like twenty-two. Married with two sons and a grandchild on the way, Alex still went out and enjoyed his life. Doug was always more comfortable at home or at work. Yet he would never admit to being lonely.

Instead he threw himself into the business, plodding along day by day, week by week, month by month. Working long hours added to the stress he was under regardless, but he lived for the job.

Feeling clammy all of a sudden, he loosened his tie and undid the top button of his shirt. Alex gave him the sheet back and sat forward to discuss it. Then he frowned.

'Are you okay?' he asked. 'You've gone a bit pale.'

'Yeah, I'm fine. Had a takeaway last night; it's left me with indigestion.'

Doug was being economical with the truth. He'd been having pains in his chest on and off for a few hours. But he thought it was nothing serious. He suffered from acid reflux, so was used to it. He rubbed the middle of his chest.

'Are you sure?' Alex didn't seem convinced.

'I'm good.' Doug nodded.

'You need to take it easy. I know you've been pulling double shifts to get this job finished on time. It's not a problem if we run over a little.'

'I'm fine.' Doug waved his comments away. 'You don't have to worry about me.'

'When do I ever stop worrying about you?' Alex shook his head. 'You're working too hard.'

'I'm telling you, I'm good to go. About this spreadsheet. I'll let Karl know that...' A rush of heat rose through his body, pain shooting up his left arm at the same time. He hung onto the desk for support as he slid down his chair.

Alex reached across to him. 'Doug!'

But Doug was already on the floor, gasping for air as he clutched at his chest. The throbbing was like nothing he had ever experienced, a vice squeezing the air from his lungs. With his spare hand, he reached out to his brother.

'Help... me... I—'

'Hang in there.' Alex got out his phone. 'Ambulance please. My brother is having a heart attack.'

Doug tried to speak, but the discomfort in his body was too much. Fear engulfed him.

Please don't let me die.

CHAPTER 3

Three months later

Home after work, Hannah slipped off her shoes. Her feet ached after standing up for a few hours, but she wouldn't swap her job for anything. Working gave her routine and a sense of purpose but above all, she had a network of friends who she looked on as family now.

She'd taken down the mirror by the front door. Sometimes it hurt too much to catch a glimpse of herself because all she saw was her mum. They had been so alike – both small in build with dark brown hair. Hannah had her dad's button nose; her mum's eyes of blue. If she looked close enough when she smiled, she could see a small part of them both, as well as her sister, Olivia. She wondered if Olivia ever glanced in her mirror and saw the same thing too.

Britain was in the midst of a heatwave, and although Hannah loved the hot weather, it was hard to work indoors when the sun was shining. She opened a few windows to let out the stuffiness, intending on making the most of the last rays once she'd changed and showered.

Her home was always tidy. There was never a cup left to

wash before she left, cushions were plumped, clothes put away. Their style had been minimal. A lot of the furniture hadn't been changed in years, but it was functional, and Hannah had lightened up the rooms as much as she could with brightly coloured wallpaper, throws, and accessories.

Upstairs, she went into her room. Her mum's bed had been downstairs for a good while, but her friend Phoebe had helped her to get it back to its original place shortly after the funeral. The front half of the room had been turned back into a dining area, not that Hannah was eating much. At the moment, there was a jigsaw she'd just completed spread across it. She made a mental note to pack it up and put it aside for the community centre jumble sale.

Hannah didn't know what she'd have done without Phoebe after her mum had died. She'd gone through the motions with her, getting in touch with the undertaker, the doctors, social services to clear all Mum's disability equipment. The hand and stair rails had been removed, although her mum hadn't been upstairs for the past three years. The bath seat and the frame around the toilet had gone, the commode that Martha had refused to use and the blocks underneath the armchair to lift it up higher, so she didn't have so far to sit down.

Then there were the boxes of tablets, bottles of medicines, and antiseptic rubs, bandages for the ulcer on Martha's left leg that never healed and was more like a hole when she died.

It had been a cruel life for her in the end, but Hannah hoped she'd made it a little less unbearable by being able to provide for her at home. Although Martha hadn't wanted to be a burden, Hannah couldn't see her in residential care either.

Her parents had been involved in a car accident when she was eighteen. Her father was killed outright, her mum left with permanent mobility problems. Hannah and her sister had to look after their mum. But Olivia had left for university two years later, leaving Hannah to be the sole carer. All her dreams and ambitions had ended in one act of stupidity by an uninsured drunk driver.

Until now she hadn't realised how much time she'd devoted to caring for her mum. All those free days in front of her without hospital appointments, visits from health care workers, doctors, and physiotherapists.

With a heavy heart, she lay down on her bed, slid her hand underneath the pillow and pulled out the letter that she kept there. Mum had written it: there were two for her and one for Olivia too, if she ever came back so that she could give it to her.

Dear Hannah,

If you're reading this, my time with you is over. I can't say I'm sorry because I was in so much pain. But I wanted to thank you for looking after me the way you did. Without you, I would have been left to end my days in some dreadful nursing home, full of people so much older than me.

I want to leave you a list of things to remember but as you've looked after me and the house for so long now, it feels disingenuous. But at least you don't have to wash and iron for two, clean and cook as well as work. You'll be able to go out of an evening, make new friends. Even go and stay with Colin. Just don't think you have to stay in this house if you don't want to.

I know it hasn't been easy for you, giving up a lot of your dreams and aspirations, especially with Olivia leaving you to deal with it all. The guilt ate me up inside. You haven't had the chance to see the world, explore outside of Somerley even, and that has been my fault.

Anyway, I digress. I wrote these letters a long time ago. This one is self-explanatory but the second will take some getting used to. You might want to open that at a later date. And, as well as these two letters, Thelma also has something for you that may help explain things a little more.

You see, there's something I need to tell you that I couldn't say to your face. I'm so sorry that I kept it from you, but whatever you think of me afterwards, until we meet again, I will be right by your side. You'll feel me there, even though you can't see me. But always know, I was so proud that you were my daughter.

Love always, Mum x

Hannah reached for the second letter in the drawer next to her. It was still in its envelope; she hadn't found the courage to open it yet. She'd convinced herself it would tell her that she and Olivia had different fathers: what else could it be? And if that *was* the secret then she didn't want to know. She wanted to keep her mum's memory pure. She had done her best for her daughters, even if Hannah was the only one of the two who had ever been grateful.

She put the envelope away. She wasn't ready for it yet.

She wasn't sure she ever would be.

CHAPTER 4

*D*oug switched off the TV and moved through to the kitchen. Just the sight of a reality TV show made him shudder. When he'd been recuperating, he'd watched so many series about house makeovers while picking fault under his breath. Then he'd moved on to homes for sale in the country. Anything to take away the long days but to no avail. There were so many channels. Some people must happily keep themselves entertained from dawn until dusk, but he wasn't one of them. He would never understand the joys of watching programmes during the daytime, probably because he'd always been so busy until now.

He still couldn't believe what had happened to him. The heart attack had been caused by a faulty valve that surgery had, thankfully, put right. Doug had been monitored for six days afterwards before they'd allowed him to go home.

His brother had been distraught.

'It doesn't get any worse than this,' Alex had told him.

'I'm still here.' Doug had tried to make light of the situation, even though it had shocked him immensely.

'You need to take some time out. We nearly lost you.'

He'd clasped his brother's hand while they had a moment. They'd been so close all their lives. There was no rivalry nor bitterness, no feuds, nor jealousy. Just pure respect and genuine love. And it could have been all over in an instant.

On his release from hospital, Alex had insisted that Doug stay with him and the family. His sister-in-law, Vanda, had made sure he was well looked after, telling him off whenever he exerted himself. But after a few days, Doug had felt claustrophobic, yearning for his own space so he'd gone home a fortnight after the initial attack.

He'd taken the next month off yet during the third week, he'd started working online, still being in the thick of things but from the comfort of his home office. After another month he was back at his desk with Alex fussing around him.

Now, he felt much better than he had before; he hadn't noticed until he'd been taken ill how out of breath he'd been, and he was on tablets for the rest of his life. He'd been lucky.

Even so, it had shaken him to the core. At forty-nine, he was too young to die. He had *so* much to do with his life yet.

Nonetheless, even though he'd been eager to return, work had somehow become meaningless. All of a sudden, he disliked what the business had made him. More to the point, what he had lost because of it. He'd known there and then that things had to change. He'd let life get on top of him; stopped enjoying it.

So he'd decided to move away for three months. Realising how precious every day was, he needed to leave his worries behind. The slower pace in Somerley would be good for him and, with no one knowing him, maybe he could enjoy himself again, getting back to the simpler things in life.

He made a mug of strong tea and went to sit out on the patio. The garden was blooming everywhere as summer arrived. He'd mowed the lawns yesterday afternoon and filled some pots and borders with bedding plants, although he hadn't mentioned it to Alex because he'd think it was too strenuous. His gentle nagging was worse than having a wife in some respects.

But he never wanted to go through that period in his life again. It had scared him rigid, his nightmares of the event breaking his sleep pattern on a regular basis. So, whatever the doctor ordered, and no matter how much he didn't like it, he would do what it took to stay healthy and well.

'Doug?' Alex shouted as he let himself in.

'I'm outside.'

Alex came through wearing cropped denims, and a pale blue T-shirt, sunglasses tucked into its neck line. His arms and legs were a golden brown due to his time outside on the sites.

'Garden's looking nice.' He stared at Doug suspiciously before sitting down beside him.

'It is.' Doug smiled, saying no more. 'Tea's in the pot. Or there's beer if it's not too early?'

'Tea is fine. How are you feeling?'

'Good, thanks.'

'You wouldn't tell me if you weren't, would you?'

'No.'

They shared a smile, followed by a lengthy conversation. Half an hour later, after running through everything he wanted Alex to keep an eye on while he was away, Doug stretched his arms in the air.

'Are you taking the truck with you at the weekend?' Alex asked.

'Of course.'

'You should have picked something with a little class.'

'It's me all over.'

'It looks as old as you.' Alex smirked. 'Although, did they have those models nearly fifty years ago?'

Doug made to swipe Alex around the head but after laughing, they stood next to each other in silence.

'I'm going to miss you, bro.' Alex's tone was melancholy.

'I'm not going far.'

'You know what I mean.'

Doug did. He would miss his brother too. They saw each other most days; what would it be like to only have him on the end of a phone? He wasn't going to take his laptop so there would be no opportunity to Skype or FaceTime. But he would speak to him every day and come to visit once he'd settled in.

He pulled Alex into a warm embrace, clapping him on his back a few times before breaking away.

'You'd better remember to take your tablets,' Alex said. 'And get your hair cut before you go. You look like a tramp.'

'You sound like Mum.' Doug's eyes misted over as he thought of the sweet but strong woman who had been taken from them too soon.

'Good. I hope you'll listen to me. No doing too much, either.'

'Yes, sir.' Doug saluted his brother.

'And if you don't like it, you can come back immediately.'

'I'm planning on staying as long as I can. I'm determined to get back to my usual self, with no stress and a sense of life in my blood.'

'Yes, I don't want a fright like that again. You might end up giving me a heart attack too.'

Their laughter was warm.

'You'll let me know your new phone number as soon as you're sorted?'

'I will.'

'Well, at least I won't have to see your ugly mug every day for a while, loser,' Alex mocked.

Doug laughed, knowing his brother was only teasing him. But a new adventure, if only forty miles away from home, was just what the doctor ordered.

CHAPTER 5

*H*ope Street Hair was owned by father and daughter, Morris and Esther Helton. They had come up from London to the West Midlands after the previous owner, Mr Watkins, had passed away and the café that had been there for over twenty years was put on the market.

Mr Watkins had lived on Hope Street ever since he was a child. He had died shortly before his seventieth birthday, when sadly he was due to retire because the café had become a health hazard he refused to close.

The residents watched on during the renovations with a mixture of emotions due to loyalty to Mr Watkins but were ultimately happy when a hair salon had opened. The room at the front had been stripped, thousands of pounds spent renovating it into what it was today. Now the frontage was pale grey, a block of frosted glass across the middle of the picture window. The name of the business was etched into it in a fancy script. Above it was a black canopy, open to keep the glare of the sun away whenever necessary. Inside was tastefully decorated with pale lemon walls and grey padded chairs, black ornate mirrors and silver accessories.

When the Helton's had returned to London, only coming back once a month to check in on things, Phoebe Marshall was left to manage the business. She was a real asset to them. And when it was time to hire part-time staff, Phoebe had looked no further than her best friend. Hannah had worked there for the past five years.

Hannah remembered when she'd first started working with Phoebe. She'd done the sweeping up, manning the phones and reception, washing hair and replenishing supplies. But gradually, by going on the relevant courses, she'd learned how to perm hair, do basic cuts, and add colour. She enjoyed what she did, but it was Phoebe who was the head stylist. Everyone wanted to book her. She hardly ever had spare appointments.

Hannah arrived just in the nick of time for her shift that day after a quick visit to Thelma next door.

'Morning.' She smiled when she found Phoebe in the back room getting ready to open up.

'You're glowing.' Phoebe frowned. 'Have you been a wanton sex goddess all night, like our good friend Bridget Jones?'

'I wish.' Hannah rolled her eyes. 'Just another sleepless night – I feel like I'm starting the menopause. It's so blooming hot.'

'Tell me about it.'

Phoebe lived at 41 Hope Street and had moved in shortly after her marriage to Travis fifteen years ago, staying on when they divorced three years ago. A tall blonde, she was lithe and extremely athletic. When she wasn't at work in her stylish grey uniform, she'd either be wearing gym or running gear, or skinny jeans and a figure-hugging top.

She and Hannah had known each other since they were five years old. They'd met hanging their coats up on their first morning in nursery class. Hannah had chosen a duckling sticker and Phoebe had picked the apple one next to it. They'd smiled at each other tentatively and then Phoebe had taken Hannah's hand and dragged her to the sandpit. At that age, they didn't care about life. They just wanted to get on with the art of playing. But Hannah realised she'd found a friend for life when Phoebe thumped David McIlroy on his arm after he'd pinched her.

'Are you still coming over tonight?' Phoebe asked.

'Definitely.' Hannah began to make coffee. 'I might have to shower at yours though.'

'You've had no luck with the landlord then?'

Hannah was having problems with her boiler. It was only heating the water sporadically, no matter how much she swore at it. There was nothing worse than a lukewarm shower, even in this warm weather.

'No, but I did speak to someone from Regency Property Management. According to Mike, *we* now have to pay one hundred pounds before they'll even look at any repairs.'

'You're joking?' Phoebe turned to her as she grabbed a fresh batch of towels to put out.

'I'm not. He said it was part of the new tenancy agreement. I argued the toss, but he wasn't having it.'

'So, we all have to fork out that much before we can get anything done now?'

Hannah nodded. 'It'll have to stay temperamental for a while longer.'

'Bloody typical. Tossers. Why don't you ask Robin to have a look at it?'

Robin Marriott was a friend of theirs, and the owner of RM Training. Well known in Somerley, he was in his mid-forties and had been running the business for the past twenty years. In and out of trouble himself when he was at school, he'd been taken under the wing by a local businessman and taught how to lay bricks and plaster walls. Those two skills alone had made him a lot of money.

After a few years of working for himself, and with the help of a community grant, he'd set up the training centre. Now he had a team who trained teenagers, mostly from the large estate a mile away, how to paint and decorate and tend gardens and erect fencing. The business had gone on to win awards both locally and nationally, and with a number of staff working for him now, he'd helped hundreds of young men and women over the years.

'He does so much for us already,' Hannah replied. 'I don't like to impose.'

'He'll be cheaper, that's for sure.'

She nodded. 'I'll ask him later, see when he can fit me in.'

The door opened and their first customer came bustling in, putting paid to any more conversation between them.

Ellen Savage lived at 19 Hope Street. Married to Gray for nearly twenty-five years, they ran Somerley Stores on the high street. Ellen came in for a blow dry every Friday, popping in early morning while Gray minded the shop and the staff. It was her treat to herself, she always said, but really, they all knew it was to get out of the open-all-hours shop.

She down in a chair. 'Are you looking forward to your party?'

'Yes, but not to being forty.' Hannah draped a cape around Ellen's shoulders, encouraging her to pop her arms through the sleeves. 'Besides, I'm working on the day itself.'

Ellen gasped, her eyes wide as she looked through the mirror in front of them.

'You can't have the day off? Oh, that is a travesty.'

'Hey! I'm not the slave driver.' Phoebe pouted as she

rushed to answer the phone. 'This one here chose to work. I didn't have a say in it.'

'Why would you do that?' Ellen frowned.

Hannah sighed. 'You know I don't like a fuss and well, it's the first birthday without my mum. Most of my friends will be coming to have their hair done for the party. So, I thought I'd buy some wine and cakes and celebrate while I work.'

Ellen nodded. 'That sounds a little better.' She patted her hair. 'Just the usual this week. Make me look like a supermodel.'

'I'll try my best.' Hannah grinned.

Ellen roared with laughter. 'I'm not sure anyone can work that kind of miracle.'

'Oh, behave. You always look lovely.'

Whereas, Hannah thought, *I always feel dowdy. I need a miracle too.*

CHAPTER 6

*H*annah grabbed her shopping bag full of wine and goodies and went on a hefty night out across the cobbles. When they were teenagers, Phoebe had lived over on the other side of Somerley Square. They would meet by the church; Phoebe would sneak out the odd bottle of lager and a couple of ciggies and they'd sit in the park out of sight. Hannah remembered feeling so grown up. Luckily neither of them had got hooked on anything. The cigarettes had gone for good and the drink was only around for social occasions.

Phoebe's husband had left when her children had been eleven and four. At the time Phoebe had been devastated. Travis had just upped and gone one evening, leaving her to tell the kids. It was three months later she learned he'd moved in with a woman eight years younger than him. It took her less than ten seconds after that to realise that the new girlfriend was carrying his baby.

Staying in had reduced the need to find a babysitter and meant that Hannah was still close to her mum if she needed her. And besides, Travis was often the one out on the town on Fridays, even before he left, so Hannah had spent most weeks across the road, regardless. Phoebe's house was her second home.

'Hello,' Hannah shouted as she let herself in, the front door on the latch.

'I'm in the kitchen,' Phoebe shouted back. 'In a mass of cheese and onion crisps. I was a bit too energetic tearing the bag open, and it exploded.'

Hannah grinned as she spotted her friend on all fours. Phoebe's long blonde hair was tied in two plaits at the side of an oval face. The twinkle in her kohl-lined eyes matched the brightness of the red-cherry lipstick smile on full lips.

Phoebe's home was almost as loud as her style. Each room was painted cream but there were dashes of personality throughout. A deep purple three-piece suite in the living room, navy blue and white in the bathroom and shades of burnt orange in the kitchen. And she had a thing about striped rugs, scattered around every floor. Hannah knew if she tried to replicate it in her home, it would look atrocious, but here it gelled. She loved its sense of togetherness.

A young boy with a mop of blond hair and the bluest of eyes popped his head around the door.

'Hannah, have you seen the mess Mum's made?' He covered his mouth with his hand as he stifled laughter.

'Whatcha got in the bag?' Phoebe asked. 'Ooh, peanut butter cookies. Better than an orgasm.' Then she grimaced, realising Elliott was still there.

'Mum!' Elliott protested. 'I don't want to know about your sex life, thank you very much.'

Phoebe ruffled his hair. 'Good, because I'm never going to tell you about it. Not that I have much of one at the minute,' she muttered to Hannah out of his hearing range.

'I'll be in my room if you need me,' Elliott replied, putting on a posh accent. 'I'm not one to join in with the shenanigans of the local riff-raff.'

Phoebe and Hannah glanced at each other and rolled their eyes in unison.

'He doesn't get that charm from me,' Phoebe sniggered.

If Hannah hadn't known the children's father, she might have said the young boy had been planted on Earth by an alien force. He was the sweetest but the weirdest seven-year-old. Level-headed with a wisdom beyond his years. But a credit to his mother. Whereas his elder sister seemed to mirror what she and Phoebe had got up to during their teens on every turn.

'Is Tilly in?' Hannah asked as she emptied her bag out on the kitchen table.

'No, but she'll be back soon. She has to be in by eight every night for a week. She came in from school with another letter and I have to go and see her form teacher on Monday.'

'Again?'

'Yes, a-bloody-gain.'

'Oh dear.' Just lately, Tilly seemed to be in more and more trouble at school.

Phoebe sighed. 'Why won't she talk to me, Han? I'm her mum.'

Hannah harrumphed. 'Did we ever talk to our mums when we were that age?'

'You have a point there.' Phoebe grinned. 'We did get up to some fun though.'

'And that's what Tilly's doing now. She's testing boundaries, learning how far she can go before getting into trouble. I bet it will be typical teen stuff.'

'I hope so.'

A text message came in on Hannah's phone.

I might make it back this weekend. Fancy hooking up?

Hannah put down her mobile without replying.

'Colin?' Phoebe raised her eyebrows.

'Hmm-hmm.'

Colin was someone Hannah had known almost as long as Phoebe. Divorced with three children, he spent most of his life on the road as a light and sound engineer for a rock band. It wasn't nearly as exciting as it sounded. The group went from small club to even smaller pub, with no more than a handful of people in the audience, but it was how Colin liked it.

They'd got together one night after Hannah had finished a shift at the Hope and Anchor, way too many years ago for her not to be embarrassed about how long it had been going on. Colin came back to Somerley every few weeks, and they often shared a bed – okay, the settee mostly – whenever they could. But in reality, neither of them wanted anything else, or he would have moved in with her soon after Mum had passed. They had become complacent, used to each other. Well, the closeness of another body, really. The sex wasn't all that great if she was honest.

Twenty minutes later, the wine was flowing. Hannah was lamenting about missing her youth.

'I feel as if I have nothing to look forward to now, I'm going to be forty soon,' she admitted.

'Aw, come here, my friend.' Phoebe slung an arm around her shoulder and gave her a cuddle. 'What you need is a good holiday. Get yourself away from Hope Street for a few days.'

'I wish I had some spare money to blow on one. It must be great not to worry about it. I don't even have enough to pay to get my boiler looked at.'

'I don't think anyone can ever have too much money, do you?'

'Millionaires can.'

'Oh, yes. They have *way* too much. It should be shared out.'

'I'd just like a bit of security.' Hannah took another

handful of crisps from the bowl on the settee in the middle of them. 'I'm happy with a roof over my head but it would be great not to have to worry about it.'

'I'd like to be rich enough to hire someone like Daniel Craig.' Phoebe reached a hand in the bowl too. 'He could be my butler.'

Hannah roared with laughter.

'I'm serious.' Phoebe pouted. 'He could wait on me hand and foot and… I'm sure he'd come in useful for a lot of other things.'

'I'd buy a new bed,' Hannah said. 'The one I have is too old for—'

Phoebe giggled.

'Too old for me to get comfortable now because it dips so much in the middle, I *was* going to say. I'm never too old for some loving.'

'You see, there is definitely a purpose in life.'

Hannah raised a glass in the air for a toast. 'To Daniel Craig and new beds.' She laughed. At least Phoebe had made her stop feeling sorry for herself, even if only for a few hours.

Two more glasses of wine later and in came Tilly. 'Ah, good. The adult of the family returns,' Phoebe announced. 'Had a good time at Jack's?'

'Jack's?' Hannah sat forward inquisitively. 'Do you have a new boyfriend?'

'Jacqueline,' Tilly explained. 'We've been watching *Mamma Mia*.'

'Again?' Both women spoke in unison and then laughed. For some reason finding this funny, Hannah clinked her glass to Phoebe's.

'I've seen it about five times, but it's SO good,' Tilly added.

'It is,' Phoebe agreed, beginning to sing *Mamma Mia*.

Hannah joined in as they sang their own version of the next line. 'My my, feet are covered in blisters.'

Tilly rolled her eyes as the women burst into laughter again. 'Is Elliot asleep?'

'The last time I looked he had his head under the covers reading by torchlight,' Phoebe told her.

'Why can't he use a lamp like everyone else?'

'At least he doesn't keep you awake.'

Tilly sighed. 'Have you any idea how embarrassing it is to be fourteen and still sharing a room with your brother?'

'Needs must, I'm afraid,' Phoebe replied. 'Unless you can sleep in the bath, there isn't anywhere else.'

Tilly sighed again, then jumped to her feet. 'I'm going to make myself a hot chocolate.'

'It's too hot, woman.'

'It's never too hot for chocolate.'

'See what you're missing out on?' Phoebe waved a hand in the air after her daughter.

'I have your children to mother,' Hannah replied.

'Yes, you are their godmother. You can move them in with you now if you like.' They shared a smile, knowing Phoebe's words were empty.

'I'm not sure if I want any children. It sounds really selfish of me, but I've looked after Mum for so long that I think I'd like some "me time" now.'

'That isn't selfish. It's sensible, if you ask me.'

Hannah nodded. Ms Sensible. Yes, that was her all along. Why couldn't she be Ms Adventurous for once?

CHAPTER 7

*I*t was Sunday afternoon when Doug turned into Hope Street after making his way through the city of Hedworth and finally reaching Somerley. The area had a village feel to it with most things set out on the high street. There was a range of shops and amenities including a chemist, a hairdressers, and a pub, The Hope and Anchor.

His friend Robin had told him rumour was if you moved into Hope Street, you'd never want to leave. He wasn't sure about that, but he could understand why people would like it here. There appeared to be a sense of pride everywhere, as if the street welcomed you with open arms. "Come on in and take a seat," it seemed to say. "Let me get you a cup of tea."

He drove past cars parked on either side of two rows of brightly painted doors that opened out onto the pavement. There were window boxes and hanging baskets festooned in a riot of colours, and full of aromas he could imagine even though he couldn't smell them.

In front of the wall that blocked off the bottom of the street, a seating area had been made stretching over several metres of decorative slabs. A couple with a young baby were sitting there, two small children on bikes pedalling around them. An elderly man sat on a stool outside the end house, leaning on a walking stick resting between his legs.

Doug felt eyes on him as he manoeuvred the truck round to face the other way. It was a tight squeeze, so he was grateful to do it with quite a respectable seven-point turn. Then he drove back down the cobbles, squeezing in between a red and white Mini and a taxi.

He removed a holdall from the passenger seat, got out of the vehicle, and slung the bag over his shoulder. It was quiet down here, although he reckoned, give it a day or so, and everyone would know he had arrived.

Pushing the front door open, Doug's heart sank when he realised his new digs were pokier than he'd remembered from his one visit all those years ago. It had seemed a good idea to come here at the time. Now he wasn't so sure.

The house seemed clean, he'd give it that. But it was sparsely furnished, with drab cream walls and a beige carpet. The two rooms downstairs had been knocked through into one large open space with a staircase going up its middle.

He walked through into a galley kitchen to see standard cheap white units in a row topped by a black replica marble worktop. Another door led on to a tiny vestibule that contained the boiler and at the back of the house was the bathroom.

Walking back into the living room, Doug recalled the first home he and Casey had purchased after they married. They had saved hard and bought a run-down house similar to this one, when they'd hardly had anything to call their own. It had been more of a wreck than he'd bargained for but between them, they'd managed to do it up on the cheap. They'd had a good few years there but as soon as the kids came along, it had been too small and they'd moved on. And on again. And then they'd grown apart.

Sometimes he yearned for those simpler times when he'd played football in the yard with his son. When his wife and daughter had moved deck chairs around every half hour to catch as much sun as possible. Where having a barbecue had involved having half the street and their kids around too.

How had he become such a bore?

Upstairs, he found a bedroom either side of a tiny landing. They were more or less the same size, the back one having a cupboard built over the stairs. He walked the few steps to the window and looked down on the yard, noticing that the guttering over the kitchen needed clearing. There was also a pile of rubbish by the wall that could pose a fire risk. He would shift it as soon as he could.

All in all, 35 Hope Street was fine for him to lay down low. It would be a small sacrifice, getting used to the simpler things in life again.

Pushing all the gloomy thoughts aside, he made a coffee while he planned what to do before the day was finished. He'd called in at the shop on the high street for the essentials, but he'd need to do a supermarket sweep as soon as he could.

First, he switched off his smartphone and placed it out of sight in a drawer, not even stopping to check for correspondence. Then he took out the pay-as-you-go phone he'd brought with him. Once set up, he messaged Alex so that he had his new number.

These houses are really small but I'm sure there's at least three miles between the bedroom and the loo!

The reply came back a few moments later.

Get yourself a potty, ha. Stay safe, bro.

Doug smiled. Then he popped the phone into his pocket. He wasn't going to share the number with anyone else. Neither was he going to turn on that smartphone for at least a week. He needed to switch off too. He would lie low for a while, recover and rest without too much hassle. Then he could go back home with fresh vigour, a jump in his step. Maybe things would improve if he didn't push himself too hard. Being away from Alex would be tough but worthwhile if his health improved.

Over the next few minutes, Doug fetched his few belongings from the truck. As he took the last bag from the cab, he sensed eyes on him again. He looked across the street. An elderly woman was in the window of number thirty-two. He raised a hand; found it quite charming when she returned his greeting.

There could definitely be worse places right now than Hope Street.

CHAPTER 8

The weekend had been long and sunny but still Monday morning came around too quickly. Without the heavy routine now that her mum no longer needed caring for, Hannah dreaded the beginning of another long week. She checked the time, saw it was two minutes to eight and located her phone. She and Phoebe rung each other most mornings. It was Phoebe's turn today.

Bang on time, the ringtone went off.

'Hey, Phoebs.' She tried to inject a little joy into her voice. 'You good?'

'No time for small talk. Go to your front window.'

'Why?'

'Just go!'

'Okay, okay.' Hannah did as she was told. She paused, then frowned. 'What am I looking for?

'You mean you can't see the dirty big truck parked right across from you?'

'I saw that yesterday.' For some reason, she thought Phoebe would have been talking about something a little more exciting. But that was Hope Street for you. 'Someone must be having some work done.'

'No, it looks like we have a new neighbour. The man driving the truck is a dish.'

Hannah imagined Phoebe now, peering behind the curtains as she was. 'But you can't see him from your side of the street.'

'I've had to fetch some milk. Elliott used it all for his cereal, so I went to the shop. I saw him on my way back. Mr Wendover is going to be so pissed when he sees someone parked in his space.'

Phoebe had one of those raucous laughs, sounding very much like a seal. Throughout the years they'd been friends, it had always made Hannah giggle. It had made her very nearly wet herself on lots of occasions too.

Ralph and Iris Wendover had lived at number thirty-three for six years now. From that day, Ralph had instantly created Car Wars, reserving the right to park outside his door. Hope Street had always been first come first served. Some residents didn't have cars so there was room for everyone, but not necessarily by your house. Ralph, however, insisted it was his space. She and her mum had spent many a time laughing about his antics as they'd watched through the windows, before Martha had become bedridden.

'Is that *all* you have to say this morning?'

Phoebe laughed. 'You know I always get my priorities right. You need to check out the *owner* of the truck.'

Hannah looked again but there was no one there. 'Can't see him at the moment. Why?'

'Well, my lovely, I suggest you do like the rest of the women on the street and stand on the doorstep waiting for him to come out again.'

'You're not standing on your doorstep? Are you?'

'Of course, I'm not, numpty.'

'What age is he?'

'Early forties, I reckon.'

Ah, now she understood.

'You want me to fix you up with him? We're not kids anymore. You can ask a man out yourself at our age. I'm sure he'll be—'

'Not *me*. You.'

'Me? Oh, behave.' Hannah paused. 'I wonder what he does for a living, though.'

'With a truck that size, I bet he has big tools.'

'Ooh, a handyman.'

'Yeah, he might come in… handy. He could rub his hands over me any day.' Phoebe's laugh was intentionally dirty this time.

Hannah checked her watch again. 'We'd better get going. See you soon.'

She disconnected the call, thinking of Phoebe's words. It might be nice to have a new neighbour. And it was thoughtful of Phoebe to try to fix her up with someone new, knowing how low she was feeling. But, really, another man in her life was the last thing she needed right now.

~

On her way out, Hannah popped in to check on Thelma. Often, if she had time of a morning, she called to see how she was. She'd always got Mum's care out of the way first. Sometimes that hadn't taken long; sometimes it had taken forever, depending on how much pain Mum had been in.

Thelma was seventy-eight, with the sharp mind of a twenty-year-old. She got out and about as much as she could but, just lately, Hannah had noticed her slowing down.

Still, the thought of losing her independence hadn't

stopped Thelma. With Hannah's help, she'd sourced a mobile phone and a laptop, learning how to shop online and use social media in record time. Now she sent Hannah a text message if she needed anything urgently.

'It's only me,' Hannah shouted as she closed Thelma's front door. Then she shook her head. She must stop saying that: it reminded her so much of her mum, she almost thought she'd be sitting waiting for her to return.

'Good job I'm decent,' Thelma replied.

Hannah couldn't recall a time when her neighbour hadn't been dressed and made-up. She would worry if she wasn't. Today, Thelma wore a sleeveless top and wide-legged trousers. Her arms were thin, a mass of wrinkles with a hint of a tan. During the past few weeks, she'd been sitting in the yard they'd made into a colourful terrace together. It hadn't taken much, a few potted flowers, a couple of acers, and the odd conifer, and a row of plastic bunting bought in Hedworth. There was a comfy chair, as long as Thelma remembered to bring in the cushion of an evening, and an outside light that Raymond had fitted the last time he'd visited.

Raymond was Thelma's nephew. He lived in London, and for Hannah's part, the less he visited the better. Although Hannah hadn't seen him for a while, Thelma was often tetchy once he'd left.

Something didn't seem right about his visits. Hannah reckoned he was fleecing his aunt of money, but she couldn't prove that and she certainly wouldn't ask her about it, no matter how much she cared about her welfare. Thelma felt like family to her, but she had to remember many times that she was someone else's relative. Still, she was a good neighbour to have and always showed her appreciation at Hannah popping in.

'How are you?' She noticed that the older woman looked

better than her in terms of perkiness. Thelma's short grey hair was thick and shiny, her crowning glory she called it. It was styled in a short chic cut.

'Your nails look nice,' she added. 'Has Bernice been to do them for you?'

'Yes.' Thelma splayed her fingers out to reveal ten blobs of bright purple.

Hannah made fists to hide her own. They used to be lovely until her mum died and she'd bitten them away.

'What plans have you for today?' She moved through to the kitchen to flick on the kettle.

'Don't you worry about me, Hannah Lockley.' Thelma pushed herself to her feet.

Hannah ignored the sound of creaking bones behind her, resisting the urge to rush and help.

'It's your day that's much more important.' Thelma joined her in the kitchen, a well-placed hand on the sideboard for support on the way. 'Are you doing anything nice?'

'Oh, you know, the usual.' Hannah popped two teabags into the yellow teapot that Thelma had used for years. 'I'm meeting Ryan Gosling for brunch at eleven, then I have an appointment with Reese Witherspoon to talk about the latest blockbuster of mine she's adapting to the big screen.' She poured in water and gave the tea a stir before putting the lid on and then placing the teapot on the small table Thelma had sat down at. 'Then I might have time to play tennis with Andy Murray this afternoon.'

'Such a wonderful life.' Thelma smiled. 'So you're off to work, then?'

'Something like that.' Hannah grinned.

CHAPTER 9

 oug had been pleased when Alex had set him up to work with Robin Marriott. His first port of call was to pick up a young lad from a neighbouring street and head on round to Somerley Community Centre.

After finding his way to the address he'd been given, he pulled up outside a red brick council-owned property, keeping the engine ticking over. When no one came out after a minute, he papped his horn.

'Keep the noise down!' A woman hung her head out of the upstairs window. 'You'll wake the baby.'

'Sorry,' he shouted in a loud whisper through the open cab window. 'I'm after Dylan. Is he around?'

'Dylan! Someone to see you. Work, I think.'

Doug sniggered under his breath: she was noisier than him.

Another minute passed and Doug was about to drive away when someone finally emerged from the house, pulling on a navy T-shirt. The lad looked about sixteen with shorn hair. A silver stud in his left eyebrow caught the sunlight. His stride was long, his legs even more so. He jumped in the cab and surprised Doug by smiling wide and holding out a hand.

'Sorry about that,' he said. 'My sister's had a baby and I can't for the life of me put him down. He's named William, after Prince William because Sheryl has a crush on him. He's three months old now, getting quite a porker. He threw up on my T-shirt, so I had to iron another one. Want to see a photo of him?'

Doug had no choice as Dylan thrust a phone under his nose. The image was of the woman at the window, looking tired but grinning as she held her newborn son.

'Your sister's first child?' She didn't look much older than Dylan, barely a woman in fact.

'Yeah. And the last she says, but I know she'll change her mind.' He swiped the screen and showed him another. 'I can't wait to have my own kids. You got any?'

'Two, but they're mid-twenties now.'

'Yeah? So, what do they do?'

'Buckle up. We're already late.' Doug started up the engine, ignoring the question. How could he reply if he didn't know the answer?

'Where are we off to, boss?' Dylan fastened his seatbelt.

'Somerley Community Centre. Robin's already there.' Doug pulled away from the kerb. As Dylan shouted goodbye to the woman who was still hanging out of the window, a smile played on his lips. They obviously didn't realise how noisy they were.

'Have you worked with Robin for long?' Doug asked as he drove.

'Since I left school last summer. Before that I did work experience with him. He's a great bloke. Did you know he owns the community centre?'

'Yes.' Doug concentrated on the road as Dylan explained everything to him, anyway.

'The council put it up for sale and were going to demolish it until Robin stepped in and saved the day. He owns the building now.'

'Good man,' Doug said.

'Yeah. Lots of people use it. It's never usually empty – everything has to be done on a rota. They even hold weddings and christenings at the weekends. Toddler Tots on Tuesdays, bingo on Fridays, lunch club on Mondays and Thursdays.' Dylan counted things off with his fingers. 'Oh, yeah, and the slimming club on Monday night. Scouts and brownies too. It's a den of iniquity. And all run by volunteers.'

'Sounds… busy,' Doug replied.

'It is. We help to maintain the building.'

Ten minutes later, he turned into a car park and pulled in next to a white van with a red company logo splashed across its side, *RM Training*. Somerley Community Centre was a single-storey building with waist-high windows along one side, and double doors leading inside. Cream rendered walls had hardly a mark on them, a new roof standing proud.

Dylan jumped out and joined him.

'Robin will be around the back,' he said. 'I bet he's on his phone. He's always on it.'

'Like you will be, no doubt.'

Dylan laughed. 'His is practically glued to his ear. A fiver says—'

'Not a betting man,' Doug told him.

'Yeah, you're wise to watch the pennies.'

When the man in question sauntered over, Doug saw he did indeed have a phone to his ear and was talking energetically into the mouthpiece. They waited for him to finish his conversation.

Robin Marriott was a stocky man with a trim grey beard. His T-shirt bore the same logo across his chest as the one on the van, and he revealed a bald head when he removed his safety helmet and wiped his brow.

Doug was looking forward to working with Robin and his team, remembering back to a time when he'd been sixteen and a know-it-all. Him and Alex were always getting into scrapes. Their parents had spent a lot of time with complaining form teachers, and they'd completed hours in detention. He'd been eager to finish school too.

Robin disconnected the phone and shook hands with Doug. 'Did you get here okay yesterday? I know we're not too far from the motorway, but it can get rammed at times.'

'Yes, sorry I'm late today though. Took a wrong turning on the estate when I picked up me laddo and had to double back on my way here.' He glanced surreptitiously at Dylan who grinned at him. 'What do you need us to start on?'

'We're trimming the hedges at the moment. I'm laying a patio area this year, by the double doors at the back so I need an area clearing. There'll need to be a ramp too. Have you used a chainsaw before?'

Doug nodded. 'I sure have.'

'Great. We'll set you up with the safety gear and get cracking. We should get a good bulk of it finished for lunchtime.'

'And if we're lucky, we'll be invited to eat with the luncheon club,' Dylan enthused. 'The company will be an average age of ninety but it's bangers and mash today.'

Doug felt his stomach roll even though he'd had breakfast less than an hour ago.

'Apart from our Hannah, who's only thirty-nine. But she can sure cook a mean sausage.' Robin licked his lips. 'And her gravy is to die for.'

'Hannah?'

'I'll introduce you to her later. First, come and meet the team and then we'll get started.'

CHAPTER 10

*H*annah hadn't been in the luncheon club for longer than twenty minutes when Robin shouted her from across the room. She and him went back a long way. They'd met at high school and he'd dated Phoebe for a few months. When they broke up, they all lost touch until he'd walked into the Hope and Anchor a few years ago, where Hannah had been working behind the bar. He and his team often came in from work after that and they'd have a good old natter. Most of the time, Robin knew more gossip than she did.

Hannah didn't know many men she could talk to like Robin. He was a considerate soul, even offering money whenever she told him how broke she was, which she never took, and advice if she felt inclined to ask, which she sometimes acted upon. He'd plastered the bathroom ceiling that time it fell down after the property management firm failed to send anyone out to it too.

'Have you lot finished already or are you only after my bangers and mash?' she teased as she walked across to them.

The man standing next to Robin had eyes that smiled a

fraction of a second before he did. At a quick estimate, she put him around mid-forties. He was clean-shaven, with wavy blond hair and a toothpaste ad set of white teeth. She could see the bottom of a faded tattoo popping out from his short sleeve as he stretched his arm towards her.

'Hi, I'm Hannah.' She smiled. 'Nice to meet you.'

'Likewise. I'm Doug. Doug Barnett.'

His large hand was rough wrapped around her own and it hurt when he shook it. She tried not to grimace and let him know.

'Doug's new to the area,' Robin told her. 'He's going to be working with me for the next three months.'

'That's right.' Doug nodded. 'I'm staying in Hope Street.'

Hannah's eyes shot across to him. Was this the mystery man Phoebe was talking about?

'I live in Hope Street,' she said. 'Have you moved into number thirty-five?'

'Yes.' He beamed. 'What number are you?'

'I'm at thirty-four. Right across from you. I'm sure you'll be able to see straight into my windows.'

'I don't think I'm the type of person who does that sort of thing.'

'Well, obviously not.' Hannah heard herself laughing like a banshee.

There was an awkward silence as if everyone around had stopped to listen to what she was going to say next.

'So, you're a handy man,' she added buoyantly. 'Well, I need my boiler fixing, if you're up for it?'

Robin burst out laughing even before Hannah's hand had covered her mouth. She felt the heat rising up her face.

'That is NOT a euphemism.'

But Doug laughed too. She tried not to stare at the curling hair escaping from the ribbed collar of his T-shirt.

'You'll tell me anything.' His gaze fell on her again. 'But I could pop across after work and have a look at it for you.'

'I was only joking.'

'I wasn't. Tomorrow about six?'

'Thanks.' Hannah raced away, stopping to pick up Mary's magazine that had slipped to the floor. She handed it back to her.

'What are you blushing for?' Mary shouted.

Mortified, Hannah waved a hand in front of her face. 'It's hot in here, isn't it? Shall I open another window?'

She counted to sixty in her head, not daring to look back for a minute. When she did, they'd gone.

Her heart returned to normal but something inside her had stirred. Something she hadn't felt for a long time.

She sighed, wishing things weren't so complicated right now.

∾

*D*oug followed Robin and Dylan to the back of the car park again, but not before he'd stolen another quick look at the woman who had caught his attention. She was slight with layered brown hair to her shoulders, wearing a bright orange T-shirt, a faded denim skirt, and trainers.

As she chatted to the elderly man he'd seen in Hope Street yesterday, she straightened up his tie, pulling the knot a little tighter. Then she patted him on the shoulder before turning to the window and waving when she saw him looking in.

Almost immediately, Doug wished he was years younger but as wise as he was now. Because he might not make such a hash of things the second time round.

∾

*T*hings are only as complicated as you make them,' Phoebe said, as Hannah spoke to her over the phone that evening.

'I guess,' she replied. 'He seems really nice, though.'

'Has he said why he's come to Hope Street?'

'I didn't ask.'

'You mean you haven't given him the third degree?' There was a tut down the line. 'You could have found out his back-story. He's old enough to be married with a family.'

'Yes, but—'

'He's definitely good-looking enough not to be single.'

'Yes, but—'

'*And* he has a trade behind him. So why on earth would he end up here?'

Hannah gave up trying to tell Phoebe that it wasn't any of her business. As she let her friend rattle away, she went over to the window to see if Doug was home yet. His truck was parked outside, and she laughed when she spotted Mr Wendover's face in the window of the house next door. The way he was gesticulating she knew he was moaning to his wife.

'I feel like one of the properties on Hope Street, Phoebs,' Hannah said. 'Old and outdated on the inside; drab and boring on the outside but trying my best to look attractive.'

'Hannah Lockley, will you listen to yourself? You're thirty-nine, not seventy-nine. You have lots of years in you yet, and you're still a babe.'

Hannah smiled. You could always rely on a best friend to cheer you up, even if you didn't agree with what they were saying all the time. But if she lived to see Thelma's age, she was almost two-thirds done with her life already.

She went through to the back of the house, opened the

airing cupboard door, and looked inside to see if any switches had tripped. But there was nothing out of place.

'At least my boiler will be fixed soon,' she said. 'Though at what cost, I'm not sure.'

A dirty thought popped into her head and she chastised herself. But Phoebe had the same thought.

'Perhaps you can barter for sexual favours. I know I would.'

'I'm sure you would. But I'm not as confident as you.'

Hannah remembered Phoebe's words long after they'd finished the phone conversation. She didn't look too weatherworn for her age, but she certainly felt it at times. Maybe it was because her birthday was coming up. She closed her mind to the thought of getting to the big four-o next month.

And the fact her mum wouldn't be there to share it with her.

CHAPTER 11

The following evening, Doug walked across the road to number thirty-four. There had been a thunderstorm and the air was sticky, puddles on the road and pavement, but now people were starting to come out to enjoy the evening.

Several doors were open onto the street, and Doug realised that without any frontage, the cobbles were their front gardens. People sat with legs outstretched on steps, some on chairs next to their front doors. Laughter and chatter could be heard. It was like stepping back into the sixties. Not that he'd been anything but a baby then.

He knocked on the door, pleased to have an excuse to get to know Hannah better. Although he wasn't so sure her proximity to him was a good idea. Really, was it the best of things if she lived right opposite him?

Dougie, you're only going to fix her boiler, not drag her to bed.

Although that was rather a nice thought, he mused.

Hannah came to the door, thankfully without the ability to read his mind.

'Hi.' She smiled. 'Come on in.'

'Sorry I'm a bit late.' He stepped inside as she held the door open for him. 'Couldn't get away.'

'That's fine. Would you like a cup of tea, or something cold?'

'I could murder a tea, please. One sugar and a spot of milk.'

Hannah's home was laid out the same as his, two rooms knocked into the one, but it was much brighter. It was mostly down to decor – white papered walls with a delicate lilac floral pattern, pale floorboards, and a coffee-caramel settee with a matching armchair.

There were a group of photographs on the wall, mostly of Hannah and another woman, a few of a family of four. A bookcase stuffed full of paperbacks and a large canvas above the fireplace that read '*The best journey always takes us home*'.

He followed her through into the kitchen, the walls painted a sunflower yellow with accessories to match.

'Your house looks the same as the one I'm staying in.' He pointed to a door. 'So, the boiler is through there?'

'Yes. Unfortunately, the landlord doesn't know where *anything* is. It's his job to fix it but the company he uses have decided we have to pay one hundred pounds before they'll start any work.'

'What?'

As Hannah explained about the surcharge, Doug shook his head in annoyance. That wasn't on any agreement he'd seen. Was she being ripped off?

'I swear the house could fall down around me and no one would care.' Hannah broke into his thoughts.

'Is it always hard to get jobs done?'

'I hope you aren't touting for business.'

'No, not at all.' He shook his head vehemently, embarrassed by her claim.

'I'm joking.' She held up her hand. 'It's just that if anything goes wrong, don't expect anyone to come out to you. It will be a good job then that you're handy with tools.'

As she stood next to the sink, adding water to the kettle, Doug clocked her sagging shoulders. She seemed so burdened about something. But in a moment, she turned to him and smiled again. He looked away, humiliated about being caught.

'I'll just crack on, then.'

Ten minutes later, he had stripped off the front of the boiler and located the problem. He'd also found something else stuffed behind it. He pulled it out and popped it inside his bag while he finished his investigation.

'The clock isn't working,' he said. 'That means your timer will be out, if it allows the boiler to come on at all. Have you been manually switching it on?'

'Yes, when I could get it to work. It's been very temperamental.'

'Well, I can't fix it this evening, but I can order you in a clock and then replace that, if you like?'

'Will it cost a lot?' Hannah looked on with a worried expression.

'Not much I expect, but I won't know until I price it up. I might even have one to hand. I won't charge you for fitting, if that helps. New neighbours and all that.'

'That's very kind of you. I must find a way to return the favour.'

He knelt to put his tools in his bag before he said something flippant that might sound inappropriate. 'Oh, I found this padded envelope.' He handed it to her. 'It was wedged at the back of the boiler.'

Hannah opened it, gasping as she pulled out a handful of ten-pound notes. Her eyes filled with tears.

'Are you okay?' he asked.

'My mum must have put it there,' she explained. 'Although

I don't know when.' Hannah looked up at him through watery eyes. 'She died three months ago.'

'I'm sorry to hear that.' Doug exhaled. 'I've lost my mum too. She had a long illness, cancer. It's tough to go through.'

'Isn't it just? I'm at the stage where I'm still shouting, "it's only me," when I come in through the front door, and then the realisation sinks in that I'm alone. Now, I'm doing the same when I visit Thelma next door.'

'What happened to your mum?' Doug always liked to be upfront, unafraid to talk directly about death. Most people either skirted around the issue or didn't mention it at all. He had never decided which was worse.

'She had a stroke and died three weeks later of complications.'

'That must have been dreadful.' Doug leaned against the worktop. 'My mum died three years ago now. Still feels like yesterday at times. Others it seems like forever.'

'It was on February fifteenth,' Hannah went on. 'She was only sixty-four.'

Doug tried to keep his face straight, feeling that familiar rush of fear coming over him as his thoughts went into overdrive. It was just before he'd had his heart attack.

Hannah opened the fridge and pulled out a half-full bottle of rose wine.

'Do you fancy joining me for a glass of something chilled?'

'Yes please. Happy to prolong the evening in such delightful company.' Doug pointed to the sink. 'Let me wash my hands and that's a definite.'

CHAPTER 12

*H*annah fanned herself while she poured the wine. She wasn't sure if it was the weather or the company that was making her hot. She pulled out a bag of ice from the freezer and added it to the wine. It was a trick she'd got from Phoebe, admonishing her at the time for doing it but enjoying the end result.

'What's it like living on Hope Street?' Doug asked once they were settled in the living room, him on the settee and Hannah on the armchair. 'From first impressions it seems a nice place to live.'

'Nice sums it up quite… *nicely*.' Hannah smiled. 'We have great neighbours who help rather than hinder, and it's an environment where everyone knows everyone else. Not that it's a blessing all the time.'

'It sounds like *Coronation Street*.' Doug grinned.

'It can be *very* much like a soap opera. There's always something going on. Someone falling out, someone leaving, someone returning. Someone retiring, someone giving birth. Someone dying sadly. But it has a really great community spirit. I don't think I'd want to live anywhere else.'

'Don't you find it a little claustrophobic?'

'No.' She shook her head. 'I suppose it's all I'm used to. How about you?'

He looked at her quizzically.

'Robin said you were here for three months. Do you have a home elsewhere? Family? Wife?'

'A home. Manchester.'

'Posh Manchester or poorer Manchester?'

'Salford. Do you always ask so many questions?'

'Sorry. It's just there hasn't been anyone new on the street in a good while. Everyone will want to know your business so you might as well come clean. Mind you, I can't guarantee that the rumour mill won't start up and the reason why you're here could probably end up as you've murdered your wife and are lying low from the police.' She paused dramatically. 'You haven't, have you?'

'Done a runner, or murdered my wife?'

'Both.'

'Well, my ex is on the other side of the world.'

'Ah.'

'So there ends the rumour.'

'But not the intrigue.' Hannah raised her eyebrows inquisitively, waited for him to speak again.

'We're divorced. She moved to Australia when her new man got a job there. They're married, and the kids seem happy enough.' Doug nodded. 'Natalie is twenty-seven and Mikey is twenty-five. I haven't seen them since they were in their teens.'

'Why not?'

Doug paused to gather himself. Why not indeed? He'd been able to afford the airfare; it had been harder to find the time. But he couldn't tell Hannah that. Besides, he knew that was only an excuse. It was the guilt that had kept him away.

'It's expensive to get there. It's hard to keep in touch when you have twenty-four hours of travel and a huge lot of jet lag to cope with if you want to visit. Aside from that, they have their lives out there now.'

Hannah held back a frown. In this day and age, it was easy to keep in touch via social media. Hannah had set up a few Skype calls with her mum and the hospital staff rather than go in for an appointment and it had seemed so personal, as if the consultant was in the same room. Maybe there were other reasons why they didn't keep in touch.

'Do you have grandchildren?'

'Not yet.'

'Pity, I would have enjoyed calling you granddad.'

He smiled at her.

'You really should make an effort to visit them,' she added. 'Life's too short, as we know.'

'Maybe.' He was non-committal as a silence grew between them. 'How long have you volunteered at the community centre?'

'A couple of years now. I used to take my mum and then I started helping out more regularly. We do lots of fundraising too, to make sure Robin doesn't have to fork out money all the time. It's my way of giving back a bit. I lend a hand at the luncheon club and other times if I can.'

'So, once you've been in the hairdressers tomorrow, everyone will know my business, right?'

'Hey, I'm no tittle-tattle.' She gave him a stern stare. 'Maybe I'll leave it a couple of days first, see what rumours have started, anyway.'

He laughed. 'Have you always worked there?'

'No, but I've been part time for a few years now. It was easier to fit around Mum, and we needed the cash.'

'Have you ever wanted to do more?'

'Like what?' She felt a bit patronised that he would think

she was worthless. 'I don't have qualifications to be a doctor or the like.'

'Oh, no, I meant perhaps take some evening cases, broaden your horizons.'

'Around here?' She huffed. 'There's nothing to do.'

'You're, how old… thirty-two?'

'I'm forty next month.'

'Really?' Doug's eyes widened in disbelief. 'You see, you have age on your side.'

Hannah smiled at his compliment.

'Do you have plans to celebrate?' He went on.

'There'll be something going on at the pub. Whenever we have a birthday, we have a big do with a buffet and cake.'

'Sounds like fun. I'm fifty next year.'

'You don't look forty-nine either.'

'I feel it. I had a heart attack three months back.'

'Wow, I'm sorry.' It was Hannah's turn to look flustered. 'There's me going on about my troubles. How are you now?'

'It was cured with surgery, luckily. I need to be careful obviously, and it made me re-evaluate certain things in my life. Who knows if I'll go back to Manchester.'

'Maybe you'll fall hopelessly in love with Hope Street.'

Hannah blushed as soon as she'd said it. They shared a look.

'Maybe I will,' Doug replied.

'Well, as long as you're good with your hands and can do your own repairs, you'll be fine here.'

'Yes, there is that.'

'Bloody landlord. Whatever you do, don't try to get anything fixed.'

'I can do most things for myself, and anything else you might need doing?'

'My boiler should be fine soon.' Hannah smirked. 'But Thelma next door is having trouble closing a few of her doors. They need rehanging or something. Would you be up for doing that?'

'I sure would.' Doug put his glass down. 'I'd best be off. It's been great getting to know you this evening, Hannah. And about that rumour? Maybe I should kiss you passionately on the doorstep. Now that would get everyone talking.' He put his hand to his mouth, eyes widening in disbelief. 'I'm sorry, I don't know where that came from.'

Hannah giggled.

At the front door, Doug pointed to the bookcase.

'You have a huge collection.'

'I hate to throw anything away. Thankfully, I borrowed a lot of books from the library. Mum and I often read the same ones before I'd return them. Do you read?'

'Yes, when I can find time.'

'Take something with you, if you fancy any. They might not be to your taste though.'

'I'm not all sci-fi and westerns.' He smiled. 'I like to get lost in the story. I love unique voices.'

'Me too.'

He ran a finger along the shelves for a few moments, choosing a crime thriller and popping it in his bag.

Hannah showed him to the door which involved taking three steps across the floor.

On the pavement Doug turned back, reached forward for her hand and kissed her knuckles.

'Might as well get the neighbours talking.' He winked and turned, walking across the road.

She watched him go into his house, waving to him before he did, laughing inwardly at the fuss they may be causing. Smiling as she realised she'd made a friend.

And maybe a little something more than friendship could evolve. She would certainly welcome a fling, if he fancied staying in Hope Street. As long as he was good with his hands in that department too.

She giggled, her mind going off on a tangent again. But it was good to end the night with a smile for a change.

She picked up her phone and sent a message to Phoebe.

You're right. Doug is SO hot. And he was flirting with me, I'm sure. I feel like a teenager again.

CHAPTER 13

*S*omerley Cemetery was a beautiful place despite the fact it held so much sorrow. Everything seemed to be pristine no matter what time of year it was. Hannah made her way to visit her mum. Her father was buried there too – Mum had gone into the same plot – but she couldn't imagine him there. She'd never felt able to talk to him like she had her mum. It seemed strange but, although she could remember him, it felt as if she'd never known him in some ways.

A young woman pushing a pram walked past on the main pathway. Hannah smiled at her as she passed, just able to see a newborn baby. A toddler ran behind, laughing as he played with a paper aeroplane.

To her left, she noticed an elderly man standing over a grave, a bunch of flowers in his hand and tears pouring down his face. She looked away knowing he didn't want to share his intimate moment with anyone.

At the grave, she busied herself clearing away last week's flowers, polishing the stone, and adding a fresh bunch of chrysanthemums. They had been Martha's favourites.

The grass was dry due to the weather being warm, so she dropped to her knees.

'There's someone new in the street, Mum, and he's causing quite a stir. He's called Doug, and he's forty-nine. I met him when he came to mend our boiler – the one you shoved a whole pile of money behind.' Hannah shook her head and then smiled as her eyes focussed on her mum's name engraved in the stone. 'You're so thoughtful. I don't know how you managed to do that without me knowing.

'Anyway, he said it was the timer, and he was right. It's been working okay since he changed it. He wouldn't take any money for it though. That's really kind of him, isn't it?'

Posing questions was her way of seeing if her mum was listening. Looking for signs – a leaf blowing over and landing on the grass next to her, the breeze through her hair, a feather from a bird. It was silly, but it was comforting.

'This letter you left for me, Mum,' she went on. 'I'm really scared of opening it. You and I never had any secrets and it hurts that you kept something from me. But I guess until I see what it says, I'll never know, will I? And you want me to know for some reason.' She paused. 'Just bear with me, I'll open it soon.'

Again, she wondered if it was about her sister. Hannah thought she'd spotted Olivia in the crowd at the funeral but she couldn't be sure. One minute she'd seen someone; the next time she looked there was no one there. She wondered if she'd even recognise her now.

It had been eighteen years since Olivia had gone and Hannah still wasn't sure why she'd stayed away. She didn't understand why she'd never come back, not even for a visit. At first there had been birthday cards sent, and Christmas cards. Then nothing at all for the past two years.

Hannah was three when her sister was born. They'd been so close growing up together. Hannah had always been the wiser sibling, in years and manner. Olivia was the one who got into trouble and Hannah was the one who always covered for her, often taking the blame herself.

She remembered when Olivia had snuck out of the house when her parents were in bed to meet a boy from school at the bottom of the street. She was only gone half an hour, but Hannah had been terrified that she'd be found out. She was also concerned her sister might be walking into trouble as the boy she was meeting was older than her. But everything had worked out okay.

When they were very little, she'd make up stories for Olivia before they went to sleep. She would read her *My Naughty Little Sister* and could still remember Olivia's cries of delight as she'd laughed at the antics of the characters.

They were so close until the day of the accident. And then everything turned horrible within a few months. The relationship that Hannah valued was challenged and the drama it caused won the day. She never thought for one minute that her little sister would let her down.

She'd found it hard to deal with at the time, but she'd pushed it to the back of her mind over the years. She doubted either of them would forget how their lives changed in a flash.

Well, how *her* life changed. Olivia pretty much did what she'd always done. Look out for herself. That was Olivia all over. Perhaps if Hannah had exerted her authority a little more, she might have been more of a sister to her. The accident was hard on everyone.

Hannah had been taking her A levels when it happened. Olivia was fifteen and in her final year at high school. Hannah had plans to move to Manchester or Birmingham, maybe even London if she was brave enough and found the right job, to pursue a career. She knew she wanted to get out of Somerley and spread her wings wide and far, see more of a bigger city. But she'd been called out of her lecture and met by two policemen who'd told her there had been a car accident.

Her parents had been coming home on the motorway when a lorry had veered into their lane and forced them off onto the hard shoulder and headfirst into a barrier. Their father hadn't survived, their mum was in a coma.

No one then had known the extent of Martha's injuries. It had been touch and go for the first few days on the intensive care unit. Then slowly Martha had come round. She had spinal complications, a broken pelvis and femur on her right side, and both ankles had been crushed. Further tests revealed she had severed a main nerve which rendered her unable to lift her right foot without dragging it. She would have trouble walking for the rest of her life. It meant everything changed in an instant.

Not only did the house need to be adapted, it had come down to the sisters to be carers. Compensation had taken years to come through and hadn't been as much as they'd expected.

The funeral for their father had taken place while Mum was still in hospital. She came out for a few hours on the day itself, but it had been down to Hannah to organise everything. She didn't have time to grieve for herself. What she'd lost, missed opportunities now that they couldn't leave their mum.

But things for Olivia didn't change that much. Hannah put it down to her age. She was a schoolgirl, getting used to what had happened. But she went out more and more, leaving Hannah to do the bulk of the work towards her mum's care, and then arguing when she should have been helping. Sometimes she realised that Olivia wasn't just being childish; she was being selfish.

And then something changed. Olivia had an argument

with Martha, which neither would tell Hannah about. But she could sense the unease building up. Then Olivia told them she'd got on a course at Manchester Metropolitan University and left, never coming home again.

Hannah always hoped that one day Olivia would write a letter, send an email, pick up the phone, or even knock on the door. She would still be welcome, no matter what. Family was important to her, especially now she was on her own. She didn't want to talk to dead people all the time.

CHAPTER 14

*D*oug gazed through the window out onto the back yard. It had been drizzling on and off all morning, giving the summer day a cooler feel. The weather over the past few weeks had been glorious so no one could really complain.

He glanced at his watch. After visiting Hannah last week, he'd wanted to check out the damp patch over the kitchen window before it got any worse and they charged him for it when he left. The guy from Regency Property Management was already an hour late, and this was the third appointment he'd made after twice having no one turn up. It riled him because he'd had to book time off. Doug detested unreliability.

There was a knock on the door at last. He put down his copy of the paperback he had borrowed from Hannah and went to answer it.

The youth standing on the pavement was barely out of his teens. He was lanky, with wavy dark hair that was in need of a wash and a comb through it. His uniform of black T-shirt with the company logo and black trousers looked as if they hadn't seen a washing machine in quite some time.

'Mr Barnett?' the lad sniffed, wiping his nose with the back of his hand. 'Sorry, hay fever at its worst. Mike Dentford. I'm here to look at the damp patch, for Regency Property Management.'

'You're really late,' Doug said as he showed him through in to the kitchen. 'I was about to give up on you.'

'Yeah, well, you know how these old biddies can chat when you get stuck with them.' He laughed. 'Last one insisted on making so many cups of tea. Before I start, can I use your bog?'

Somehow Doug managed to stop himself from answering back. The guy was a disgrace. He only hoped he knew what he was doing when it came to property maintenance.

Mike threw a thumb over his shoulder once he'd come out of the bathroom. 'Your boiler looks old. We're checking them all at the moment to see if they need replacing. I'll have a look while I'm here, shall I?'

'Be my guest.' Doug pointed to the ceiling over the sink. 'That's where the water is coming in.'

Mike looked up and nodded. 'Is your guttering okay?'

'I'm not sure.'

'Shall I have a look while I'm here?'

'Yes!' Doug held in a sigh. He was supposed to be doing the job, not asking if he wanted him to do it.

They trouped out to the yard where Mike glanced up at the single storey extension at the back.

'That's your problem,' he said. 'Flat roof. It'll be knackered.'

'And you can tell that without looking?'

Mike nodded. 'These properties are all the same. Been built so long ago that they're falling apart.' He did the classic rubbing of the chin.

'But you can fix it for me?'

'It will cost you.'

'*Me?*'

'I'm afraid so. According to your rental agreement, you have to pay the first one hundred pounds of any repair.'

'But that's absurd.' Doug was trying his best to stay civil but how many tenants were they conning like this? Would any of them know to look at the rent agreements they were signing to see that this wasn't part of the deal?

'Company policy. Which is why it's best if I look to see if you need a new boiler as well. You can get it done without paying any more then.'

'Do you have a copy of my agreement?'

Mike looked confused. 'No, sorry. Don't you have yours?'

'Not to hand. Do you have a blank one I can look at?'

Mike shook his head. 'There'll be some back at the office. I'll get them to post you one.'

Doug had a feeling he probably wouldn't bother.

'I'll leave you to whatever you need to do then,' he said. 'Shout me when you're done.'

'Sweet.'

Doug went upstairs and watched him from behind the curtains. After a five-minute conversation on his phone, Mike fetched a small stepladder from his van, and began poking around in the guttering. Once he'd cleared a few leaves, he got back down to ground level. His phone went off again, and he spent another couple of minutes talking about what he'd got up to the evening before.

Doug went back down to the kitchen. Mike hadn't as much as looked at the roof to see if there was a problem. Now he was peering inside the airing cupboard.

'This boiler is definitely on its way out, mate,' Mike said when Doug drew level. 'It's lucky it hasn't exploded.'

'Is it that bad?'

'Yep. It needs pulling out and replacing. Haven't you had any problems with it?'

'I've only just moved in.'

'Ah, okay.' Mike closed the airing cupboard door. 'Right, I'll be on my way then.'

'What about the roof?'

'I'll log a job for it when I get back to the office.'

'You're not doing anything now?' Doug frowned. 'I've taken the morning off work.'

'We don't do anything until we've got the proper tools for the job.'

'You don't bring them with you?'

'Of course not.' Mike laughed. 'I'm the maintenance officer. I see what needs doing, order in everything, and then get one of the workers to come back. Don't worry, we'll give you plenty of notice.'

'Any idea when it will be?'

'A few weeks, I reckon.'

'That's a long time.'

'Sorry, can't do it any quicker. We're so busy with work. Between you and me, the fella that owns this house, and others in this street, is a cowboy. I wouldn't trust him as far as I could throw him.'

Doug couldn't believe he was badmouthing someone so much to take the blame away from himself.

'Do you need me to sign anything?' he asked wearily.

'Not right now. We'll get the job done and then send you an invoice. Like I said you only need to pay the first hundred pounds.'

When Mike had gone, Doug shook his head in wonderment. This was a scam. There was nothing wrong with the roof; he'd checked it out as soon as he'd moved in. There was also nothing wrong with the boiler either. He'd just wanted to test Hannah's theory, that the property landlord wasn't doing a good job. She'd been right.

Someone was fleecing the residents of Hope Street out of their well-earned money. And he couldn't have that.

CHAPTER 15

The past fortnight had gone by quickly and so far, the hot water system had behaved itself. Hannah had bumped into Doug a few times at the community centre. They'd passed the time of day, chatting about the weather, the heatwave that was still giving. She liked that he made her smile.

She liked that she kept looking out for him too.

Doug had mentioned he was going to the Hope and Anchor that evening. She and Phoebe were going as well. Hannah was really looking forward to it.

So when her phone rang and her friend's name flashed up, she knew their plans were about to change.

'I hate to be the bearer of bad news, Han, but Twitface has cried off from picking Elliott up for the night so I have no one to look after him.'

'Oh, Phoebs.' Hannah sighed on her behalf. "Twitface" was Phoebe's name for Travis. He was erratic at the best of times, often cancelling at the last minute. Hannah had never really warmed to him, but Phoebe was desperate to let her children have access to their father after a painful divorce with her own parents had left her scarred.

'How's Elliott?' she asked.

'In his room trying not to cry. He's had his bag packed ready since last night. I could really kick Travis in the balls. He isn't the one who's left with an inconsolable child, thinking that his daddy doesn't love him.'

'Twitface indeed.' Hannah sympathised. 'So this means I'm coming across to keep you company?'

'No, you go to the pub.'

'It's no big deal. Really. I'd rather talk gossip and watch trashy TV with you.'

'We can do that any time, Han. It's Friday night. Go out and enjoy yourself. Have a large one for me.'

'I suppose.' There would always be a friendly face, someone she could sit with and not feel as if she was hanging on.

'You'll be fine.'

'Are you sure?' Hannah was still hesitant. It wasn't the same when she went without Phoebe.

'Yes, but you'd better tell me any gossip in the morning. Especially about Doug!'

'You old tittle-tattle, you.'

'Oh, don't give me that, you want to know everything too.'

'I do now.'

Phoebe giggled. 'Annie Merritt may be the eldest resident in the street but I'm the one who *needs* to know. It's my job to inform all my regulars.'

'It's your job to be nosy, more like.'

'Someone has to do it. Otherwise life would be bloody boring around here.'

Hannah had to agree with that. Although she wasn't sure that gossiping counted as a hobby.

She took a shower and then raced upstairs to get ready. After Doug found the envelope that her mum had left for her, she'd hummed and ahhed a lot about spending some of it on herself. She needed money to save for bills, but she desperately wanted something new to wear too. So she'd gone to Hedworth Shopping Centre and treated herself to a few new clothes in the summer sales. Coming back to Somerley, she'd bagged a gorgeous pair of strappy heels from Chandler's on the high street as well. Riley, who lived across the street from her, was the manager of the store and had given her a discount. Riley had moved in with her partner, Ethan, two years ago.

Hannah was looking forward to feeling bright, not dowdy as usual. Twenty minutes later, she was good to go. As she gave herself the once over in the wardrobe door mirror, she remembered how Olivia used to watch her getting ready to go to the pub before the accident.

Even after all this time, she still missed her. Hannah had tried to find her sister on several occasions, more recently when her mum had died. But it was hard after so long. She wasn't even sure if they still shared the same surname.

It had broken her heart when the Christmas cards had stopped. Mum had tried to console her, but she couldn't help thinking that something had happened. Olivia had never missed a year. But when there had been nothing last year as well, she'd had to realise that either her sister didn't want to keep in touch or there was some reason for not sending any more cards. The thought that she might have died was beyond her comprehension. That couldn't have happened.

She reached for her bag, popped her phone inside it and gave herself one last look in the mirror. Checking her teeth for lipstick, she pouted.

'Not bad, Lockley.' She twirled around to see all of herself. 'Not bad at all.'

~

*D*oug was meeting Robin and Dylan in the Hope and Anchor. He hadn't been out to a local pub in such a long time, and for a while wondered what to wear. Knowing Hannah would be there had thrown him into a spin. It seemed to matter more to him how he would look now.

Should he go casual in a T-shirt and jeans or wear trousers and a shirt? He wanted to make a good impression but not stick out in the crowd. In the end, he settled on dark jeans and a short-sleeved white shirt with a thin navy stripe.

He hadn't expected to be invited out that evening, nor had he planned on meeting so many friendly people since arriving in Somerley. He'd thought he'd be grabbing a take-away and watching some trashy film like he'd done the week before. Going out would be like a breath of fresh air.

He tried to remember the last time he and Alex had gone out for a pint but shook his head with regret when he couldn't recall. For some reason, he'd always been too busy with work. He supposed it was all part of having responsibil-ities, but when did having a night out with your brother become less important than everything else?

He thought about his mum for a moment as he stood up after fastening his laces. Would she be looking down on him now, urging him to take his time, be gentle on himself, ease back into work? He'd done a lot of manual labour these past two weeks, his body was aching, but he felt invigorated all the same. Even a weak heart needed help to become strong again.

Would she have approved of what he was doing? Of course, she would. Although he was taking it easy as advised by the consultant, it didn't sit well with him not to be in the thick of things. But he'd left a pressure cooker behind and knew the stress might kill him if he continued to work as he was.

Yet until now, he hadn't realised how much he'd missed the hands-on labour. Being in a large group of men again was fun too. The camaraderie and the banter had meant he'd never laughed so much in a long time. It had shocked him to see how much was missing from his life.

He'd enjoyed supervising too, especially working with Dylan. The lad had the makings of a gaffer himself. He was keen, eager to learn, and quick to adapt. He was always cracking jokes, but an avid hard worker too. Doug had told him to slow down a few times as he'd put him to shame. He was an asset to the company, something he had mentioned to Robin on the quiet.

It still took a lot of getting used to not knowing what was happening in Manchester. Then again, he hadn't realised until now how much of his time was spent sitting down, going to meeting after meeting.

He stepped out of the house onto the pavement and turned to lock the door. Two teenage girls were sitting on the benches at the end of the street, heads together looking at something on a mobile phone. A few doors down a man in his late twenties was washing his car, a woman the same age standing on the step holding a small baby.

As he drew level, Doug recognised them as the couple he had seen the weekend before sitting at the top of the street. He was tall with wavy blond hair and a crooked smile. She was blonde too, long hair in a ponytail, blue eyes, and a scattering of freckles. Doug reckoned she'd just about reach the man's shoulders.

'Evening,' the man said, stopping what he was doing. 'Great night, isn't it?'

'It is,' Doug replied.

'Are you settling in okay?'

'Yes, thanks. Everyone has been so welcoming.'

'I'm Emily,' the woman told him. 'And that's Sean.'

'Doug.'

'We know.' She smiled. 'Are you off to the pub?'

'Yes, just for a swift half.' He smiled back.

'I'll be along shortly,' Sean said. 'Our sitter has let us down but I'm coming regardless. My missus is a star.'

'That's because he's promised to buy me a pampering package at the hairdressers,' Emily explained.

Doug had no idea what a pampering package would be but replied with enthusiasm. 'Sounds like fun.' He then turned to Sean. 'I might see you later.'

'I'll buy you a pint to welcome you to the street.'

Doug nodded and continued on his way. There were front doors open all the way along as people tried to get cool. The night was still warm, full of vibrancy, so he decided to leave his nerves right where they were during the short distance left to walk. At least he wouldn't have far to go on his return.

CHAPTER 16

The pub was rowdy as he pushed the door and entered into the lively atmosphere. It was packed wall to wall with people. From what he could see of the decor, it was modern mixed in with traditional. Creams and beiges, the odd flash of orange and yellow. Circular tables and stools, rectangle tables with chairs. The bar along the back wall was three deep with customers.

He made his way through the crowd, seeing all ages as he scanned it. There were a few people he recognised from the street and the community centre. Then Robin spotted him and beckoned him over.

'What's your poison?' he greeted, patting him on the back.

'Let me get these.' Doug's hand was already retrieving his wallet.

Robin shook his head. 'You can get the next round in.'

'A pint of Carlsberg then, please.'

'Dawn, when you're ready?' Robin waved for the woman's attention. Then he took a gulp from his own pint. 'So, how's your first fortnight in Somerley been?'

'It's been… different,' Doug admitted. 'I think I've met

more people in two weeks here than during the past year altogether.'

It was true. Back at home, it was only ever small talk, shallow promises of catching up for a drink or having dinner somewhere. Here, it seemed to Doug, people kept to their word. Several had invited him along to the pub and every one of them had turned up. No one he knew in Manchester had made him feel this welcome.

Dylan was standing next to Robin, looking all grown up in a shirt and faded jeans. He was pleased to see him after enjoying his company at work.

As his pint was held out, Doug took it and raised it in the air.

'Cheers, everyone.'

They chatted amicably, the banter jovial, and it didn't take Doug long to relax. There was no one trying to impress or outdo each other, except in jest. It was all so chilled, he seemed to fit in here without trying.

He was on his second pint and roaring with laughter when he noticed Hannah coming in. She'd put a wave in her hair and was wearing a vampy red lipstick. Together they made her look...

Hot.

He waited for her to catch his eye. She smiled when she did and came over.

'Evening, gentleman,' she addressed them. 'How are you all this fine Friday evening?'

'Good and dandy.' Robin smiled.

'Can I get you a drink?' Doug offered, knocking back his own. 'It's my round – unless you're meeting someone?'

'No, I'm on my own. So, yes please,' Hannah nodded. 'I'll have a G&T. Need a hand?'

'Sure, thanks.'

Doug went to the bar, Hannah behind him. Pretty soon

she was off saying hello to people she knew. As she stood talking, he could see much more of her from here. A slinky red top, skinny jeans, and painted toenails peeping out from white strappy heels. Large hoop earrings and a thin silver chain around her neck finished off the outfit.

She really was beautiful, and yet either she didn't realise it or she didn't make a fuss about it. He watched as she had everyone listening to her every word, speaking animatedly about something.

Turning to him, she smiled, and then came over.

'Haven't you been served yet?'

'It seems a popular place.'

'You bet. Everyone loves the hope and grope.'

Doug looked on in confusion.

'When we were younger, if we could sneak in on the premise of having a soft drink, it was the only pick-up place around, so it was like snogging pass-the-parcel. Everyone ended up necking in any dark corners they could find.' Hannah raised her eyebrows. 'And the odd toilet cubicle. And then we'd spill outside into the tiny yard.'

'I'm liking the sound of that.'

'Doug, how rude!' she mocked. 'You just can't get away with it nowadays, unless it's New Year's Eve.'

He smirked.

'I like to try things out when I'm staying in different places. I'll meet you at cubicle three in half an hour.'

'I hope you mean in the ladies'? I'm going nowhere near the gents.'

His order ready, Doug passed Hannah her G&T, grabbed hold of the three pint glasses in a triangle, and made his way back to the group. After handing out the drinks, Hannah was still at his side. He turned slightly to chat to her.

'Do you come here often, love?' His tone was cheesy.

Hannah giggled. 'Yes, unless it's Friday Night Club.'

When Doug looked confused again, she explained. 'My friend Phoebe has two children and can't always find, or afford sitters, so I go across to her house. We have a great laugh, mostly moaning about men. How we can't live with them. How we can't live without them.'

Doug's face creased up again. Hannah burst out laughing.

'I'm teasing. And every so often you'll find me in here. It's the only place I feel comfortable walking into on my own, where I'll know someone I can join, rather than looking at four walls and talking to myself. Phoebe comes when she can, but her boy, Elliott, is at home this weekend. His father was supposed to be collecting him but cried off at the last moment.'

Doug's face crumpled a little as he thought of his divorce, hard on his children too. Then he gained his composure. 'Well, I'm glad to see you, anyway.' Again, he lifted his glass in the air. 'Here's to new friendships.'

'New friendships.' She smiled, clinking her glass against his. 'Do you feel settled in yet?'

'Like I've lived here all my life.'

'I told you.' She smiled. 'It's like having a welcome hug.'

'Isn't there anyone I need to steer clear of?'

'I don't think so. Apart from Harry of course.' Her eyes flicked over to an old man who was sitting at the table in the corner. Doug reckoned he must be late seventies, one of the brigade who wore blazers, shirt, and tie despite the high temperatures. He liked that though.

'He seems all right?'

'He's always coming home drunk and trying to get into the wrong house. He wakes you up banging on the door demanding to be let in.' She nodded her head in the direction of the woman sitting next to Harry. 'You should get Alma's telephone number so you can ring her in case it happens to you.'

'O-kayyy.' Doug pulled a face. 'So what—'

A man came up behind Hannah, his arm wrapping around her waist. He looked about her age, with a barely there crew cut and a ribbed white T-shirt stretched to bursting across a muscly torso.

Hannah turned round, a look of surprise on her face as he kissed her on the cheek.

'Colin!' she cried. 'I didn't know you were coming.'

'I can see that.' Colin glanced at Doug, almost making him feel like a naughty child. 'Thought I'd surprise you as I'm in the area.'

'Well, you have.' Hannah turned to Doug, clearly trying to hide her embarrassment. 'Colin, meet my new neighbour, Doug.'

The two men shook hands and then Colin rubbed his together.

'Get us a pint in, Hannah. I'm bursting for a piss.'

CHAPTER 17

*H*annah couldn't believe it when Colin turned up unannounced. She knew he'd only appeared in the pub because he had nothing better to do and was after a quick booty call. And he hadn't even complimented her, nor noticed she'd had a new outfit.

Annoyed that she'd been enjoying herself talking to Doug before he'd flounced in like an action hero, she silently fumed as the two men chatted by her side. Colin was making a big fuss about her being his woman when in essence she was nothing of the sort.

But she didn't want to make a scene. She couldn't tell Doug that Colin was just a friend because he was more than that and he'd be hurt. And she couldn't say why they were more than friends without inferring they were a couple.

Frustration seeped into her. Already she'd realised that she'd like to get to know Doug just as much as Colin.

And the thought of sleeping with Colin later, as that's what he'd expect, didn't exactly enamour her. Especially when Doug was now living right across the street. She wouldn't put it past Colin to make a song-and-dance about that fact, showing her off, which would be highly embarrass-ing, not to mention insensitive.

She was in a pickle, and that even depended on Doug actually *wanting* to spend time with her.

Finally, Colin moved away to speak to friends, leaving Hannah and Doug alone again.

'Sorry about that,' she said. 'He can be really embarrassing at times.'

'It's fine. I hadn't realised you were seeing someone.'

'Oh, I'm not. Me and Colin… well, we… we're a little more than friends every now and then.'

'You don't have to explain.'

But Hannah wanted to.

She wanted to say she was sad they couldn't continue what they'd started.

She wanted to say it had made her aware that they'd both like more from the evening.

She wanted to say it made her realise that she was coming out of her shell, having feelings she hadn't had for a long time. And certainly not with Colin.

But she said nothing, glad of the noise in the pub as their silence stretched out. Fury tore through her. Why did Colin have to come and spoil everything now?

When Colin rejoined them, Doug slipped to the bath-room. Colin tried to kiss her, and she pushed him away before anyone shouted, "Get a room".

'What's up?'

'Nothing.' Her tone was churlish, but he didn't catch it.

'You ready for the off yet?' He put a protective arm around her. Hannah checked the clock on the wall behind his head. It was just past eleven, but she didn't want to leave.

'Let's have another first. My shout.' She reached for her purse, but he stopped her.

'I fancy an early night.'

She held in a sigh. She could either hang around awkwardly or call time and get it over with. The good mood she'd come out with had evaporated, anyway.

She nodded. 'Okay.'

They said their goodnights and trundled down Hope Street. As Colin prattled on about the gig he'd done the previous evening, he didn't even notice she'd tuned out as soon as her feet hit the pavement.

Back at home, Colin flung himself onto the settee and switched on the TV. So much for a romantic interlude, she fumed, even if she'd wanted one.

She sat down next to him. Near to, he wasn't even that nice looking. His eyes were small and close together and his chin stuck out at a weird angle that she'd dismissed until now. There were hairs on his neck where he'd missed with the shaver, a few red spots where he'd caused a rash.

'What are we, you and me?' she asked.

'What do you mean?' He glanced at her before flicking through the channels once more.

'Well, are we more than just friends?'

'Of course we are.'

'But you turned up at the pub this evening without telling me you were home.'

'It was a surprise.'

'How did you know I'd be there?'

'I didn't. That's why it was a surprise for me too.' He rolled his eyes as if she'd said something stupid.

'That's beside the point. Why do you think it's okay not to ring, or send me a message? I haven't heard from you in two weeks. So, I ask again, where's this going?'

'*This* is going exactly where it always goes.' He placed a hand on her thigh, moving it upwards. 'The bedroom.'

'No.' She slapped it away. 'I'm going to bed – *alone.*'

'I've driven for two hours to see you. And I've got nowhere else to stay. I can't wake my mum up this late.'

She folded her arms.

He held up his hands in surrender. 'If you don't want to have sex, fine. Just let me crash on the sofa until you're in a better mood.'

Hannah knew she was too soft. But she wasn't in the state of mind for an argument.

'I'll get the spare duvet.' She stood up. 'You can stay here tonight but you and I *are* going to talk in the morning.'

'You're the boss,' he shouted after her as she stomped off.

Hannah cursed under her breath with every step she took. She walked across to the window in her bedroom. Then she froze. Across the road, Doug was on the pavement, making his way home. When he glanced up, she drew the curtains quickly, as if she hadn't seen him.

She flopped onto the bed with a sigh. Was she reading too much into things? Did Doug like her or was he just being friendly?

Either way, she couldn't be with Colin any more. It was as if her desire switch for him had been turned off. That part of her life was done and dusted.

She should have told him to leave. It hadn't been the same between them since her mum had died.

~

*D*oug hadn't wanted to stay in the pub after Hannah had left. Colin turning up had put a dampener on his evening too, so he'd said his goodbyes after finishing his drink. He'd been having such a good evening getting to know Hannah better and now it was all over.

As the light caught his eye when he drew level with his

front door, Doug looked up at Hannah's window. Then he wished he hadn't as he saw her closing the curtains. Images of her and Colin invaded his head. Him pushing her down onto the bed, removing her clothes slowly, pressing himself into her.

Where he wanted to be.

He let himself into the house, went straight through to the kitchen and made toast. Afterwards he took himself to bed with a frustrated grumble. He tossed and turned for ages. All he could imagine was Hannah across the road having sex. *He* should be pulling her red top up over her head, shimmying down her skinny jeans. *He* should be running his hands over her body, kissing those warm lips, running his fingers through her hair, kissing her neck, her chest…

He groaned loudly. He must be tipsier than he'd realised for his thoughts to go off at such a tangent. He did have it bad.

He'd known Hannah Lockley less than a month and already he wanted all of her.

CHAPTER 18

he next morning Hannah was sitting up in bed on the phone to Phoebe.

'I tell you it was bizarre,' she said. 'Usually when I see Colin, I'm fine about him being my bit on the side.'

'I wouldn't be.' Phoebe's voice was laced with sarcasm.

'Don't interrupt me when I'm moaning. Anyway, I wasn't sure why but him turning up out of the blue and expecting me to drop everything for him made my blood boil.'

'And did you?'

'Did I what?'

'Drop everything for him.'

'No. That's what I'm trying to tell you. I didn't want to.'

'Oh.' A pause. 'Why not?'

'I don't know.' Hannah sighed. 'It felt too much like hard work, I suppose.'

'I can see why. But surely it doesn't take him long. He looks as romantic as a frog.'

'You're supposed to be on my side.'

'I am. But what I really want to know is did you see Doug?'

Hannah pushed off the duvet: it had been so hot last night she was surprised to see it still on the bed. 'I was having a lovely time chatting to him until Colin turned up.'

'Ooh, tell me more.'

'Nothing to say except I'm sure my restlessness last night was because I was dreaming of Doug for most of it. What am I going to do, Phoebs?'

'Dump Colin.'

'But what happens if I've read the signs wrong with Doug and he doesn't want to know?'

'I'd still dump Colin.'

She laughed. 'You really are no lover of my lover, that's for sure.'

'That *is* for sure. I just want you to be happy and he's no good for you. Go and tell him now before you can change your mind.'

'He might have left. I told him it was over last night.'

'He'll be there. He'll be waiting to use up his morning glory.'

'Ugh, stop it.'

In the background, Hannah heard a commotion at Phoebe's house. She pulled the phone away from her ear until Phoebe had finished shouting.

'What's up?' she asked.

'I have to go – Elliott can't find his trainers. Speak later, and don't forget, sack that loser. And then I want to hear all about it. Good luck.'

The call was disconnected before Hannah could reply. She threw her phone down on the bed. She was dreading the next few minutes. Seeing Doug walking home last night had made her think about what would have happened if she'd been with him. She wasn't sure she'd ever dreamed about Colin. Nor felt frissons of electricity when he'd stood close to her, talked to her, touched her arm. And that made her realise that she and Colin were a habit that needed breaking.

She pulled on leggings with her T-shirt, feeling the need to cover her bare legs. Colin was still asleep when she went downstairs. She walked past him and made herself a coffee. He hadn't stirred by the time she sat down across from him, so she shook him awake.

He sat up, his hair sticking up in tufts. 'What time is it?' He stretched his arms above his head.

'Time you were on your way,' she couldn't help snapping. 'I have to be at work soon.'

He screwed up his eyes as he yawned loudly.

'I meant what I said last night,' she said.

'About what?'

'About you and I being over.'

He was wide awake now. 'Oh.'

Silence followed.

'Are you sure?' He broke into it.

'Yes.'

'But we'll still be friends?'

She had to stop from laughing aloud. They had never really been friends. All they'd shared was sex.

'Of course,' she lied. 'We'll no doubt see each other around. Somerley isn't a place you can hide.'

Her attempt at a joke was wasted. Colin pulled back the duvet and put his feet on the floor. 'Suppose I'd better go then. I've obviously overstayed my welcome.'

'Oh, don't be like that.' Hannah sighed.

'What do you expect me to be like? You're breaking up with me. It's not exactly the happiest day of my life.'

'I'm sorry. But it's…'

'It's not you, it's me?' He glared at her.

'I wasn't going to say that.'

'No?'

'No.'

They sat in silence while he waited for her to say something. She shrugged, knowing there was no point in continuing. They'd only end up arguing and she didn't want to end things like that.

Colin slipped his feet into his Chelsea boots, pulled on his T-shirt and tucked it into his jeans. 'Can I at least use your bathroom before I go?'

'Of course.'

As he left the room, Hannah threw back her head and sunk into the chair with another sigh. The relationship was over so why did she feel so guilty? Mind, she hadn't been dumped since she was twenty-one and Dave Jarviss had told her he was fed up of taking second fiddle to her mum, and she'd told him to go away in no uncertain terms. There had been a "selfish bastard" in the conversation too.

A few minutes later, Colin came out of the bathroom and she let him out without him uttering another word.

'Bye then,' she said as he stepped out onto the pavement.

'You're really sure?' He made one last attempt.

She nodded.

He leaned forward and kissed her full on the lips, taking her by surprise. She tried not to squirm, wanting to give him his moment.

'I'll miss you,' he said afterwards. 'It was fun.'

Hannah pulled away from him, stung by his words. Fun? Is that all he could say? But then again, she didn't really want him to put up a fight.

She couldn't close the door quick enough. But she did glance across the street to see if a certain neighbour had seen her. Luckily, she couldn't see any signs of life at number thirty-five.

CHAPTER 19

'So what were you and the delightful Doug talking about last night?' Phoebe shouted over to Hannah once her lady in for a perm was under the dryer.

'Just general chit chat. It really was going great until Colin turned up.'

'I said he's a loser. I'm glad you told him to sling his hook at last.'

'I hope he doesn't think I'll change my mind.'

Phoebe gave her the evil eye.

'Don't worry, I have no intentions of getting back with him. It felt so wrong when he was at my house last night. It's never felt like that before.'

Phoebe reached for a bottle of shampoo from the shelf next to her. 'Were you dreaming of the delightful Doug instead then?'

Hannah, who had been folding towels, flapped one at her. 'Stop calling him that. You sound as if you're sixteen.'

'You're blushing as if you were.'

'I am not.' But Hannah could feel her skin burning. She

had enjoyed herself with Doug much more than with Colin last night. And now that Colin was out of the equation, well, maybe Doug might ask her out. He seemed interested enough at the beginning of the evening.

'Did you wear that new red top you bought?' Phoebe wanted to know.

Hannah nodded. 'For once I felt really nice.'

'I bet he was drooling over you. Actually, I bet everyone was drooling over you. Was Robin there?'

It was said oh-so-casually, but Hannah knew what Phoebe really wanted to know was if Robin was on his own. Robin had recently divorced his wife after finding out she'd been having an affair for several years with a friend of his. He was still bitter from her betrayal, but he'd been on the dating scene for about a year now. So far, they'd seen him with two women, neither of them lasting longer than a few weeks.

Hannah knew that Phoebe was still interested in him, no matter how much she kept denying it. It was clear to everyone that their torches still shone for each other. But neither of them seemed to want to move things forward. Which was a shame, Hannah thought, as they suited each other.

'Yes, Robin was there, with the lads from work.'

It was enough for Phoebe to know that he was on his own, yet she tried to hide her face as she blushed now. Hannah nudged her.

'What are you like? Just ask him out.'

'I don't want to go out with him,' Phoebe insisted. 'He's just a friend.'

'Yeah, right.'

Their conversation was interrupted when the front door opened. Tilly came in, followed by Elliott doing jerky movements and keeping his arms and legs straight.

'I am a robot. I am a robot,' he cried.

'You are an idiot, more like.' Tilly rolled her eyes.

'Morning, my darlings,' Phoebe grinned. 'Elliott, I hope you brought enough with you today to keep you entertained. I don't want a repeat performance of the "I'm bored" thing that happened last weekend, okay?'

'Well, I do get bored. It's not fair that I have to come to work with you. Why can't I stay at home? It isn't far and I am seven.'

'Which is way too young to be home alone.' He went to protest again but Phoebe pushed him towards the back room. 'Go on, spread out on the table and the day will go faster. Tilly, darling, do us a favour and make a round of drinks.'

Tilly had helped out for a while in the hairdressers now. She came in for a few hours after school on Fridays and all day on Saturdays.

'Let me help, Tils,' Hannah offered, giving both of her arms a quick squeeze as she followed behind her.

~

Tilly loved that Hannah didn't treat her like a slave. Not like her mum who thought she was a skivvy and a babysitter. Sometimes she wondered if she loved Hannah more than her own mum. Hannah had always been around. Tilly had called her auntie Hannah until it wasn't the cool thing to do.

Hannah had been there for them all when Tilly's dad left. It hadn't been a nice time at all. She remembered when Hannah had taken her to The Coffee Stop, which had been Lil's Pantry back then, bought her coffee and carrot cake and then they'd sat under the oak tree having a long chat about things.

Tilly had been eleven and had unburdened everything that afternoon: her worries that her dad wouldn't love her anymore; that she didn't want to split her time between her parents' homes because she might not be able to see her friends; how Elliott would react and how she didn't think she could be a good enough sister to him because she was so upset herself. She didn't have enough worry in her for him too.

Hannah had listened, not butted in like Mum would have done. She had let her have her say. She remembered crying lots of tears.

Tilly had spent a lot of time with Hannah's mum too. Martha had been like her gran in a way. She hardly ever saw Travis's parents now and her mum's mum had died when she was a baby. Her pops was okay, but not like Martha.

She'd been allowed to go to the funeral and Mum had bought her a new black coat. It wasn't the same without Martha. She had been fun, even though she couldn't do much. Tilly had loved to sit and read to her.

Hannah had suggested Tilly help out more with the clubs at the community centre. But as she worked at the hairdressers, it didn't give her much time. At least she got a good rate of pay. She was saving for a new laptop at the moment. She wanted something with more graphic designing capacity. Her old one was, well, old. She needed to update it.

'Are you daydreaming there, Tilly?' Hannah broke into her thoughts.

Tilly smiled shyly. 'We all have to dream about something, don't we?'

'Indeed we do.'

Tilly glanced at her brother who was outside in the small yard with his football.

'How's school these days?' Hannah flicked on the kettle

and busied herself getting out fresh cups while Tilly loaded the dishwasher with the ones they'd already used.

'It's fine,' she replied. Was this why Hannah had said she'd help? Was she trying to get information for her mum?

'Don't worry.' Hannah rested a hand on her arm. 'I'm not fishing for anything. I just wondered, that's all. When I was your age, I hated school with a passion. In fact, both me and your mum did.'

'You wouldn't think so by the way Mum keeps going on about how lucky I am to get an education.'

'Well, she's right there.' Hannah nodded. 'Which is why you have to make the most of it. Having said that, you don't often realise that until you've left and started to work. I'd love to see you going off to university and leaving Somerley. I wish I'd had the chance.'

'I don't want to leave Somerley.' Tilly shook her head. 'I'm either going to be a roaming cupcake maker, selling them from the back of a camper van, or I'm going to set up my own online shop and sell my artwork, and design cool stuff too. You can do that from anywhere. And I don't have to go to university. I want money in my pocket when I leave school, not tons of debt that'll weigh me down for years to come. And then I might not even get a job.'

Hannah put down the kettle, smiled at her, and gave her a hug.

'Never lose that ambition and feistiness,' she said. 'It will make you proud one day.'

Tilly hugged her back.

'So, what are your short-term plans to get you to that goal?' Hannah questioned.

'I need a new laptop. That's what I'm saving up for.'

'Great. Like you said, everyone has to dream.'

Tilly could sense Hannah getting sad again. Here she was

with the equivalent of two mums and Hannah had lost hers. She really was lucky.

Today she would try not to argue with Elliott, and tonight she'd offer to cook tea for her mum, give her a rest after a hard day's work. She would like that.

More importantly, Tilly would like that. And if it took her mind off school, well, that could only be a good thing.

CHAPTER 20

*D*oug had spent a pretty miserable Saturday wondering whether to go and see Alex but found he didn't want to leave the house. He couldn't stop thinking about Hannah, how well they'd been getting on until Colin had turned up. And what a prick he seemed. On Friday evening, Doug had spent most of the time listening to him boasting, trying not to clench his jaw too much. He seemed so arrogant, or maybe it was nerves. Or trying to ensure he realised that Hannah was his.

Hannah.

Just the thought of her had his heart racing. Now he wouldn't be able to ask her out, which had been his intention at the end of the evening.

Making his way across the road on Sunday morning, he knocked on Thelma's door. Hannah had told him to wait a few moments in case Thelma took longer than necessary to answer. But from what he'd seen of her, she seemed an active woman, not a frail one.

The door opened and he was met by a fragrance that instantly took him back to lazy days spent with his grandma.

Chanel No 5 had been her favourite scent, and he remembered burying his face in her shoulder on occasions and inhaling the smell from her clothes.

He'd seen Thelma a few times at the community centre since his arrival. She seemed the kind of person who would brighten up any dull party. There wasn't a strand of her silver-grey hair out of place, and her make-up was just enough to accentuate her age rather than work against it.

Again, it reminded him of his grandmother although she, to his knowledge, had never worn a heel, not even a slight one. And never nail varnish.

'Doug.' She smiled.

In the short time he'd known her, Thelma was always dressed immaculately. But he clocked her outfit of pale blue sweat suit and white trainers in wonderment.

'I'm not interrupting anything, am I?'

'Well, I was on my way for a run around the park.' She grinned wickedly. 'Of course not. Do come in.'

Doug stepped inside. This property was still laid out as the standard two-up, two down, the stairs through a doorway in the far room. There was a large oak dining table, two carver chairs at either end with a crocheted runner and a glass bowl full of potpourri. A standard lamp with a blue shade stood proud to the left of the chimney breast. On the far wall were landscapes photos.

He followed Thelma into the next room. This one had laminate flooring and bright floral wallpaper to give the room a country-cottage feel. A deep green two-seater on one wall, a cream armchair perpendicular to it, wrapped themselves around a coffee table, a large raffia rug on the floor. The curtains were heavy at the long window, swags and tails he hadn't seen in a long time.

But he wasn't interested in the decor. The room led on to the kitchen.

And Hannah.

He couldn't help but smile when he saw her bustling about by the sink, even though sad to keep the rest of his feelings hidden.

'Cup of coffee, Doug?' she offered.

'Please. One sugar—'

'Just a spot of milk. Coming right up.' The room was filled with the sound of running water.

'You need a couple of doors sorting out?' Doug asked Thelma, wanting to get cracking. He felt awkward in close proximity to Hannah now.

'Yes, please,' Thelma nodded. 'The back door is really stiff and also the bathroom door won't shut at all now. I'm terrified of someone walking in while I have my knickers around my ankles. Oh, the shame.'

'How can you be embarrassed?' Hannah joined in as she stood in the doorway. 'They're the best of M&S.'

Doug looked from one woman to the other. They were teasing him, he was sure.

'I don't mind seeing anyone in their knickers as long as they're clean,' he mocked. 'I've seen all sorts in my time.'

'Ooh,' Thelma, who was seated in the armchair now, cried. 'Tell me more. I bet you have a woman in every city, a fine-looking man like you.'

'I've had my moments.' Doug grimaced. 'That makes me sound terrible. I've always been a one-woman man.'

'Good to hear. Maybe you should take this one out on a date,' she whispered to him, 'to make her forget that loser she's just dumped.'

'Oh?'

'It's about time if you ask me,' Thelma went on. 'I never liked that Colin.'

'Are you talking about me, Thelma?' Hannah came into the room with two mugs and placed them down on the coffee table. Doug noticed she was the colour of a ripe tomato.

'No, just moaning about the weather.' Thelma had a twinkle in her eye.

'I'd better be going,' Hannah said. 'I have cleaning to do.'

No sooner had she left than Thelma started questioning him.

'Hannah says you're from Manchester, Doug. What made you come this way?'

'Oh, just helping out an old friend really, while I take a bit of time out. Did she mention I'd had a heart attack?'

Thelma nodded. 'You seem to have got over it though?'

'For now, yes. I needed an operation but to be honest, I've never felt this good for quite some time. I'd noticed I was slowing down, getting out of breath more, but I put it down to my age.' He smiled. 'It hasn't stopped you, if you don't mind me saying so.'

'Not a lot does.' She smiled. 'How long are you planning on staying?'

'About three months in total.'

'And you have family to go back to?'

Within a few minutes, Doug had the definite feeling he was being vetted, and that Hannah had already been filling Thelma in on his past. Still, it had been good to throw in a few curve balls. Like the fact that he was one of nine children and lived in a caravan until the age of ten, even though he knew she hadn't believed a word of it.

'What do you think of Hannah?'

Although the question didn't come out of nowhere, it sat expectantly in the room. Doug wondered if he'd inadvertently given his feelings away.

'She seems really nice,' he said nonchalantly.

'I don't mean in the platonic way.'

'Ah. The women in Hope Street aren't backwards about

coming forwards, are they?' He stopped. 'So, this thing with Colin, it's definitely over? She told you that?'

'Yes, she finished it yesterday. She should have done it a long time ago. He isn't good enough for our Hannah.'

As Thelma stared at him intently, he nodded his head towards the kitchen. 'I'll get on with fixing things for you.'

It took him just over an hour to sort out the two doors in question. When he joined Thelma again, she was waiting with a few notes in her hand.

'Thank you for doing that for me.' She held them out to him.

He brushed them away. 'First job is always on the house,' he answered, knowing full well he would never take money from her.

'There might not be another job that needs doing,' she protested, pushing the notes at him. Still, he declined.

Thelma sighed. 'One last chance.' When he didn't take the money, she put her hand down. 'You're a gentleman, Doug. Thank you.'

'That's what good neighbours are for.'

As Thelma let him out with a wave, Doug was almost tempted to kiss her on the cheek. That would get the neighbours talking, and him a reputation with the ladies.

She caught him sniggering to himself and pulled him up for it.

'What's so funny?'

'Nothing.' He smiled. 'Nothing at all. It's just... Hope Street. I like it here.'

'Good, because you'll need to get your strength up if Mr Malloy at number fifteen collars you for anything. He's a bit of a whiner at the best of times, an extreme moaner at the worst. He's a lot more trouble than us ladies.'

'Thanks for the heads-up.'

Doug was over at his door when Thelma shouted out to him.

'Bye, Doug. Call again, anytime.'

She gave him another wink, saucy old minx. He *was* beginning to like it here in Somerley. Which was both exciting and rather worrying.

CHAPTER 21

*H*annah hadn't caught up with Doug for a couple of days. Despite several unnecessary trips to the Somerley Store, and one for a general walk around the area, she hadn't bumped into him once. So she was pleased when she arrived home after work on Wednesday to spot him pulling up in his truck across the road.

'Hannah!'

She waved, thrilled to see him get out of his vehicle quickly, fighting with the seatbelt in his haste, and jogging across the cobbles to her.

'I wondered if you were free to join me for dinner tonight?' He pointed at his house. 'I mean a bite to eat at my place. I make a fair spag bol.'

'Will there be bread, with garlic in it?' Hannah wanted to know.

He smiled, understanding her reference to the catchphrase of a Northern comedian.

'There certainly will.'

'Then it's a yes from me.'

'Great.' He checked his watch. 'Half an hour do you?'

'As long as I have time to nip to the shop. I don't have a bottle of anything to bring.'

'That's okay. I can get one. Red or white?'

'White please. Although with red meat—'

'No, no, white it is. I have chocolate ice cream as well.' He felt his skin reddening, realising it sounded like the double entendre of the boiler.

'Right.' Hannah's eyes were twinkling, the corners of her mouth trying not to break out into a smile. 'Well, I'll see you in half an hour.'

Doug jogged back across the road before he embarrassed himself further. Then he waited for Hannah to close the door before racing along to the high street. Somerley Stores would be open; he needed ingredients. The cupboards were bare for an impromptu meal.

As he hunted out something edible, his stomach flipped at the thought of seeing Hannah again. He couldn't wait to have her all to himself. His thoughts immediately turned to dessert, and he laughed as he felt his skin reddening again. He was so out of practice.

'Are you okay there?' A voice came from behind him.

Doug turned to see a woman standing behind the counter. She was about the same age as him, with a slick, sharp auburn bob and a motherly figure.

'Ah, yes, thanks.'

'Well, if you need anything, do shout up. It's Doug, isn't it?'

He held back his smirk. 'Yes, I've moved into Hope Street.'

'I'm Ellen,' she introduced. 'I run the shop with my husband Gray. Pleased to meet you.'

'Likewise.' He took over his basket and she began to scan his items. Embarrassment flooded through him when he realised his meal could easily be for one, as if he didn't want to cook for himself. But there seemed no point in explaining he was eating with Hannah even if he'd wanted to. It would probably be all over the place come morning.

'Our Hannah is a lovely girl,' she said pointedly, as she handed him back his card.

You see?

'She is.' He popped his shopping into a bag as quickly as he could.

'She used to work in here, on Saturdays and some mornings when her mum was around. She always brought a bit of happiness to the place.'

Doug glanced around. 'You have it set up well.'

'Thanks.' Ellen beamed with pride. 'It might not be much to some but it's our little part of the world.'

'Whatever makes you happy.' Doug finished packing and picked up the bag. 'You must have worked incredibly hard, and long hours. That's no mean feat.'

'You're right. I often forget how good we've got it.'

'We're all guilty of that,' he agreed. 'I'll see you again.'

'Soon, I hope.'

He laughed to himself as he left. These people certainly made him re-evaluate his life. They worked so hard, long hours, often for such little pay. But they got an awful lot of satisfaction from the simpler things.

And Hannah had been right. Was nothing secret around here? He'd better watch what he said.

~

'*H*e's asked me over for something to eat,' Hannah told Phoebe as soon as she answered her phone. 'The handyman.'

'No! What are you wearing?'

'Nothing special.'

'Why not?'

'It isn't a date.'

'Of course not, dur.' Phoebe tutted. 'Of course it is. Your best knicker and bra set is a must. *You* might be dessert.'

She laughed. 'Might be tempted.'

'Wear your lilac dress. The one that shows off your boobs.'

'It does not show off my boobs.' She paused. 'Does it?'

'Yes, lucky cow.'

Phoebe had always been fairly flat-chested and hailed the day bras had begun to help her out. She was always going on about extra cleavage, enhancers, super padded, to name a few.

'Do you have any wine or chocolates I can IOU?' Even though Doug had told Hannah not to bring anything she couldn't go empty-handed. It seemed bad manners.

'I have both. Text me when you're ready and I'll meet you on the street.'

'Thanks. You're a lifesaver.'

Hannah dashed into the shower, excited about the evening. She *was* going on a date, with someone other than Colin. She paused. Actually, scrap that – she wasn't sure she could remember the last time she and Colin had gone anywhere.

But then again, she was only going across to Doug's home so technically did that count?

Actually, scrap that too – this wasn't a date.

Chastising herself for overthinking, she lathered herself up while singing at the top of her voice, praying Thelma wasn't sitting in the garden. She wasn't sure she'd appreciate the melody.

'I *think* I have a date, Mum,' she whispered into the empty room. 'He's really good-looking, with such perfect teeth. And very large hands, quite rough too.' She laughed self-consciously. 'But he's such a laugh and we bounce off once another. I... I know you would have liked him.'

A sadness dropped over her. It was things like this she missed sharing with her mum. Of course, she wouldn't tell her everything – that was only for Phoebe to know – but it would have been good to have a chat about it, to see her mum's face light up and wish her luck. Even to introduce them – that would have been wonderful.

She switched off the shower and put her happy face back on. Now was not the time to dwell.

'You look delicious,' Phoebe said when they met outside as planned. 'Definitely good enough to eat.'

'Oh, behave.' Hannah locked the door behind her.

Phoebe handed her a carrier bag. 'I found a box of choco-lates and a nice bottle of white.'

'You're a star.'

'I know.' She grinned.

Hannah took a deep breath. 'I'm so nervous.'

'Don't be, he's lovely. I want to hear all about it in the morning.'

'About what?'

Phoebe nudged her. 'Everything. I might even ring you later.'

'There might not be anything to tell.'

'There'd better be.'

'Well, in that case, I won't have time to answer the call.'

'I blooming hope so.' Phoebe gave Hannah a hug. 'Now, go get him, tiger.'

Hannah waved to her friend and then ran a hand down her dress. She let out a huge breath.

'You got this,' she whispered to herself before stepping across the cobbles.

CHAPTER 22

*D*oug had popped the food into the oven while taking a shower. He'd towelled himself dry as he checked it wasn't burning. He'd dressed quickly while setting the small foldaway table that had come in handy. Who said men can't multitask, he mused?

When he opened the front door to Hannah, her hair was down now and she was freshly made-up. It was hard to think she'd be forty shortly. Her dress had a fit-where-it-touched inviting look without being too clingy. She'd accessorised it with flat sandals and a huge smile.

Taken in by her, he tried not to stand open-mouthed with his tongue hanging out.

'Come on in,' he said at last. 'You look lovely.'

'Thank you.' She held up a carrier bag. 'I bring gifts.'

'You didn't have to do that.'

'I couldn't come without anything.'

He took them from her, breathing in the smell that was lingering as she passed. Her perfume was fruity with a hint of vanilla.

'But I have to make a confession,' he added.

'Oh?' Her tone was ominous.

'I don't have a stocked fridge and the only shop in quick walking distance was the Somerley Stores. There was no fresh mince and I wasn't going to con you into thinking I'd cooked a ready meal. So...'

'We're having beans on toast.' Hannah giggled.

'Not exactly. Frozen pizza and salad do you?'

'With garlic bread?' She raised her eyebrows.

He nodded.

'Perfect.'

He followed her through to the kitchen where he poured them each a glass of wine and urged her to sit.

'Dinner will be served in approximately two minutes.' He trickled the salad out of the box and onto a plate.

Hannah pulled out a chair and sat down. 'What exciting things have you been up to today?'

'We've been cleaning out a garden. Well, it was more like a jungle to be fair. We found a pathway underneath it all – and seven tennis balls, two wheels off an old bike and a deceased dog's favourite toy, which was a bit sad.'

'That *is* sad.' Hannah sighed. 'We had a dog, Bruno, but he died three years ago. With Mum how she was, it would have been too much work to get another one. I miss having a pet, though.'

'Yes, me too. The last one we had was twelve when she died. A cocker spaniel named Darcy. They're like a member of the family, aren't they? Such a terrible loss.'

With anyone else whose mum had died so recently, he wouldn't probably have said that. But Hannah knew he had lost his mum too, so he didn't think it was insensitive. He decided to go onto safer ground though.

'The woman – Marjorie, seventy-two with a useless son

and grandson, baker of delicious and rich chocolate cake – couldn't thank us enough.'

'It must be extremely satisfying teaching others your skills,' Hannah replied.

He laughed at her choice of words; found it sweet when she blushed.

'I meant work wise.'

'Of course.'

The oven timer gave out a ding. He took out the pizzas, slid them onto plates, and popped them on the table.

'Ta-da!'

Next was the garlic bread which he placed down in the middle, refilled their glasses with wine and lifted his for a toast.

'Here's to good food and – oh, well, here's to good health.'

'Good health.' Hannah tapped her glass to his. He drank in her beauty as he tasted the wine, glad he'd got her all to himself at last.

～

*H*annah checked the time to see it was nearly half past nine. So comfortable where she was sitting, she didn't want to get up from Doug's settee. She'd slipped off her shoes and put her feet up next to her side.

Doug was at the opposite end, legs outstretched underneath the coffee table. There had been chocolates with the wine, and ice cream before as promised. She felt stuffed to the brim, happy too.

For the last few nights she'd gone to bed hoping she hadn't made a mistake by finishing things with Colin. Now, she was in another man's home, feeling content after good chat, wine, and food. Somehow everything felt right.

She stretched her arms above her head. She'd been watching a police drama for the past half hour because Doug had fallen asleep and she hadn't wanted to wake him.

She stole a moment to study his features. His mouth hung open loosely. Grey flecks around his roots were coming through. Laughter lines, although relaxed at the moment, were more prominent than her own. His olive skin sported a five o'clock shadow.

She moved her eyes down towards his torso, his almost flat stomach, his… She glanced away, embarrassing herself as she felt the urge to reach a hand over towards him.

Wow, she hadn't felt this way with Colin – no wonder she'd wanted to finish things the other night. If it weren't for Doug, she might never have realised how complacent they'd become.

The ads came on and the TV suddenly went louder. Doug shifted in his sleep and woke up. He glanced around the room as if he didn't know where he was.

'Oh. Hi.'

'Hi.'

'I didn't snore, did I?'

'Like a very old dog with asthma.' She enjoyed seeing the self-conscious expression appearing on his face.

'Sorry.'

'Don't apologise. It's your house.' She put her feet down.

'I wasn't intending on falling asleep in your company though.' He glanced at his watch. 'Half past nine? What a lightweight. I have a body clock that wakes me early but shuts me down early as well.'

'I'm a morning person too. Whereas my friend Phoebe is a night owl.'

Doug stifled a yawn.

'I'd best be getting back across the road,' she said.

'Already? Would you like another drink before you leave? Especially after I fell asleep on you?'

She paused for a moment, unsure if that was talk for "I'd like you to stay longer," or "I'd like you to stay the night in my bed."

Her skin flushing as her thoughts went into overdrive, she shook her head. 'I think I'll head home.'

'I'll walk you to your door.'

She laughed. 'It's five metres away.'

'You never know who might be hanging around,' he joked.

'Yeah, it's really dangerous living in Somerley. Crime rate is shocking. Only last week someone stole a red rose from the bushes in the square.'

'Still, you can't be too certain.' He stood up, took her hand, and pulled her to her feet. She slipped on her shoes and he led her out. The air was still warm, the night just beginning, the sky a deep purple bruise.

They walked across the cobbles as slowly as they could.

'How is it still so warm?' she said. 'It must be hotter than going abroad at the moment. Not that I'd know.'

'Haven't you been overseas?'

His tone was one of shock, but she was used to it. People couldn't believe that she'd never been on a plane.

'There wasn't an opportunity after the accident. I'd been planning my first ever beach holiday with some girlfriends, but it had to be cancelled. Still, I'm not complaining when we have weather like this.'

Hannah could hear people laughing at the end of the street, but she couldn't make out who it was in the shadows. At least it had interrupted their awkward conversation.

Was it too late to mention she'd like that coffee, unafraid of what it might lead to?

But as Hannah reached her door, and Doug took hold of her hand again, she realised there would be another night for it. She could see the lust in his eyes reflected in her own. It gave her a good feeling. There seemed no need to rush things.

'I had a lovely time,' she said. 'Thank you.'

'It was my pleasure.' He chuckled. 'Although next time maybe we could go out to dinner properly?'

'So that you won't doze off?'

'Exactly.'

She smiled shyly. 'I'd like that.'

A wisp of hair fell across her face in the breeze and he moved it away with his hand. His face came towards her and he kissed her on the cheek.

Disappointed, she looked into his eyes daring him to kiss her properly, and as if he read her mind, his lips connected with hers. His kiss was tentative at first, inviting, exciting. Then it became more urgent and she felt her body responding of its own accord. She moulded herself to him, arms wrapped around him as he did the same. All those feelings she'd never thought she'd have again resurfaced, and she felt breathless when they pulled apart.

Their smiles were shy.

'I feel like I'm fifteen again.' He kissed her on the nose. 'I think this is going to be complicated, Ms Lockley.'

'This is *already* complicated, Mr Barnett.'

'So how about a proper dinner out next time?'

She nodded. 'That sounds divine.'

Inside the house, she slid down the back of the door and sat on the floor. It was good to arrive home feeling happy, and not so lonely.

For once, she relished the silence as she gathered together her thoughts. Remembering the feel of him on her lips. The touch of his skin against her own. The anticipation of more to come.

'I don't care if I've only just met him, Mum,' she whispered. 'Because whatever he's doing to me, I like it. I like it a lot.'

CHAPTER 23

*H*annah couldn't hide the dreamy look in her eye as she went into work the next morning. She knew Phoebe would be after details of the evening she'd spent with Doug but she wanted to pretend it hadn't been as special as it was. Trouble was, you couldn't do that with someone who'd known you since you were five years old.

'Spill,' Phoebe whispered loudly, pushing her into the back room while she mixed a hair colour for a client.

'I had a lovely time.' Hannah beamed, feeling a flush rise instantly to her cheeks as she remembered their kiss.

'Hannah Lockley, did you give out on your first date?'

'It wasn't a date.'

'Okay, okay.' Phoebe glared at her, eyebrows raised. 'But did you?'

'No, but I wish I had. I can't stop thinking about him.'

'Awwww.'

'It took me an age to fall asleep last night.'

'Can't blame it on your hormones this time. Oh, actually you can.'

'I felt as if I was a teenager again.' Hannah recalled how

her senses had been heightened. 'It reminded me of my first kiss with Daniel Morrison behind the garages as I fought off his octopus hands.'

'Daniel Morrison. I wonder what happened to him. I haven't seen him in years.'

'The last I knew he'd shacked up with Regan Reynolds.' Hannah wrinkled her nose. 'I didn't like her much.'

'I remember the boys did.' Phoebe paused. 'I wonder if any of those ridiculous rumours at school were true, come to think of it. You know, that certain girls did anything and everything on a first date.'

'I doubt it. Doug was a gentleman. I didn't have to fight him off. Shame, though.'

They shared a smile.

'So are you going to?' Phoebe asked.

'Do what?'

'You know.' She nudged her. 'Stick the sausage into the roll.'

Hannah laughed at her friend's turn of phrase. 'I wouldn't mind, actually.'

Phoebe nodded. 'He seems nice. But you don't know much about him.'

'I don't need to. He won't be here long. I could just have a good time until he leaves.'

'I guess you could, but knowing you, you won't.'

Hannah knew Phoebe was right. She wasn't the type of woman who would sleep around, despite being on her own for so long. That's why she'd put up with Colin for all those years.

Sensing her dilemma, Phoebe patted her on the arm. 'It won't hurt to have a fling. Lord knows we could both do with a bit of loving.'

'Shop. Anyone in?' A voice shouted through.

Phoebe rolled her eyes. 'Coming.'

. . .

*H*annah finished at midday and headed to the community centre to help with the luncheon club. Shepherd's pie would be on the menu and her job would be to dish it out to the over sixties.

Maureen Dawson was in her early seventies and another volunteer. She was already in the kitchen when Hannah arrived, along with her husband Frank, and two other women, Alma from number twenty-four and Irene from behind the square. Members of the luncheon club often took it in turns to help out with the preparation and serving, but it was Maureen and Frank who were in charge of the kitchen.

Maureen had been one of her mum's carers in the early days. Frank was the grandfather she'd never had, her own dying before she'd been born. The two of them bickered affectionally all the time.

'Hannah.' Frank gave her a gummy grin, his dentures long gone in the bin, much to Maureen's dismay. What little grey hair he had was swept back like Errol Flynn, his charm the same as the man himself. 'I'm glad you've come. You can stop this lot picking on me.'

There was a chorus of objections.

'It's a good job you know us, Hannah.' Maureen rolled her eyes. 'He'd have us sacked for working him too hard, if we were paid.'

'You *always* work me too hard,' Frank protested.

Maureen rapped him across the hand playfully with a tablespoon. She handed Hannah a box of cutlery and spoke in a whisper.

'Once the table is set, you can tell me all about your date with the handyman.'

'But how—?'

Maureen laughed, her bosom bouncing as she clutched a

hand to her chest. 'The look on your face. I was taking a wild guess that he would ask you out soon. No one has been gossiping. But I'm right, aren't I?'

'You might be.' Hannah would have tapped her nose if she were able.

She moved into the main room where the luncheon group met twice a week on Mondays and Thursdays. The club couldn't cater for anyone with special needs or with debilitating conditions such as dementia, but they did tackle loneliness; their camaraderie second to none.

The bunch they had there today were a lively group. Some of them had mild ailments; some seemed as fit as a fiddle. Hannah often marvelled about how much history and life experience was in the room, and never tired of listening to chatter about days gone by and "you young ones don't know you're born" insinuations. She always tried to get them talking. She hated thinking people felt left on the scrapheap because they were too old.

The club had also raised a lot of money doing various events throughout the year and were always first out delivering anything to the needy. Hannah was proud of them all. That's why she continued to volunteer for a few hours each week.

Half an hour later, she corralled everyone together to sit at the table. It was no mean feat. There were about twenty people in total, some moving a lot quicker than others.

She was chatting to Alf, who lived at the top of Hope Street. He'd been a regular for the past couple of years. A large man with a bald head full of liver spots, the hairiest of white eyebrows and a stout belly, his face always wore a smile.

Something caught her eye and she turned to the window. Doug was outside, halfway up a ladder. Her stomach did that childish flip of excitement that she was glad to see hadn't deserted her with age.

She opened the window, admiring the view greatly. 'Hey.' She smiled. 'What are you doing here?'

'Hi.' Doug came down to ground level. 'Dylan had a dentist appointment, so I thought I'd fix this flickering light. It's on my list to do and has been annoying me.' He raised his eyebrows. 'Although really, I'm after cadging lunch. I'm told you make a mean shepherd's pie.'

'You're not old enough to be part of the luncheon club,' she teased.

He winked. 'Save us a bit though?'

Hannah folded her arms. 'We'll have to see if there's enough to go around.'

'I'm joking but you can feed some of it to me, if you want?'

'Before you fall asleep in the chair like...' She turned to look at the group and pointed. 'Like Fred. It shows how excited he is to be here.'

Doug followed the direction of her finger and laughed. Fred's eyes were shut and his head kept lolling to one side.

'I'm surprised he can do that with the noise around him. Those women can't half natter at full volume.'

Hannah rolled her eyes but smiled at him all the same.

'How old is he?'

'Seventy-nine. He'll be eighty soon. There's a party being arranged for him, if you're still around.'

'Oh, I think I might be.'

'I have to warn you that they get very rowdy. Everyone brings a plate of food and a bottle of something. Sometimes it's like a bottle bank out in the car park after some of the parties. They sure can knock some drink back.'

'Sounds like my kind of party.'

'Ready when you are, Hannah,' Maureen shouted over. 'There's some for you, Doug if you're after a nibble.'

Peals of laughter and saucy comments filled the room.

'Calm down, you lot,' Hannah chided. She turned back to Doug and threw a thumb over her shoulder. 'I'd best be off to do my duties. No rest for the wicked.'

Once the food was dished out, Hannah couldn't help glancing at Doug surreptitiously. She'd wanted to ask him when they were next meeting, so she had a definite date to look forward to, but she didn't want to seem desperate. So instead she watched as he climbed the ladder and changed the light fitting. He didn't seem afraid to get his hands dirty, that was for sure. It was a shame he wasn't here for longer. She could set him up in business the amount of people round here that needed something doing to their property.

She turned on her heels quickly, tutting at herself. She was already setting down roots for him. She *had* got it bad.

One thing was certain, she didn't want him to leave until her itch had been scratched.

~

*D*oug had been pleased when Dylan told him about his dentist's appointment. He was hoping he might bump into Hannah. Because he couldn't stop thinking about her. It was wearing him down, that adolescent longing to kiss her again. If he had his way, he would take her in his arms right now, sweep her down almost to the floor, and press his lips to hers, long and hard until they were both breathless.

He stifled laughter, wishing he was lithe enough to do that. And he was supposed to be here to *mend* his heart not give it away. Still, he couldn't think of a better person to be the recipient of it.

Through the window, he'd watched as Hannah laughed and chatted to the club members, getting them seated at the large dining table, tucking paper napkins into the mens' shirts and laying them out on the ladies' laps. Everyone seemed to love Hannah. She had such a charm about her.

He looked away as she bent over to pick up a napkin she'd dropped, the longing to go over and wrap his arms around her waist becoming too much. If he wasn't careful, he'd need to adjust his trousers. What was that woman doing to him?

'Everything good, Doug?' Hannah popped her head through the window. 'Because you keep looking over this way as if you're expecting me to come out and hold the ladder for you.'

'Yes,' he cried, turning away quickly, embarrassed that she'd caught him daydreaming.

When he'd calmed down, he beckoned her outside.

'I was wondering if you're free tomorrow evening?' he said as she drew level with him.

'Sure.' Hannah beamed. 'Although I'll have to put off my knitting class until the following week.'

He grinned and took a sneaky grasp of her hand, lacing his fingers through hers. 'I was thinking about dinner, in a restaurant this time, cooked by someone else.'

'Dinner the other evening was cooked by someone else.'

'I meant fresh, not frozen.'

She giggled. 'That would be lovely.'

'Great, come across at… seven?'

'Perfect.'

He watched her move across the room again, aching to kiss her once more. But he would hold that thought. At least he had another date set up.

CHAPTER 24

'*I* have a date with Doug,' Hannah told Phoebe over the phone. 'We're going to Georgie's Bistro.'

'I know. Doug called to see me first for recommendations on where was the best place to go. It was me who suggested the venue.'

'Aw, thank you.' Hannah loved the restaurant. She and Phoebe went every few months if they could get a night together.

'So what are you wearing?'

'I don't know. Most things in my wardrobe are practical, loved but well-worn.' The furthest Hannah had been in a long time was to the pub and there was no need to dress up formally to go there. And then she didn't want to dress *too* formally.

She sighed and sat down on her bed. 'Everything seems… old. Do you want to pick me something?'

'Wait there.'

The phone went dead in her hand and she raced downstairs, opening the door for Phoebe. She was across in minutes, carrying a bag.

'Here, try this,' she said.

It was Phoebe's favourite dress. She'd worn it for a wedding and it had cost a fortune.

'I can't borrow that,' she protested.

'You can, and you will, Cinderella.' She grinned. 'It's not that posh, and I got it in the sale, anyway.'

Hannah removed her dressing gown and shimmied into it. It was a shift dress, to the knee, so simple and yet so elegant. A shade of baby pink with tiny budding flowers embroidered around the neckline the only detail needed. It would go lovely with her scarlet shoes. Funnily, all those heels she hadn't been able to refuse in the sales over the years were coming in handy now.

'How do I look?' She gave a twirl.

Phoebe clapped. 'Like a million dollars.'

'You're a star.' She gave her a grateful hug, squeezing her tight.

'Call me when you get home.' Phoebe did the universal sign for a phone against her ear.

'I might be busy.' Hannah laughed at her friend's expression as she shooed her out of the door. Then she ran upstairs to finish getting ready.

On the fifteen-minute drive into Hedworth, Hannah showed Doug all the local landmarks as they drove past. Finally there, he located a parking space off the main road and they went inside.

Georgie's Bistro was two-thirds full, chatter heard above the music playing low. Wedgwood blue tablecloths with white toppers at each table, navy blue upholstery on the chairs. Pale orange walls and large mirrors gave it a Mediterranean feel. Soft lighting had been switched on, brighter lamps in each corner.

'I love it in here,' Hannah said once they were seated. She put her menu flat after a few seconds.

'You've chosen already?'

'I know what I'm having. I always have the same thing.'

'Does it come with garlic bread?'

'Absolutely.'

Once their order had been taken, the waiter left them to it. Doug was a bundle of nerves now, sitting across from Hannah. He wanted everything to be perfect tonight. Hannah deserved to be pampered.

They chatted over their food and were soon reminiscing about childhood toys.

'I loved doing jigsaws when I was younger,' Hannah said, her eyes sparkling at the memory. 'My dad used to help me. He'd always buy me one with about 2,000 pieces in it and we'd set it up on the dining table. Mum would go ballistic when it was time for tea, but we were never made to move it. So for weeks we'd eat off our knees, and then we'd all sit around the table and do a bit each night until it was done.'

'Ah, thatched roofs and water scenes,' Doug said. 'I remember them well, although I can only actually recall finishing one. Too fiddly for me. And I was more interested in the girls back then.'

'This was before we found boys.' Hannah laughed. 'I was about nine and Olivia would have been six. Dad always bought us challenging images though. The worst one was of a large plate of beans. It took ages to complete it.' She smiled. 'Funnily enough, I'd just packed one away that I'd finished. I had the desire to complete one when me and Phoebe put the dining table back up after moving Mum's bed.'

'Was it sudden when she died?' he asked.

'Yes,' she replied. 'She was eating her breakfast. I was pottering about in the kitchen, chatting away, shouting through to her when I heard her choking. I rushed in to see her face reddening and her hands at her throat.' She paused for a moment. 'It turned out she'd had a stroke, and it had taken away her function to swallow. It was lucky I was there or else she'd have choked and died horrifically.'

'How awful.' Doug shook his head.

'She was admitted to hospital and put on a drip. Obviously, she couldn't eat or drink and a few days into her stay, they wanted to get solids into her through a tube but it wasn't successful.'

'So she starved?' Doug grimaced.

'Not exactly. They kept her on the drip, then she caught a chest infection. From that she got pneumonia and then slowly deteriorated. At least I was there when she passed.' Hannah gave a small smile. 'I remember the day before she died. Phoebe and I visited and we were sharing anecdotes from when we were kids and Mum had told us off. Mum never spoke, her eyes were closed but she kept chuckling. It's the last thing she did but I treasure that memory. My mum was in pain for most of her life, yet she never lost her sense of humour. She was a remarkable woman.'

'Hey, now, I didn't want to upset you.'

'You haven't.' Hannah took a sip from her wine. 'It does me good to get it out now and then. Bottled up, it makes me maudlin.'

'She sounded like an extraordinary woman.'

'She was, so brave. My dad died outright in the accident.'

'Oh no. I'm so sorry.'

Hannah shook her head to indicate she didn't mind. 'People don't understand why I never left home, like my sister.'

'You have a sister?' Doug was shocked.

'Kindof. When she was eighteen, she went to university, leaving me to deal with Mum.' Hannah looked away momentarily. 'It was so much easier when there were two of us, even though I had to drop out of college. I hardly had any time for myself after Olivia had gone. If you haven't been a carer, you'll never know how much you sacrifice. I never had time to live my life like she did.'

'That was unfair. I have a brother and we're very close. I'm not sure what I would've done if that had happened to me. How is she with you now?'

Hannah sighed. 'That's the thing. I haven't seen her since she left.'

'She never came home?'

'No.' Hannah twirled the stem of the glass in her fingers. 'At first I was worried and said we should check up on her but Mum said it was best we left her to come to us. But she never did. We got the odd card to let us know she's safe but there's been nothing for the past two years.'

'Wow. It makes me appreciate my brother all the more.'

'You're very close?'

Doug nodded. 'He was devastated when I had my heart attack. And he became such a nag afterwards. "Don't do that, be careful of this." Honestly, I was glad to get away.'

Hannah smiled.

Doug glanced at the clock behind them, the restaurant nearly empty. 'It's getting late.'

'Oh, I had thought we'd be going on to a nightclub?' she teased. 'I'm told Rembrandts will let old-timers like us in but we might feel a tad out of place.'

'I was thinking more along the lines of a coffee. Perhaps back in Hope Street?'

CHAPTER 25

$\mathcal{H}$annah didn't want the evening to end. She hadn't had so much fun in a long time. She and Doug had laughed so loud at one point that they'd had to apologise to a couple on a romantic interlude. Luckily, they'd smiled back, resulting in the two of them sniggering like two schoolchildren.

Considering she hadn't known him long, she felt so comfortable with him. It was great that he knew Robin before he arrived because at least that put her mind at rest that he wasn't an axe-wielding murderer under the guise of a handyman. If Robin could trust him, she could too.

It had been wonderful spending time together, just the two of them. Already she was hoping that he'd want to see her again. As they drove back towards Somerley, she prayed tonight wouldn't end like the last one. The anticipation of what was to come was driving her crazy, and she was certain Doug felt the same.

She'd even worn her best knickers just in case. Stuff big pants on nights like these. If they were going to have sex for the first time, she wanted to look her best. Mind, after all the food she'd eaten she'd probably look like a stuffed pig, anyway.

So his invitation for coffee was very welcome. She remembered his eyes staring at her from across the table, seeming to say the things she wanted to hear from his mouth. All she'd wanted to do was lean forward and kiss him.

Back in Hope Street they'd barely set foot on the pavement when they heard a commotion behind them. A man a few doors up was cursing loudly as he staggered around. He was trying to fit a key into a door.

'Oh, great,' Hannah said. 'That's Harry from number twenty-four, you remember? The old guy from the pub, with his long-suffering wife.'

'But that's number fourteen he's trying to get into.'

'Exactly. I won't be a moment.'

Hannah ran across the road. 'Harry,' she cried. 'You're at the wrong house again.'

'Is that you, young Olivia?'

'No, it's Hannah.' She took his arm. 'Why don't I get you home?'

'I am home, you silly girl.'

Hannah heard footsteps and turned to see Doug jogging across to her.

'Need a hand?' he offered.

'Mind your own business,' Harry slurred. 'Who are you, anyway?'

'No use introducing yourself. He won't remember anything in the morning,' Hannah explained.

'He's pissed as a fart.' Doug wafted a hand in front of his nose. 'Is this really a regular occurrence?'

She nodded. 'He wakes us up quite often.'

'Come on, Harry.' Doug took him by his elbow. 'Let's get you home.'

'Take your hands off me, you lunatic.' Harry tried to shirk him off.

'Strong for an old boy, isn't he?'

'I heard that, you cheeky feck—'

'Nothing wrong with his hearing then.'

Together they managed to manoeuvre him towards the right house. Hannah knocked loudly on the door, but as they waited for it to be opened, the old man went limp in their arms.

'Are you all right, Harry?' she asked.

Harry muttered something and then projectile vomited. Doug was in the firing line. Huge bits of goo landed all over the bottom of his trousers and shoes as he stepped back, trying to avoid it.

Doug retched behind his hand. Hannah tried not to as the smell hit her.

'Oh, no, I'm so sorry,' Alma cried as she opened the door. 'Look at you, you old eejit. I can't leave you alone for one minute before you're rushing off out of the house. What a state you're in – again. Have you no shame?' She manhandled Harry into the house. 'Thanks, Hannah.' With another embarrassed apology, she closed the door.

Hannah and Doug stood on the pavement, the earlier anticipation dissipated in an instant.

'I think we'll have to defer that coffee for another evening,' Doug said.

Hannah grimaced. 'I think so.'

When they got to her door, Doug pecked her on the cheek. 'Not exactly the ending I'd planned, but I had a lovely time until now though.'

'Me too.'

Hannah watched him walk across the road, waving as he closed his door. Then she gave out a huge sigh. What an abrupt end to the evening. She'd really been looking forward to that coffee they'd talked about for so long.

'Great timing, Harry,' she muttered before going inside. She got out her phone and threw down her bag.

There was a message from Phoebe.

How did it go with the handyman?

She was about to text back when a message came in from Doug.

I had a lovely evening. Sorry it ended so abruptly.

I know. Me too. Thanks for dinner. It was lovely.

I had big plans for afterwards.

She sat down, a huge grin on her face. Dare she admit to him that she was sad they hadn't been fulfilled? She typed away, with a little bit of mystery.

Hold that thought.

I won't be able to control myself much longer.

She roared with laughter in the empty room.

Well, you'll just have to. Thanks to Harry.

Yeah, thanks, Harry.

They chatted a bit longer and then she put her phone down. It was late and she needed to get to bed. Phoebe would have to wait until the morning. From the sound of her message, she assumed she and Doug would be tucked up in bed together, anyway. It would be fun telling her otherwise. Or not so much, come to think of it.

Patience is a virtue, her mum used to say. As she switched off the light downstairs, she looked back into the room, imagining her mum sitting up in her bed. She would have wanted to know all about her evening, and Hannah would have enjoyed telling her. She would have laughed so much at Harry's antics.

Hannah prayed she'd never forget the sound of her voice.

'I wish you were here to share all this with me, Mum,' she said. 'Because I think I might be falling in love. And I think I quite like it.'

CHAPTER 26

*H*annah let herself into the house, her arms fit to burst with all the paraphernalia. She'd been over at Phoebe's house all evening after her friend had arranged a surprise get together with some of the women on the street. It was a pre-birthday treat before her fortieth the next day.

The evening had been so much fun, even if she was full of cake, and she'd quite enjoyed being pampered. There were early presents to open too. She ran a hand over the silver bracelet Phoebe had given her, tracing the fine detail of the belcher chain, and the charm in the shape of a heart. Tilly had given her chocolates from Elliott, who was with his father that weekend, and a funky journal from herself.

In the kitchen, she placed the cards and presents on the worktop before she dropped them. There were so many of them, she felt humbled people had made such an effort. And there was the party at the pub tomorrow too.

Covering a yawn with her hand, she frowned when there was a knock at the door. She wondered if she'd left something behind and someone had called on their way home to drop it off. Or maybe it was Doug come to see how she was.

She was still annoyed about Harry ruining the end of their evening in such a dramatic fashion.

She opened it with a huge grin on her face. But it was soon swapped with a look of surprise. Colin was standing there, holding a huge bunch of flowers in one hand and a bottle of champagne in the other.

'Colin! What are you—'

Without being invited, he stepped past her and went through to the living room. She followed him quickly, eyes widening when she saw him drop to the floor on one knee. What the hell was he doing?

Oh, no.

'I've been thinking about things since we split up and I – I can't stand being without you. This past fortnight has been torture. You're all I've thought about and I had to do something about it.'

No, no no. Please don't say he's going to...

'I'm nothing without you.' Colin put down the flowers and champagne and pulled a small velvet box from the pocket of his jeans. Flicking it open, he revealed a ring inside it. It was a gold band with a single small white stone. 'Hannah Lockley, will you marry me?'

Hannah's mouth opened and closed like a goldfish. What was he thinking, pulling a stunt like this?

'Hurry up and say something,' Colin cried. 'My knee is killing me. It'll seize up if I'm not careful.'

Hannah ignored the box and pulled him to standing, thankful they were alone. Imagine if he'd chosen to propose at her party.

She studied him for a moment. He didn't smell of drink so he hadn't done this on a whim. The flowers were a lovely touch and looked expensive and the ring, well. Even a cheap engagement ring wouldn't be that cheap. But marriage?

She took a deep breath.

'Colin,' she began.

'I know it's a bit sudden,' he exclaimed, pushing the ring at her again. 'But we've been together for so long now and I hadn't realised how much a part of my life you were until you were no longer there.'

'We hardly ever saw each other.'

'We can change that.'

'And you haven't been in touch since we split up.'

'I've been working.'

'Too busy to pick up a phone? And you'd never be home anyway.'

The words were out before she'd had time to think about them. She didn't need to reason with him. There was going to be no engagement.

'I'll get a proper job, settle down. We could even think about having some kids.'

'You have three already,' she taunted. 'You hardly ever see them so I don't think that would be a good idea.'

'Okay, that's no big deal. I thought you might like them. I'd be happy for it to be just you and me. Growing old and grey together.' He paused for dramatic effect. 'So, how about it?'

She put her hands to her head. 'You can't just barge into my house like this and expect me to say yes.'

The look of dejection as the smile dropped from his face made her gasp. With a creeping sense of horror, she realised he had thought *exactly* that.

'I love you, Hannah. Always have and always will. And neither of us is getting any younger.'

What?

He made it sound as if it were the last chance saloon. She sat down across from him.

'Colin. I—'

'We can have a trial,' he interrupted her. 'I'll move in for a month and we can see if it'll work.'

She shook her head. 'I don't want you to move in.'

'Okay, then we can do this the old-fashioned way. I can move in after we've got hitched. Although I'd want it to be quick then, a couple of months at the most.'

Hannah couldn't speak. What part of no didn't he understand? Did he really think she'd be happy getting married to him, living the same life on her own, just because he thought it was a good idea rather than losing her? And he wouldn't be satisfied, nor would he change his lifestyle. Besides why should she settle for less than she deserved?

She started to pity him then. He was a decent man, but he didn't set her heart on fire. And the way she felt right now about Doug, she knew that Colin couldn't be a part of her life moving forward. It wasn't fair.

'I don't want to marry you,' she said in a firm tone. 'I meant what I said. It's over.'

'But why?'

'Because we're not even a couple. We never have been.'

'We've been together for years.'

'For whenever you wanted a booty call.'

'That's not fair. It went both ways.'

She nodded in agreement. 'It was easy for us that way. Neither of us wanted to be tied down.'

'You used me.'

'You used me too.'

Colin paced the room.

'Sit down for a minute, will you?' she moaned. 'You're doing my head in.'

Colin paced again, then sat next to her. The silence grew uncomfortable as neither of them knew what to say.

'This is about him, isn't it?' He snapped then.

'Who?'

'The man across the street. I saw the way you looked at him in the pub.'

'I was only talking to him.' Hannah shook her head. 'And don't be ridiculous. This is about you and me. Doug happens to be a nice man who—'

'Pretty defensive, aren't you? You were all over him. It was a good job I turned up.'

'I was not. I—' Hannah stopped. He wasn't going to listen to her so there was no point arguing.

Colin snapped shut the jewellery box and clasped his hand around it.

'Keep the flowers. Happy birthday, by the way.' He marched out of the room without a second glance.

'Colin, wait!' The front door slammed behind him.

Hannah flopped back on the settee. She was *definitely* glad he didn't think to do that tomorrow at the party. Thankfully, she should be able to keep the episode to herself because he'd come so late at night. She wondered if he'd been sitting out in his car, waiting for her to come home. It was a good job she hadn't been with Doug, although a fight similar to Daniel Cleaver and Mark Darcy Bridget Jones style would have been hilarious.

Or maybe not. No, she didn't want anyone getting wind of that or else it would be all over Hope Street.

Although, she did have to tell one person.

'He did what?' She heard Phoebe gasp down the phone.

'Talk about being put on the spot. It was excruciating.'

'But I thought you'd finished things with him.'

'I did. He obviously thought I didn't mean it.'

'Well, when they say life begins at forty... a new man on the scene, a marriage proposal. What next?'

'Nothing, I hope.'

There was silence, then Phoebe bellowed with laughter.

'It's not funny.' But Hannah was laughing too. It could only happen to her.

'Oh, *Hannah*.' Phoebe caught her breath. 'Your life is a riot. Happy birthday, doll.'

CHAPTER 27

*H*annah woke up shortly before her alarm was due to go off. She yawned, opened her eyes, and promptly pulled the covers over her head.

Was she supposed to feel different today?

'I don't want to be forty, Mum. And it seems weird without you here to celebrate.'

She recalled some of her earlier birthdays. Her eighteenth had been good because it had been just before her parent's car accident. Her twenty-first had been awful because Olivia hadn't been there. When it came to her thirtieth, Hannah had thought she was having a quiet one until she'd turned up to meet Phoebe at the Hope and Anchor and found a surprise party had been arranged. That had been the start of the big birthday bashes.

Forty felt so old. If she'd asked her sixteen-year-old self what she wanted from her life, she would never have forecast this. She had no high-flying career, no husband or family – despite Colin's proposal last night.

Still, there was nothing she could do about the day, or her

age, so she might as well enjoy it. Her friends would make sure, anyway. And last night had been fun.

Her phone began to buzz seconds later as she lay in bed.

'Happy birthday to you!' Phoebe sang badly down the line. 'So how does it feel to be so old?'

'No better or worse than yesterday,' Hannah replied. 'At least the weather is good.'

'You'll have a great day. We have so much planned for you.'

'We?'

Last night, Tilly had given Hannah an agenda of what would be happening throughout her birthday. She had designed it on her computer, surrounding the A4 sheet of paper in cupcakes and hearts. So Hannah knew she'd be having bacon butties brought in at work first thing, that people would be dropping into the salon so there would be more cake. But what else did Phoebe mean?

Then she remembered the line at 11 a.m. that had been blank. When she'd questioned Tilly about it, she'd looked all coy and walked away.

'Wait and see,' Phoebe replied.

'You know I don't like surprises.'

'Like your party last night?'

'Because you're awesome, I can make an exception for that.'

'Or like your proposal?'

'I hope Tilly can't hear you.'

'Don't worry. She and Elliott are in bed. I still can't believe he asked you to marry him. What a knob.'

'Hey.'

'Oh, I didn't mean for proposing to you. I mean in general. Anyway, back to surprises.'

'Oh?'

Phoebe laughed and the line went dead.

Hannah sighed, then her eyes brimmed with tears. Whatever happened today, she knew her friends meant well. But this would be the first birthday there would be nobody from her family there to share it with. She'd given up on Olivia coming back a long time ago, even more since she'd been unable to tell her about Mum's death.

Would her sister even think of her today, on her birthday? She wished she could find out. It would be wonderful if she popped up unannounced at the party this evening, just like Colin had last night. That surprise she *would* welcome.

Again, she wondered about the letter her mum had left for her. Should she open it, now it was her birthday? Well, maybe tomorrow. She didn't want anything to spoil today.

A message pinged in from Doug.

Happy birthday old un. x

For some reason it made her giggle when she saw a kiss on the end of the message. It was something that she'd done automatically but she hadn't been expecting him to pick it up. Only women added kisses to the end of everything, didn't they?

She sent him a message back.

Very funny, but thanks! x

See you tonight. x

She grinned, wishing he would pop into the salon before that. She was hoping he would be her treat later too.

Arriving at work, she was welcomed by Phoebe and Tilly with a rapturous rendition of the birthday song again.

'I've purposely not booked anyone in for the first hour to give us time to celebrate,' Phoebe told her.

'Aww, you sweetie.' Hannah gave her a hug. 'Thank you so much for everything today, despite me not knowing about all you had planned.'

'Don't worry, you'll enjoy it all.'

After a quick coffee, an order of bacon butties was delivered but Hannah hardly had time to eat. There were people calling in every few minutes to wish her many happy returns. Thirty minutes after they'd opened, she already had over twenty cards and numerous gifts.

'I can't believe people have been so kind.' She smiled as she held up a Tote bag that Emily from number seven had bought her. 'I think I do like being forty after all.'

'Happy birthday, Hannah.' They'd only been open a few minutes when Thelma burst in. She was holding several balloons with 4-0 written on them and blowing a paper trumpet. 'Tilly, come and take these from me, please, darling. I feel as if I want to sneeze and I'm scared of going up in the air like Mary Poppins if I do.'

Tilly came over and unburdened Thelma of the balloons.

Hannah, who had been on the phone taking a booking, finished the call. Thelma thrust a gift bag at her.

'Only the best bubbles will do today.'

Hannah pulled out a bottle of champagne.

'Thelma, you shouldn't have.' Her face lit up. 'But thank you all the same.' She pointed to a table at the far end of the room that had been bought in especially. 'Have you seen the cake Tilly made for me? It's amazing.'

Tilly blushed as Thelma cooed over her creation. It was in the shape of a shoe box, two red stilettos on the top and Hannah's name iced across it.

'Tilly made it all by herself,' Phoebe shouted over.

Hannah could hear the pride in her voice.

'A super talented, miss,' she replied. 'I love it.'

'You should make all the big birthday bash cakes, Tilly,' Thelma said to her. She sat down in a chair next to Phoebe, who was teasing Bev from number twenty-three's hair into a French plait. 'You could get a good little sideline going there.'

'I'm going to study catering when I leave school,' Tilly told Thelma as she helped her into a gown.

'What a good idea.' Thelma winked at her through the mirror as Hannah took over. 'Now, just the usual for me, ladies. I don't want any old woman's rinse either. I know the trend is for dashes of pastel colours but for me, it's all about the grey.'

'You will never go out of fashion, Thelma,' Phoebe shouted. 'I think women should follow you.'

'Oh, get off with you.' Thelma waved her comment away but Hannah could see she was secretly pleased. She reached for her scissors.

'So how are things between you and the delightful Doug?' Thelma asked. 'I didn't want to mention anything last night. He's such a dish, isn't he?'

Hannah laughed at the saucy look on Thelma's face. 'He certainly is.'

'Are you meeting up with him again?'

'Perhaps.'

'Excellent.' Thelma tweaked Hannah's cheek as if she were a baby. 'I'm so happy for you.'

'Thelma, what are you like with your matchmaking?'

'When they're as easy on the eye as the handyman,' Phoebe joined in, 'I'd say she'd be a fool not to.'

'It's a good job I have you all to discourage me,' she said with sarcastic affection.

'Any time, my darling.' Thelma touched the tip of her nose and stared at Hannah. 'Maybe he'll be your birthday surprise.'

Hannah's laughter was as raucous as Phoebe's. 'Maybe he will.'

Thelma beckoned her closer.

'Whatever you do, don't throw love away,' she whispered. 'Grasp it while you have it and keep it close. And live your life with no regrets.'

Hannah frowned. There was more significance to that sentence, she was sure.

'What do you mean, Thelma?'

'Just that if I had my time over again, I know I wouldn't make the same mistakes.'

Hannah wondered if Thelma would ever open up to her about the secret that haunted her; why she'd come to Hope Street alone twenty years ago. She didn't think it was simply because Thelma was a lonely widow. There seemed much more to it than that.

When Thelma said nothing else, Hannah didn't press her. Thelma was only a neighbour, but she cared about her so much. She hoped one day she'd be able to share whatever it was that was burdening her.

Then again, surely everyone was entitled to have a secret or two. She certainly wasn't about to tell anyone about Colin's proposal.

CHAPTER 28

*H*annah was halfway through rinsing Ellen's hair when Doug came into the salon.

'Happy fortieth to my favourite birthday girl.' He strode over and dropped a kiss on her cheek.

"Oooh" rang out around the salon.

Doug's cheeks reddened in an instant. 'You're not one of those women who are offended about being called a girl, are you?'

'Not now I've reached the ripe old age of forty,' Hannah replied.

'Forty is the new twenty, apparently.' Doug nodded knowingly. 'I think fifty is supposed to be the new thirty but try telling my aching bones that in the mornings.' He held up a large pink and white striped gift bag. 'I've been told you can be spared for half an hour.'

'I'm in the middle of a rinse.'

'Don't mind me.' Ellen tried to look up at her as she sat with her head in the basin.

'Tilly's taking over, once she's ticked off your agenda.' Phoebe switched off the blow dryer for a moment. 'Cake for your birthday, I'm told.' She raised her eyebrows. 'Another double entendre, if you ask me.'

'Go on.' Tilly gently shoved Hannah out of the way.

No sooner had she dried her hands, Doug reached for one of them and pulled her out of the door.

'Later, ladies,' he shouted over his shoulder.

'Where are we going?' Hannah walked with him down the street, happy that his hand was still in hers.

'To the place that makes the best coffee in Somerley.'

Off the high street, a large square opened on to a row of properties, a church to its left and their only coffee shop situated near to its middle. The Coffee Stop was a special treat for the people in Somerley because they often forgot they had something so quirky on their doorstep. It sat around forty people and Hannah had never seen a time it was empty.

Inside, the decor was shades of lilac and cream. The counter was situated the length of the left wall, mirrored tiles behind it doubling the feeling of the space.

Two settees were arranged in an L-shape almost inside the large bay window. There were several people huddled around them this morning, a laptop on the coffee table as a woman gave a presentation.

Hannah chose one of only two empty tables and they sat down. Doug placed the bag on the spare chair beside him and picked up a menu.

'They do all sorts of coffee here,' Hannah told him. 'All the fancy stuff.'

'Yes, I know.'

'Ah. You've been before?'

He nodded. 'Which cake is your favourite?'

'Homemade carrot cake is a must for me today.' She smiled. 'Well, it is my birthday.'

'Hannah!' A woman with auburn curly hair came over to them. 'I hear it's your special day. Happy birthday.'

'Thanks, Chloe.' She pointed to Doug. 'Have you two met?'

'Yes, it's Doug, isn't it?'

'It sure is.' He smiled.

'How's Kate doing?' Chloe and Kate run The Coffee Stop. Hannah knew Kate was around six months pregnant, if she'd remembered correctly.

'She's *supposed* to be taking it easy.' Chloe shook her head. 'That's not in Kate's vocabulary. Still, little Denzil is doing well.'

'Denzil?'

'She's having a boy. That's my name for him because she and Will won't tell anyone their choice. Now, what can I get you?'

'A cappuccino for me, please,' Doug said.

'Me too please.' Hannah nodded.

'And I know your carrot cake is to die for.' Doug closed the menu with a bang. 'So two slices of that would be great too.'

'Coming up.' Chloe turned on her heels.

Doug placed his bag on the table. 'Pressie time,' he cried.

'You're like a child,' Hannah admonished, but even so pulled the bag towards her. She lifted a large but thin parcel out. She shook it, hearing it rattle. 'It sounds as if it's broken.' She looked a little worried until she realised by its shape what it could be. She ripped the paper away eagerly and grinned. 'A jigsaw.'

The picture was the skyline of New York.

'You said you wanted to visit the Big Apple one day, so I thought this would keep you going until you get there.'

She laughed. 'It will have to do for a long time. But thank you, that's very thoughtful.' She dived into the bag again. There was a card with a birthday badge on it, a box of chocolates, and a bottle of her favourite perfume.

'I asked Phoebe what you might like. I hope you don't mind.'

'Not at all, thank you.' Hannah beamed, feeling a little overwhelmed by the day already.

'There's one more.'

Hannah looked inside the bag to see a small, thin present she'd missed. She unwrapped it to find a blue hardback notepad. On the front in bright red lettering it said, "My Bucket List".

'It's just a bit of fun, really,' Doug explained. 'But to make dreams come true, you have to write them down.' He opened the notepad for her. 'I've written something in it for you.'

NEW YORK NEXT YEAR

Hannah smiled. 'If I could choose my time,' she went all dreamy, 'I'd visit at Christmas. I would love to see the Christmas tree in Times Square.'

Doug leaned forward and reached for Hannah's hand. 'I know you've had a sad time lately, but I think maybe today should be declared a happy day. No crying, hmm?'

Hannah nodded, although feeling tears welling because of his words. 'Sounds good to me.' She only hoped she'd be able to contain her grief until tomorrow. Parties were a huge affair in Hope Street.

She gazed out of the window at the large oak tree that was the centre piece of the square. The seating around it was empty at the moment, but she and her mum had sat there for hours some summer days, she reading a book, Martha doing a crossword. Her mum loved watching the world go by, and Hannah would push her in the wheelchair, and they would have a morning out of the house, stopping at Somerley Stores for an ice cream on the way back. It was the simple things she missed.

She turned back to Doug.

'Mum used to love it in here,' she said quietly. 'I miss her more today than ever.'

'That's only natural.' He reached for her hand and gave it a squeeze. 'The first year of anniversary dates and special occasions is always the worst. And that's without a big birthday.'

Chloe returned with a tray. One slice of cake had a lit candle in it.

'For the birthday girl.' She smiled. 'On the house.'

Hannah thanked her before blowing the candle out. A round of applause rang around the café and she smiled, blushing too. She tucked into the cake and gave a satisfactory sigh.

'This is delicious,' Hannah said, trying not to let the tears brimming in her eyes fall. She *was* going to have fun today.

No matter how difficult that was going to be.

CHAPTER 29

'Y ou look amazing,' Phoebe cried as Hannah let her into the house.

'Why, thank you.' Hannah had decided on a plain black shift dress that she loved and always felt comfortable in, and red wedge sandals. She knew she'd be made to wear a garish badge, so nothing would clash with black. 'So do you.'

Phoebe did a twirl in her outfit of skinny white cropped jeans and an azure blue vest top.

'I hope it goes well tonight for you, Han.'

'Me too. I want everyone to enjoy themselves and have a laugh; to drink, eat, and be very merry. I'm really looking forward to chilling out in the pub.'

'What are you going to say if Colin turns up?' Phoebe was checking her mascara in her compact mirror, making sure it hadn't gone rogue.

'I'm hoping he doesn't.' Hannah shuddered. 'You're not to tell anyone about it, do you hear?'

'Of course not. I'd never ruin your big birthday. Speaking of which, let's get going.'

They went along the road together, chatting nineteen to the dozen.

'We must have walked this street to the pub a thousand times over the years. Phoebs.'

'And we would have been in the pub a lot more if we could have got served before we were eighteen. That's the trouble with everyone knowing everyone else.'

When they went inside the Hope and Anchor, a huge roar came from everyone.

'Happy birthday!'

Hannah was given more gifts and cards as she made her way through the room. It took her a full twenty minutes to get to the bar. By the side, there was a table of food set out, next to another huge cake. The HAPPY BIRTHDAY banner had been brought out and hung up, and a handmade "Hannah" tagged on underneath it. In the background, she could hear her favourite music playing.

Finally, she clapped eyes on the one person she wanted to see. Doug was politely pushing his way through to her.

'Happy birthday, again.' He kissed her on the cheek. 'I didn't want to come over as soon as you arrived. But I would like you to myself for some time this evening. You look amazing.'

Hannah smiled at him. Really, she didn't need anything else for her birthday. All she wanted was standing right in front of her.

'Thanks, everyone,' she cried, hating being the centre of attention but grateful that people had made an effort.

A few hours later, she was beginning to feel the effects of all the drinks she'd been bought. It was the downside of the big birthday bashes, everyone dropping off a glass of your favourite tipple at your table.

Hannah looked around the room with a big goofy grin. Most of Hope Street were here to celebrate with her. Over in the far corner, heads together, were Ethan and Riley from number thirty-nine, chatting to Emily and Sean. Alma and Harry were sitting in the opposite corner – at least he would get home to the right house tonight.

To her right, she spotted Alf sitting in his favourite seat by the fireplace. Laughter burst out from a group by the bar and she looked up to see Ellen and Gray who'd nipped in for the last hour. There were so many people she knew that she lost count.

Phoebe was sitting next to her, Doug across from them with Dylan and Robin. Thelma had been with them until a few minutes earlier when she'd left "the young ones" to it and headed home.

'There you go, Hannah.' A man stopped at her table and plonked down a G&T. 'What's it like to be forty?'

Hannah laughed with him, thanking him before he left. Then she turned to Phoebe.

'If one more person asks me what it's like to be forty, I'm going to scream. I'm twenty-four hours older than I was yesterday. Nothing has changed.'

Phoebe, who had drunk some of Hannah's drinks as she'd passed them over to her, was in Hannah's face, almost touching her nose. 'Stop staring at him,' she whispered loudly.

'Who?' Hannah looked around, trying to focus.

'Doug. You have it bad, my friend.'

'No, I don't.' Hannah shook her head but didn't take her eyes from Doug. 'Do I?'

Phoebe nodded.

'I've only had dinner with him.'

'Twice. And if it wasn't for Harry puking all over his shoes…' Phoebe nodded knowingly. She pulled Hannah into a hug, sloshing her drink over the table. 'Oops. I love you, Hannah Lockley.'

'I love you too, you numpty.'

'And don't worry, all your secrets are safe with me.'

'I *do* worry about that,' Hannah grinned. 'Only joking, Phoebs. You might be the biggest gossip on the street but you're also the best friend a forty-year-old woman could ever wish for.'

'Aww, thanks, Han.' Phoebe raised her glass. 'What's it like being forty?'

They burst out laughing as they clinked their glasses together. Afterwards they sat chatting. Hannah kept gazing at Doug as he was talking to Robin. But then her mind kept wandering and that feeling-sorry-for-yourself-bout-of-maudlin began to set in.

She peered at her watch. It was close to midnight. She threw back her drink and banged her glass down on the table.

'I'm going home,' she declared before standing up. 'I need my bed and a good night's sleep. I'm forty now, you know.'

'I'll come with you,' Doug offered, downing the last of his drink.

'I'm more than capable of walking home in a straight line.'

'Sure you are.' Doug held his hands up in mock surrender. 'But I'm done in too. I'm away to my bed.'

'Oooh.' Phoebe's laughter sounded dirtier than ever as she nudged Hannah. 'Whose bed are you going to be sleeping in, though?'

Doug smirked and stood up. 'Never you mind.'

Hannah felt herself swaying and held onto Doug's arm as he reached a hand out to her.

'Come on then, stud,' she said, and then in the manner of Meg Ryan in *Top Gun*, 'take me to bed or lose me forever.'

Phoebe waved them off as everyone laughed.

As soon as Hannah hit the fresh air, she almost felt twice as drunk. They had less than a minute to walk but she tottered on her heels, stepping off the pavement twice and onto the cobbles. Doug kept her upright on both occasions.

'I wish I could fly.' She wafted her arms up and down like wings. 'I'd be home in a flash.'

'You *are* home.' Doug stopped outside her door.

'Oh, so I am.' She laughed. 'Are you coming in?'

'If you'd like me to?'

'Only for coffee, you naughty boy.' She waggled a finger in his face. Then she grappled with her handbag, finally finding her door key.

Doug took it from her when she couldn't fit it into the lock. She laughed again and almost fell on the carpet when the door opened.

Once they were inside, she reached for Doug's hand. 'You are a very, very nice man.' Leaning forward she kissed him. As she tried to pull out his shirt, he pushed her hands away gently.

She frowned.

'It's late and you're very, very drunk,' he explained.

'So? It's my birthday.' She giggled. 'Thelma says you should be my birthday treat.' She kissed him again but once more he removed her hands when she tried to undo his belt. Pulling away, she glared at him.

'I'm not good enough for you, am I?' She wailed.

Doug frowned. 'Of course you are.'

'You don't want to sleep with me.'

'Hey, that's not fair.' He tilted her chin up so she had to look at him. 'I just think it would be better if we waited until we're both in a fit state to enjoy it.'

'I should have stuck with Colin. At least I'm good enough for him. He proposed to me, you know. He asked me to marry me last night.'

'What?'

'It doesn't change anything. I don't love him. I don't even

like him that much. He only wants me because he can't have me. And that's because I want you. But you.' She tried to point at him. 'You don't want me.'

'Oh, Hannah. You're so wrong. Of course I want you.'

Tears welled in her eyes, then rolled down her cheeks as she began to cry.

'Yeah, right.' She let go of him and walked away, bumping into the door frame. 'Ow.'

Doug reached for her hand but she pulled it away.

'Leave me alone. I don't want to be with you. I don't want to be with anyone. Because everyone leaves me eventually, anyway. And that hurts so much.' She let out a loud sob. 'I hate my mum for leaving me but I hate my life even more. I gave up everything for her and she left me all alone. I was the one who looked after her for all those years. I've missed out on SO much of my life that I'll never get back. Even my sister doesn't want to know me. We used to be so close and now I don't even know where she is.'

She took a deep breath. 'What's wrong with me? I like you, Doug. I like you a LOT. It's as if I've known you all my life. I feel so comfortable with you – we fit together. But you,' she pointed a finger at him almost taking out his eye, 'you don't want to be with me. Why doesn't *anyone* want to be with me?'

'Of *course* I want to be with you,' Doug insisted.

But she wasn't listening. She fell to the floor in a heap. Doug pulled her into his arms as she broke down.

'I'm just a nobody who's done nothing with my life.'

'That's not true.'

'But you don't want to be with me, do you?'

'Yes, but—'

'You see. You said but. You're making excuses up.'

'No, I'm not. You're too emotional and I'll feel as if I'm

taking advantage of you. I care about you too much to do that.'

'Do you love me, Doug?'

He sighed. 'Don't put me on the spot.'

'You didn't answer my question. Do you love me, Doug?'

'Yes, if it makes you go to sleep.'

Hannah curled up a finger and beckoned him to follow her. 'Come on, then. Let's go to bed.'

'I'm going home, Hannah.'

'No!' She burst into tears again. 'I don't want to be alone. Not on my birthday.'

'Okay, okay, I'll stay. But I'm sleeping on the settee.'

CHAPTER 30

*D*oug woke early the next morning. For a moment, he didn't recognise where he was, the tiny lilac flowers on the wall seeming unfamiliar. He turned his head to the right to see Hannah asleep in the armchair. He was on her settee, a duvet thrown over him although he couldn't remember covering himself.

Slowly he lifted a corner of it. He still had his clothes on. Thank goodness for that. He was only human with needs and he'd have hated himself for taking advantage of someone as drunk as Hannah. Even if she *had* wanted to take advantage of him.

It sounded sloppy even thinking about it but if they *were* to get together, he wanted it to be special. She was something to him already and everything needed to be perfect. Not that first time sex with someone new was ever perfect, but he wanted to smile at Hannah afterwards and not have her fall asleep halfway through. Or himself, come to think of it.

He thought back to the night before. Mention of Colin's proposal had shocked him. Why had Hannah kept it from him? Did she not want him to know? She'd told him she had said no.

'You awake?' Hannah said, interrupting his thoughts.

'Yes, good morning.'

'Good morning.'

'How's your head?'

'Rough.' She yawned loudly. 'Yours?'

'Not as bad as yours will be, that's for sure.' He sat up.

'Did we...' Hannah asked, eventually.

'I don't think so.'

'What do you mean?' Her voice went a little louder.

'I can't remember, but I'm thinking not.'

'Oh.'

'Can you remember?'

'No.'

'Well, that's that, then. I guess we'll never know.'

Hannah paused. 'We could pretend and think it was amazing?'

'We could, I suppose.' A smile played on his lips.

She threw a cushion at him. 'You *can* remember.'

'Of course I can. And no, we didn't do anything because I wouldn't take advantage of a drunken trollop.'

'Charming.' Another pause. 'Was I *that* drunk?'

'Yes.'

'Oh lordie.'

'Can you remember anything that happened?'

Hannah was quiet for a few seconds before pulling a face. 'I can remember being in the pub.'

'That's a good start. Anything else?' He grinned as he watched a blush appear.

'I was an idiot, wasn't I?'

'You were a tad emotional.'

'Sorry.'

'Don't apologise. Birthdays do that to you. Besides, I like

the fact that by the time I leave here this morning, Hope Street will think we've been bonking all night.'

'And hanging from the chandelier.' She stretched her arms above her head and sat forward.

'If you had a chandelier.'

'I have a wardrobe. We could say you were hanging on the wardrobe door.'

'It doesn't have quite the same ring to it.'

'I guess not.'

They smiled at each other.

'So, you reckon we'll be the talk of the street today?' Doug broke the silence.

'I do.' Hannah flopped back again. 'I would have felt better if we had at least done the deed.'

Doug laughed. He couldn't help it.

'What?'

'Nothing.' He pulled back the covers and swivelled his legs around. 'Do you mind if I take a shower?'

'Not at all.'

Doug let the water wash over his face. He had a thumping headache but even so, he had more of a problem now than ever. He was falling for Hannah. And it looked as if Hannah was falling for him. He wasn't certain; of course she hadn't said. But they were pussyfooting around the issue, trying to take things slowly. Trying to make things special, it seemed, just in case.

He needed to come clean with her. After her breakdown last night, it was as if she felt everyone had let her down.

Hannah. Hannah.

'And there you have it,' he muttered. That was the real reason he hadn't wanted to sleep with her. It was because if she found out the truth about him *afterwards* and wasn't happy about it, he was sure he wouldn't be able to walk away as easily.

Hannah was still curled in the chair when he went back into the living room.

'I made coffee.' She pointed to one for him. 'I'm surprised I managed it.'

He sat down on the settee again. 'Do you have plans for today?'

'I'm going to eat a whole box of chocolates before going to Phoebe's for lunch. Would you like to join us?'

'Yes, thanks, I would.'

He smiled at her, feeling his stomach tighten. He knew what else he'd like to do right now. He wanted to reach across and whip that dressing gown off and drag her to the floor but he had to resist.

They drank coffee and made small talk about the night before.

'I'll be off,' he said afterwards, taking both mugs through to the kitchen. 'I'll let myself out and come back in a couple of hours. If I go now, I can run across the cobbles and perhaps no one will see me.'

'Are you kidding?' Hannah laughed, then held on to her head as she winced. 'Phoebe will be standing in the window staring at my door, waiting for it to open.'

'Really?'

'No.'

'Oh, *very* funny.'

He was at the front door before she shouted through to him. 'But someone will spot you. You can never do anything in secrecy on Hope Street.'

Doug found himself peeping out to see who was around and then shook his head. He stepped out, closing the door behind him. Head held high he walked the few metres to his front door with a swagger. He hadn't felt this good in ages.

~

*H*annah didn't want to move from the chair. Not so much because of her hangover, but because she didn't want to stop thinking about Doug. Was it possible to fall in love so quickly? She had known him less than a month, yet she'd never felt like this with anyone else. Sure, she hadn't had many boyfriends when she was younger, but she knew a beating heart and a fluttering stomach, and that lurch you felt as if your heart was in your throat. The smile that came to your lips when you thought of someone when they weren't with you. The giddiness taking over you as soon as you saw them again.

Her phone rang. It was Phoebe.

'My head feels like it's split in two,' she told her.

'Mine too.'

'What time did you stay until?'

'Only half an hour after you. Robin came back to mine and we had a chip butty.'

Hannah snorted. 'Is that what you call it nowadays?'

'I keep telling you, we're just friends. Anyway, I'm calling about you, not me. Did Doug put you to bed last night?'

'You're changing the subject.'

'I'm not, I want to know. Put me out of my misery.'

'I don't have to tell you everything.'

Phoebe tutted. 'Of course not, but—'

'No, he didn't.'

'No?' A sigh. 'Why not this time?'

'Because I was so drunk I started crying.'

'You didn't.'

'And then I told him about Colin proposing.'

'Eek.'

'And then he spent the night on the settee while I passed out in the chair, I think.'

'You think?'

'Well, I must have gone upstairs at one point as he was covered in the spare duvet.'

Laughter down the phone.

'It's not funny. I really wanted everything to be perfect and I failed miserably.'

'Hannah Lockley, you really *are* falling for the man across the street.'

'No, I'm not.' She was lying but it was fun to wind Phoebe up too.

'How exciting. There hasn't been a wedding in Hope Street since – I'd have to think about it. I can't remember. I'll have to buy a hat.'

'You're marrying us off already?' She sighed dramatically. 'Why did you let me drink so much?'

'I didn't force the liquid down your throat.'

'I know but I didn't mean to get so drunk. I thought it might happen because it was my birthday.'

'Oh, Hannah, it will happen when it happens. Although this "will they, won't they" thing is quite frankly rather annoying. Are you still coming over for lunch?'

'Yes, but with an extra guest, if that's okay?'

'Of course.'

Finally, Hannah dragged herself into the shower.

'I'm going soft in my old age, Mum,' she said to her reflection in the mirror over the sink. 'And I am *never* getting drunk again.'

CHAPTER 31

*H*annah yawned. She couldn't believe it had been five days since her birthday. She wasn't sure she was looking forward to the next weekend after the last one. Anything she did would be a letdown after the birthday pampering.

It had been the longest birthday celebration ever. Even her drunken interlude, and the proposal by Colin, felt like small blips on the horizon. Riley Flynn had arranged another surprise for Tuesday evening, where she'd cooked dinner for her, Phoebe, Ellen, and Thelma. Hannah was lucky to have so many good friends close by to share it with. It had made it much more bearable.

She spotted the post lying on the mat and bent down to scoop it up. There were three envelopes for her. One was a credit from the gas company after she'd switched the account over to her own name. The other was a letter from the community nurse asking if she could visit her mum. She sighed, wondering why their records weren't up to date after so long.

The third was a pink envelope. It looked like a belated

birthday card. She'd been having them for the past few days, mostly hand delivered.

It was. Hearts and flowers and a large four-o in the middle. She opened the card.

Dear Hannah

Happy fortieth birthday to my big sister.

Lots of love

Olivia xx

Hannah looked at the envelope again to see the postmark. Edgbaston. She checked the back for an address but there was nothing. Neither was there anything on the card. A rush of emotion came over her. At least she knew her sister was still alive.

She stood it on the bookcase where it wouldn't stand out and remind her they hadn't seen each other for so long. Hannah had over fifty cards now. They were everywhere. She'd leave them up for a couple more days and then take them down. She was never one to save birthday cards but these she would.

She decided not to say anything to Phoebe straightaway. Her friend never had a good word to say about Olivia.

But all day she kept thinking about why her sister had sent the card after two years with no contact. And still she didn't know where she was living. It was so frustrating. It was as if Olivia wanted her to know she still thought about her but didn't want to see her. And it hurt, because she couldn't understand why.

Was this a sign that Hannah was ready to read the unopened letter from her mum? Was it time to open the envelope now? Was she strong enough to hear about the secret that had been kept from her?

She laughed to herself. Actually, it was more that she was curious enough now to open it. It was getting to her if she admitted it, the not knowing.

But what if it ruined everything?

～

*O*n Friday evening, she went across to Phoebe's as planned. Doug had gone home for a couple of days for some check-up appointments. He wouldn't be back until tomorrow afternoon. She'd missed him being around already. But she didn't want to talk about him straight away. Over coffee, she told Phoebe about Olivia's card.

'I didn't want to mention it at work,' she said. 'We were too busy to grab a chat.'

'Are you okay about it?' Phoebe shook her head in disgust.

'I think so.' Hannah flapped a hand in front of her face. 'I don't know what's going through her mind but at least she's okay.'

'She's an idiot, if you ask me.'

Hannah frowned. It was okay for her to think that but not for anyone to say, not even Phoebe.

'I'm sorry, Han, but she is. She should have come home, at least for the funeral.'

'Maybe she doesn't know Mum has died.'

'She should have kept in touch though.'

'I know but there's no point moaning about that now. It won't change anything. I just wish she'd pick up the phone, or at the very least let me know where she's living.'

'Edgbaston isn't far.'

'But I don't have an address. I'd gladly go to her. I really miss her at times.'

'I don't know why.'

Hannah didn't expect Phoebe to understand. They'd had this conversation several times over the years since Olivia had gone.

'I just want to know she's okay. Especially after losing

Mum.' She paused. 'It's made me think about opening the other letter she left for me. I'm worried about what it will say, yet I need to know.'

'Good on you.'

'But what happens if it's something terrible?'

'This is your mum we're talking about. The sweetest, most inoffensive woman I ever met. She didn't have a bad bone in her body.'

'I suppose.'

'So, what are you going to do?'

'I don't know. Do you think I should open it?'

Phoebe exhaled loudly. 'You've always been dead set against it so far.'

'You're right.' Hannah shook her head vehemently. 'I don't want to know.'

They sat quietly.

'What are you so afraid of?' Phoebe said after a moment.

'Everything changing once I've read it.'

'Surely it can't be that bad? What happens if it contains a cheque for a million pounds?' Phoebe rubbed her hands together.

'Do you really think we would still have been living in Hope Street for all this time if she was rich?'

'No one leaves Hope Street unless in a box, do they?'

'I guess not.' Hannah paused. 'Would you like to have a lot of money? I know it would be great to be able to pay the bills, decorate the house, and have nice things now and then. But I'm not sure I'd like everything handed to me on a plate. Where's the sense of purpose? Pride in earning it, working hard for it?'

'Well, I for one would much prefer to have money in the bank and *own* Hope Street Hair, rather than be the manager.'

'Really?' Hannah looked dubious.

'Of course! That's why I play the lottery every weekend. You have to be in it to win it.'

'I guess, but I think I'd keep *that* secret if I won.'

'You don't have any secrets.'

'I know, I'm so boring.' Hannah turned to stare at Phoebe.

'I stole ten pounds from my mum and spent it all on pick 'n' mix from the corner shop when I was nine.'

'I was with you then!' Hannah laughed at the memory. 'We were sick afterwards, I remember.'

'I was grounded for a week and never nicked another thing.'

'But that's not a *secret* secret, is it?'

Phoebe paused for thought. 'But sleeping with Stuart Matthews while he was married to Sheena Latimer was.'

Hannah caught her breath. 'You told me you never.'

'That's because I shouldn't have. I've always felt guilty about it.'

'You dirty cat.'

'But it was worth it.' Phoebe roared with laughter. 'Haven't you got *anything* hidden away?'

'You mean any illicit shags I'm ashamed of?' Hannah smirked. 'Every one of the times I've slept with Colin. It was such a bad habit but I suppose it's better than going without.'

'I suppose.'

Hannah stared at Phoebe. 'I'm going to fetch it. The letter. I've decided.'

Back at home, she ran upstairs and retrieved the envelope from her bedside cabinet. Then she sat on her bed with a thump. Was she strong enough to cope with the consequences if it was something she didn't like?

But this was a letter from her mum. How terrible could it be?

She took her phone from her pocket intending to ring

Phoebe, tell her she'd changed her mind. But impulse took over.

She ripped open the envelope.

Inside was a piece of plain white paper, folded over at the middle. Her courage deserting her, she shoved it back in the envelope and pushed it into the drawer. Then she sat on the bed for a whole five seconds, took it out again and ran back to Phoebe's house before she could change her mind.

She was out of breath as she flopped back onto the settee. Holding the envelope up, she grimaced.

'I'm not sure I have the courage to read it, so I brought it across with me.'

Phoebe grabbed their mugs. 'I'll fill us up while you do.'

Hannah gnawed at her bottom lip. Then, before she could change her mind again, she pulled out the letter.

CHAPTER 32

My child,

You won't ever read this letter because I will never send it. Besides, I don't have any address to send it to. If I did and you saw it, you might think worse of me than you already do and I can't stand that thought, so it's better that I don't know either way.

I am your birth mother.

It was such a long time ago when I held you in my arms, that I cried as I ran a hand over your head, tiny bits of dark brown hair almost there. You clasped onto my finger so tightly. I didn't want to let you go. But I had to.

I hope that you have never felt rejected because of it. I couldn't have looked after you, cared for you like I should. I was a very young girl.

My parents brought me up well, I was loved and cherished, and I know they thought they were doing the right thing, for me and for you.

Had I known how my life would have turned out, I would never have let you go. I would have cherished you as my own.

I regretted ever putting you up for adoption. I am truly sorry for that. But I do hope that you have a wonderful life. I hope you find peace and love with your new family.

Yours sincerely

Martha FitzJohn

Hannah's hand flew to her mouth.

'What's wrong?' Phoebe quickly put down fresh mugs of coffee and sat down next to her again. 'Hannah, don't cry.'

'I... I...' Hannah passed the letter to Phoebe while she tried to digest its contents. But she couldn't think straight at all. Instead she sat and waited, watching Phoebe's frown mirroring her own from a few minutes earlier.

'What does this mean?' she asked.

'I'm adopted, aren't I?'

'But you can't be. You look the image of your mum.'

Hannah couldn't dispute that. 'Do you think it could have been during my early years?'

'We've known each other since we were five. And wouldn't you have at least a few memories of living with someone else and then coming back to your mum? And where would Olivia fit into everything? Then that wouldn't mean you were adopted. That would mean... what would that mean?'

'That she had me as a young child and gave me up for adoption?' Hannah suggested. 'Then got me back and never told me?'

'So why tell you now?' Phoebe shook her head. 'It doesn't make sense. Could it have been Olivia?'

'Don't you think I would have remembered?'

'Possibly not. I suppose if she was only gone a little while, you'd be too young. Is there a birth certificate or anything? Photos?'

Hannah rechecked the envelope, knowing it was empty but praying for something to be there.

'No, there's just the letter, but Thelma has a box for me.'

Her shoulders dropped. 'She's away until tomorrow afternoon. I'll have to wait until she gets back.'

'Unless… who else has been in this street longer than us?'

'Annie Merritt.' They spoke in unison.

'She would know.' Phoebe's voice came out in an excited squeak.

'She would.'

Even so, Hannah wondered now if she really did want to find out. Everything was happening so quickly.

Blimey, they say life begins at forty but she wasn't expecting so much to change so dramatically as soon as the clock struck midnight.

CHAPTER 33

*D*oug sat up in bed and fluffed up the pillows. It was so hot, the fan in the bedroom whirring around over his pounding head. He'd stayed with Alex to catch up with the family, only popping into his house to see if everything was okay.

Alex had arranged a barbecue and even though Doug had caught up with a few people, there had been too much wine flowing in between the cooking of burgers.

He put his hand behind his head and sighed. It would have been even more fun if Hannah had been with him. Alex and their friends would love her warmth, her vitality, how she made him smile.

He thought back to the women he'd met since his split with Casey. There had been no one for the first year. Then he'd met divorcee Andrea and her three teenagers. The kids had been fine; it was Andrea who'd been the stroppy one. She was a first-class gold digger, moving in within a few months and then trying to get him to sell and find something bigger to suit them all. Even her eldest daughter had told him to end the relationship. He'd hung on way too long but finding her out on a date with one of his friends had been the excuse he'd needed to finish it.

Before that it had been Sasha. Doug cringed as he thought back to their tumultuous relationship. Well, hardly a relationship at eight weeks but she'd been half his age. He'd chosen her to get back at his wife when she told him she was marrying Nigel; regretted using her ever since. It served him right that she became possessive and clingy. It had taken him a while to get over that too.

He'd done a lot better with number three. Dana had lasted two years but in the end things had fizzled out of their natural accord. Dana was seven years younger than Doug and had eventually wanted to start a family. Doug had told her from the beginning of their relationship that he didn't want to have any more children and she was fine with it at first.

But much to his dismay, her biological clock had started to tick far louder than she'd wanted it to and she'd left him when he wouldn't change his mind. She was now married with twin boys, and even though he missed her at times, he knew they'd made the right decision for both of them.

He wondered now what would happen if Hannah wanted children. Forty was fairly old in new-mother territory but not unheard of nowadays. Lots of couples divorced and married new partners, children from those relationships appearing as a result.

He groaned loudly as he ran a hand over the space beside him, wishing she was there. He wanted her so badly. But he knew she was fragile and so needed to be patient. There was no point charging in with his size tens and ruining things. And really, this waiting around lark could be fun at times. It certainly upped the sexual tension between them.

Doug felt as if he'd known Hannah forever. Already he knew the shape of her face, the curve of her back when he'd drawn her in closer. Her hair was so soft as he'd bunched his fingers in it. Their first kiss had been over in seconds, but the memory had lingered on. He was already worrying about coming home when his time was up.

Home is where the heart is, or so they say. Maybe it was time to move on for good?

Who was he kidding? He had a house, a business, and a family here.

Maybe Hannah would come and live with him.

He laughed into the emptiness. He was pairing them off, already. But he found he quite liked thinking about it, regardless. He couldn't wait to get back to Hope Street to see her again.

He really did have it bad.

It was turning out to be the summer that kept on giving. The sun was blazing through the window marking the start of another fabulous day. He wondered what Hannah had planned. If he went back earlier, he might catch her in. He decided to text her, see if she fancied doing something together.

Hey you. Do you fancy lunch with an old fella? x

When she hadn't replied back within a few minutes, disappointment flooded through him. Had that ex of hers turned up and won her back? Was she poorly, because he'd very much like to look after her if so? Or was she feigning it because she'd changed her mind about him?

'Stop with the childishness,' he scolded himself.

'You talking to yourself in there?' A voice came from the landing, and the door opened.

'I'm going mad in my old age. You look – fresh.'

'Well, I didn't polish off as much as you.'

'Lightweight.'

'Loser.'

They grinned at each other. He had really missed Alex but

Doug hadn't mentioned Hannah to anyone here yet. For now, he wanted it to be secret. Maybe he'd then bring her home one day, unannounced.

Where was home exactly? Because right now, he wasn't quite sure where he belonged. Although he knew where his heart was leading him.

'Are you decent?' A woman's voice rang out.

'Yes.'

Vanda, his sister-in-law, popped her head around the door frame. 'Morning, would you like breakfast?'

'Yes please.'

'You joining us for lunch at the boathouse?' Alex asked.

Doug looked at his phone. Still, Hannah hadn't replied to his message. He'd been about to call her, see if she was okay but maybe it was a bit intrusive.

'Thanks, and then I'll be on my way.'

'It's good to see you looking so chilled, bro.' Alex slid an arm around Vanda's waist and drew her near.

'I agree,' she said. 'Whatever is happening in Hope Street, it's suiting you.'

Doug smiled. Yeah, he liked it too.

CHAPTER 34

*H*annah's head ached from too much coffee consumed the night before, and the restless sleep tossing and turning. She hoped her visit to Annie Merritt would throw some light on the letter situation. Her mum had never been dishonest before, never been anything but humble and kind and generous. She was trying not to let it sully her memory but was finding it hard.

Reading the letter had opened a Pandora's box and earlier memories had come flooding to her about her younger years. She could remember a Christmas when she was six, waking up to find a new dressing gown and pyjamas, a *Rupert Bear Annual* and a chocolate selection box at the bottom of the bed.

She could vaguely see herself falling from a tricycle but couldn't recall what age she would have been. And she could remember being a bridesmaid at a wedding, although she couldn't think whose. She could clearly recall her mum telling her she'd gone stomping down the aisle, arms folded refusing to carry the flowers and then sat on the floor stamping her feet. But had this been a lie?

Olivia must have been a baby then too.

Had she been adopted, or had Martha changed her mind and got her back? Were you even allowed to do that? And would her dad have known? If he did, then they'd both lived with the lie and not told her, nor Olivia.

Why hadn't their parents trusted either of them?

The more she thought about it, the more unbelievable it became. The letter couldn't be about her. And if it wasn't about Olivia, it could only mean one other thing.

~

*A*nnie Merritt had lived at number three for as long as Hannah could remember. She had been a widow for four years now, her husband George dying of stomach cancer. Hannah could still picture him in his wheelchair sitting on the pavement, a bag of skin and bones, his false teeth too big for his mouth and his eyes too large for their sockets.

They had brought up two sons on the street. Christopher was fifty-two now, married with two sons of his own and living in Birmingham. Andrew was sixty-one and had moved to Brighton with his partner after a civil marriage.

Annie was the Hope Street Oracle. She'd been living there so long that she knew everything about everyone. It always took half an hour to get past if you caught her sitting on a chair by her front door. By the time you left, she knew all there was to know. She wasn't a gossip though, she just loved to know what was going on.

Annie walked with a stick, her back arched forward. She arrived at the door in a puff of something smelling like talcum powder, her hair in curlers and a smile almost the size of her face.

'Hannah. What a lovely surprise.' She beckoned her in with a wave of her hand.

Hannah stepped inside the Aladdin's cave. Annie wasn't a hoarder as such but she'd collected many things over the years and was reluctant to let them go. Dolls, teapots, pottery thimbles, magazines and newspapers. The whole front of the house was stacked up with her paraphernalia. Then there were the bulk buys, always one for a bargain.

The house had a dusty smell to it but there was nothing dirty about it. Even though she struggled to get around, Annie was a clean person. Her step and windowsill were always being scrubbed. She just didn't like giving anything away.

'You're not busy, are you?' Hannah squeezed past a large box of toilet rolls.

'Me?' Annie laughed as she toddled into the back room, holding onto the wall as she went. 'Would you like a cup of tea?'

'Let me make it,' Hannah offered. 'You sit yourself down.'

A few minutes later, Hannah sat across from Annie on her settee. She leaned on the wooden arm rest and took a deep breath. Half of her wanted to walk out there and then, but the other half needed to understand the missing links.

'I wanted to ask you something,' she began but then faltered.

'What is it?' Annie's gnarled hands reached for her mug.

Hannah took a deep breath and began. 'You know everyone in the street, and all the comings and goings over the years, don't you?'

'I do indeed.' Annie's chest puffed up. 'I've a few tales I can tell.'

'Can you remember when I was born at all?'

'Let me have a think.' She held her chin in the air for a moment. 'It was the year after your mum and dad had moved in. Your mum had become pregnant more or less straight away.'

'Pregnant with me?' Hannah frowned.

'Of course. Who else would it be?' Annie laughed.

Hannah joined in but then her face crumpled.

'Whatever's the matter?'

Hannah shook her head, unable to explain to her yet. 'Can you remember anything about me as a baby?'

'You were a screamer, I can tell you that for nothing. George and I used to watch you lots of Friday nights when your dad would take your mum to the pub. It was their weekly treat. Martha was a real looker, had men falling at her feet. But she only had eyes for your dad.'

'And me as a baby?' Hannah encouraged, knowing if she didn't get her back on track, she'd be here for a very long time.

'Ah, yes, you were a bonnie lass.'

'So you've known me since I was born?'

'Yes, and Olivia.'

'And I – I never went missing and came back?'

'I don't understand.'

Hannah took the letter from her bag and handed it to Annie.

'My glasses, love.' Annie pointed. 'They're over there, on the sideboard.'

Hannah passed them to her and sat back in the settee while Annie read the letter. She watched her share the same expression that she and Phoebe had the night before.

'I still don't understand.' Annie shook her head and gave the letter back to Hannah. 'She never had another child. I don't know who this could be.'

'I thought I was adopted at first.'

'As far as I'm aware you're a thoroughbred, Lockley. This doesn't make sense. If this isn't you, then who is it?'

'I don't know.'

Hannah left Annie's house in a state of shock. After the sleepless night, it was a huge relief to find out it seemed she wasn't adopted, that she belonged to her mum and dad and had never been given away and returned. But it still left the mystery of who the letter was really about. Had she got a brother or another sister? She needed to talk to Thelma. There must be something in that box.

She went home and sent a text message to find out when she'd be back, under the pretence of asking her if she needed anything.

Thelma messaged back to say that she'd be home around midday. Not long to wait but every minute would be agony. She reached for the novel she was reading, but even Lisa Jewell couldn't help her forget. It wasn't long before she was in tears again.

'Why, Mum,' she sobbed. 'Why didn't you tell me?'

CHAPTER 35

*H*annah's phone went off. It was Phoebe.

'Hey, how are you feeling?'

'Okay, I suppose.'

'What did Annie say?'

'Nothing useful. She was reminiscing about me when I was a baby though. I was definitely living on the street. It isn't me who's adopted.'

'So it must be Olivia, right? Do you think she found out? Is that why she left?'

'I don't know. It's strange though. I can't think of a time when she wasn't around. I know I can't recall everything but I can remember when she was a baby. Something doesn't add up.'

'Do you still want to see what's in the box?'

'Yes. Thelma should be back around twelve.'

'Oh, Hannah, that's torture. I'm sorry I can't be with you. Typical Elliott with his go-karting.'

'It's fine. I need a bit of thinking time, anyway. It'll do me good to be on my own for a while.'

'Well, if you're sure?'

They said their goodbyes and Hannah fiddled with the jigsaw as she waited for Thelma. Just like in her life, she couldn't get many of the pieces to fit together.

As soon as she heard a car pull up, she was out of the front door.

'Hiya,' she greeted Thelma with a false smile as she got out of a taxi. 'Did you have a good time?'

'It was all right, I suppose.' Thelma took her overnight bag from the driver with a thank you. 'The hotel left a lot to be desired, though. I've a good mind to complain to the booking site for trade discrimination. The website promised a lively hotel, but I wasn't expecting the average age of the guests to be ninety-five. It was like the community-centre-does-glam.'

Tears welled in Hannah's eyes. She wiped at them quickly. But it was too late for Thelma not to have noticed them.

'Whatever is the matter, child?' Thelma bustled her into her house, fussed around her while she made tea and then sat down next to her on the settee. 'Now then, spit it out. It's nothing to do with Doug, is it?'

Hannah shook her head. 'You remember the letter I told you Mum left for me?'

'You've read it,' Thelma said, a look of understanding flashing across her face.

'Yes. Do you know what it said?'

'No.'

Hannah updated her, Thelma's hand resting on her forearm.

'It doesn't make sense to me,' she finished.

'I don't understand it either.' Thelma shook her head.

'If it can't be me, who else can it be?'

Thelma understood now. 'Is that why you were waiting for me? Do you want to see the box?'

Hannah nodded. 'I have to find out what's going on.'

Thelma pushed herself to her feet. 'It's upstairs. I won't be a moment.'

As Hannah waited for her to return, she stared out of the window. Like her own, it looked out onto a brick wall at the end of a narrow yard, with a gate into the entry behind them. But all Hannah could see now was the wall. She felt like she'd come up against it. There was no turning back, no moving forward.

Doubt began to creep in. She wasn't sure that she wanted to see what was in the box now. But she didn't know if she could live without finding out either.

'Here you are,' Thelma said, puffing as she took the last step down to join her again. This time, she sat on the armchair, placing the box next to Hannah.

It was a regular white cardboard shoe box. A small picture of a sandal on the side, size 3 told Hannah it might have been a pair of her shoes from her school days – or Olivia's come to think of it. There was a Sellotape seal around the lid.

Hannah picked it up and put it on her lap.

'Do you want to open it here?' Thelma asked.

Hannah shook her head. 'I'll take it home, if that's okay.'

'Of course. But I'm right here if you need me, any time, night or day.'

Hannah stood up. With the box under her arm, she said goodbye. But she'd only got as far as the door before turning back.

'I can't do it on my own.'

'What about Phoebe?' Thelma questioned.

'I'm not ready to share this yet. Can I open it here, with you?'

'Of course.'

Hannah found herself back in the spot she'd vacated a moment earlier. She put a nail underneath the corner of the tape and scraped at it. Then with an encouraging nod from Thelma, she pulled it all away. A deep breath and she removed the lid.

There were two envelopes again. With shaking hands, she opened the first. Inside were photographs of a baby boy. One was of a newborn wrapped in a hospital cot, his tiny hands in fists up next to his head. And in another there was a toddler filling a toy truck with bricks. Hannah ran a finger over his image, seeing herself as a child reflected back. He had her eyes, the same oval-shaped face.

'I – I,' she stumbled on her words again. 'I have a brother.'

Hannah passed Thelma the photos.

Thelma raised her eyebrows after studying the image. 'It seems as if you do.' She turned the first photo over but there was nothing written on the back. 'No clues to a name?'

'No. Oh, wait a minute.' Hannah remembered the other envelope and looked inside. There was a birth certificate. Baby FitzJohn. Male. FitzJohn was her mother's maiden name but there was a blank space next to the birth father. Hannah checked out the birth date. Nineteenth October 1970.

'She named him Christopher. He's ten years older than me.' She glanced at Thelma. 'My mum was pregnant at fifteen.'

'And there ends the mystery,' Thelma said kindly. 'I bet Martha was persuaded to have him adopted because she was too young to bring up a child on her own. She was also underage to have sex, which could be why there is no father's name recorded.'

Hannah's hand shot to her mouth. 'I still don't understand why she didn't tell me about him.'

'Too ashamed?' Thelma took a guess. 'Perhaps she thought you would judge her too.'

'I wouldn't.'

'I know that. Maybe what happened with Olivia leaving so suddenly hurt her too much. Perhaps she didn't want to inflict that sort of pain on him, or you.'

'Or Olivia found out?'

'It's possible, I suppose.'

'I wonder why Mum never wanted to look for him.'

'Maybe if she'd been well enough, she might have done. But she wasn't. She always insisted she was a burden to you and—'

'That's not true!'

'But it's how she felt.'

'Did she tell you that?'

'Yes, and being a burden meant that she couldn't ask you to help her, perhaps? You already did so much for her.'

'Did you know about this?' Hannah prayed her neighbour hadn't been keeping secrets from her too.

Thelma shook her head. 'It's as much a shock to you as it is to me.'

'There's another letter here.' Hannah picked it up. 'And a piece from a newspaper.'

Dear Hannah,

I hope one day you'll read this letter too, because I was never able to send the other one. But I also dread the moment that you do. You are my daughter and I am so proud of you and yet you might hate me when you find out what I did.

I couldn't have told you when I was alive. I couldn't bear to see your disappointment in me, not after Olivia found out and left home.

I'm so sorry for what I did but the longer I didn't tell you, the easier it was to forget about it. Now, well the choice is yours. You have a right to know, even now.

I'd like you to find your brother.

Love Mum x

Hannah opened out the newspaper clipping. It was dated two years ago. The headline read:

"Family Business going from strength to strength."

There was a large photo of several men and women, of all ages, standing in front of an entrance to a single-storey building. The business was called Parker Motors. She read the caption underneath. It said, "James Parker, 47, (centre) has taken over the reins of the business from his father, Derek (far right)."

She ran her finger over the image, quickly working out which one was James and pointed to it.

'That's him,' she squeaked. 'She wants me to find my brother.'

Then she burst into tears.

CHAPTER 36

*H*annah went back to her own house. Seeing the jigsaw spread out on the dining table, she lunged at it. With one swipe of her hand the pieces fell to the floor like confetti.

She dropped to her knees and stared at them. She felt as broken as the New York skyline she'd been creating, and the one person who she could talk to about it wasn't here anymore.

How could her mum not have told her about James? And why *couldn't* she tell her about him? She could understand the embarrassment thing, the shame her mum must have felt. But that was such a long time ago. Hannah had a right to know. She should have told her.

She picked up her house keys, knowing where she had to go.

At Somerley Cemetery, she stood in front of her mum's grave for a while, unable to speak at all. Then it all came blurting out and she dropped to her knees.

'Well, I read the letter, Mum. And then I had a look inside the box you gave to Thelma for me. I know your secret. I don't understand why you never told me. How could you be so dishonest?'

She let her tears fall until she was able to compose herself again.

'The thing is, it hurts. I mean, it really hurts. You didn't trust me enough to tell me. That's what I can't understand. And now I'm left with the pain and the anger because you deceived me.

'The fact that you're telling me like this is the coward's way. I thought your values and morals were better than that. Okay, Olivia left in a cloud because of it, but you and I were close. You should have trusted me with this. I feel pretty robbed at the moment.

'I gave you half of my life. I looked after you, cared for you, made sure you were washed, fed, and kept healthy. I did things for you as if you were my own child. In a way, you were. You were my responsibility. But you let me down.'

She stopped to take a breath, only now aware of people around her. A man a few rows down looked over but kept his distance, honouring her grief. She almost laughed aloud; shouted over to him, "It's not what it looks like. I've just found out my dead mother lied to me for years, and I have a brother I didn't know existed. What do you think about that?"

But instead she said nothing. Just like she'd done when Olivia had left. Just like she'd done when she'd been walked over by Colin.

She ran a hand through her hair, realising a storm was approaching and rain might fall soon. It would do her good. Get rid of all the tension in the air.

'Do you know what I want to do, Mum?' she went on. 'I want to hold my arms up to the sky and yell and shout to rid myself of all this anger festering inside me. I don't know what to do about James, but I feel he has a right to know that me and Olivia exist. It's the least I can do. I don't think I could live with the lie like you have, now I know about it.'

Worn out, she went to sit on a bench on the main walkway. She didn't want to leave yet. No sooner had she'd settled, she noticed a woman walking towards her, half-smiled when she recognised her. Renée visited a grave on the opposite side of the cemetery as often as she visited her mum.

Renée stopped in front of her. She reminded Hannah of Thelma, elegantly dressed, a small heel and a large handbag. Thick grey hair was tied back in a ponytail.

'Tell me to mind my own business if you want, but I've been watching you and I know something is wrong.'

Hannah shielded her eyes from the sun.

'Oh, I'm fine Renée, thanks, or at least I will be. Everything happens for a reason, doesn't it? I just haven't worked out the wherewithal yet.'

'Do you want to talk about it?'

Hannah shook her head.

'Would you like a sneaky tipple? I find a drop of whisky can work wonders.'

Hannah took the hip flask the woman offered to her and had a sip. She smiled as she passed it back.

'Thanks.'

'My Albert used to swear by a whisky tipple. "A measure a day and who cares about the doctor," he used to say. And since he's no longer with us, then it's only fair I uphold his tradition.'

'Were you married long?'

'Sixty-two years. We met when we were eighteen, had five children and eleven grandchildren.'

'Wow.' Hannah couldn't help herself.

'That's your mother you visit, isn't it?'

Hannah nodded.

'You seem angry today.'

'I am.'

'With your mum?'

She nodded.

'It's hard being a mother, you know. Sometimes you don't always make the right decisions but you're always thinking of your children. I turned one of my sons away because he was abusing his wife. I don't regret it for one moment. He's a nasty piece of work, but his wife is his ex now and those children of his are happier without him. That's all that matters.'

'Do you miss him?'

'I miss what he used to be. I don't know where the violence in his life came from. We've always been a happy family. Not much money to go around but we've done okay. I don't know if something happened in his life that he didn't tell us, but it's no excuse. He's living alone now. My eldest daughter visits him once in a while and I'm here if he needs me desperately. I'm not proud of what I did but it was for the best. Maybe your mum did something wrong in your eyes but I know she had the right intentions.'

'I don't know what to think.'

'Give it time. It *is* a healer, everyone is right when they say that.'

They sat quietly together for a while, watching the world go by. It was peaceful, the sounds of everyday life seeming to dim out. Hannah thought about what Renée had said long after she'd gone, and about what she herself had been thinking over and over.

She knew what she must do.

CHAPTER 37

*A*rriving home emotionally drained, Hannah couldn't face going into her house. She was about to cross the road to see if Phoebe was home when she heard a horn peep behind her. It was Doug.

Damn, she'd forgotten to reply to his text. How could she have done that? She wiped at her eyes. She was such a mess and couldn't get away from him without seeming rude either.

She waited for him to turn the truck around and park outside his home. But the smile on his lips faltered as soon as he stopped.

'What's happened?' He came across to her. 'Are you okay?'

Hannah managed to shake her head before her tears fell.

'It's… I—' She ran into his arms and began to sob.

Doug walked her across to his house. Inside, he sat her down on the settee and Hannah found herself telling him everything. She'd never usually confide in anyone but Phoebe, yet somehow it felt right.

Finally, she showed him the photo of James.

'I hope he's having a good life,' she said, wiping at her eyes.

'He seems as if he's been well taken care of,' Doug soothed. 'He's turned out to be a successful businessman.'

A pang of jealousy ripped through her as she thought what might have happened had he been around to help out with Martha. Maybe *she* would have been able to study, set up her own business if he'd been there to help take care of her. Instead, again, she'd got the raw end of the deal.

But then she felt awful after what her mum had been through. The pain she'd endured, the years of living within four walls, being unable to travel far. In the end, they had no transport because neither of them could drive. They didn't have enough money for a holiday. They couldn't even pay for a carer if Hannah wanted to go away. Both of them had been trapped.

But they'd been happy. Mum had made up for it in other ways. Until now, Hannah had never felt anything but special. And her mum was always telling her how proud she was of her, despite her *doing* nothing special.

'Why didn't she tell me about him?' she said, running a finger down James's image again.

'I guess we all have secrets.' Doug looked away momentarily.

'Now I'm going to wonder what it would be like to see him – see them, be part of a family, if he has a family. I might have a sister-in-law, nieces, and nephews.'

'You can easily find out.'

Realisation sunk in. She did have a way of contacting him. Parker Motors. The garage was in Scarborough, the address on the newspaper clipping. James would still be there after two years, surely? It seemed a big family concern.

'I suppose I could send him an email.' Hannah shook her head. 'No, a handwritten letter – or a card. That would be more personal.' She shook her head again. 'It would take a long time to write, and I'd have trouble finding the right words.' Then something else struck her. 'He might not know he was adopted.'

'Maybe not.' Doug paused. 'But would you like to meet him?'

'I don't know. Perhaps I should visit the garage first and scope it out?' Hannah paused. 'What do you think I should do?'

'It has to be your choice, but I'd say don't do anything rash. Sleep on it for a few days and then see how you feel.'

Hannah wiped at her eyes with a tissue. 'What happens if he doesn't want to know me? My sister didn't.'

'That's a bit different.'

'I suppose.' Hannah nodded in agreement. However, she wasn't even sure if she wanted to meet James. Feeling betrayed by her mum was one thing, but she didn't want it to happen twice.

*A*t work the next day, Hannah tried to put on a brave face as she tended to Ellen who had come in for her weekly blow dry. It didn't seem to be working though. Ellen kept asking her what was wrong and she had to fake an upset stomach.

'How's Rachel doing?' Hannah asked for want of something to say.

Ellen's only daughter was nineteen, a charismatic girl who was always wanting to do more with her life every time Hannah spoke to her. Rachel had started helping out in the shop with her parents as soon as she was able to stand up and had become a permanent fixture during weekends and holidays. But she hadn't wanted to work in the business once she'd left sixth form. Now, she was at university in Lancaster, reading law.

'She's doing fine, thanks.' Ellen sighed. 'The house isn't the same without her. It's so quiet. Not that we get to spend much time there around the shop hours. I do miss her though. But as we all know, there aren't many opportunities in Somerley so having a career means moving further afield.'

'Afraid so,' Hannah agreed. It was always something she wished she'd had the chance to do like her sister, but her mum's accident had put a stop to that.

Once she'd gone, Hannah went into the staff room. She grabbed a glass of water, drinking it greedily.

Phoebe came to find her, closing the door slightly to drown out the sound of the hairdryer that Annie was sitting under. 'You didn't have to come in today.'

'I know but I'd only be moping at home.'

'Have you decided what to do about the letter?' Phoebe's voice was low, even though their clients were out of hearing range.

'I might go to Scarborough,' she said. 'Maybe I could pretend I want to buy a car and then decide what to do. I… I want to see him first. I'm not sure why. Maybe to alleviate the shock.'

'It's wise, I suppose.'

Hannah sensed her doubt. 'You don't agree?'

'It's not that. What happens if you see him and then lose your nerve? Maybe it would be best to tell him you were coming?'

'But he might not want to see me at all then.'

'And would that bother you?'

Hannah paused. Would it trouble her? Although she knew about James now, she'd lived without him for forty years. But that was because he'd been her mum's secret.

'Yes,' she nodded. 'Yes, it would.'

Phoebe gave her a hug. 'Then you do what's best for you. You'll work it out.'

The salon door opened. 'Your next appointment is here,' Phoebe said, peering through the gap in the door. She made to leave and then turned back. 'Go home, Hannah. I'll sort Margaret out. Have some time to yourself.'

'I can't leave you in the lurch again.'

'People will understand.'

'I'm better not thinking about it, if I'm honest.'

'Well, if you're sure. In the meantime, why don't you see if Doug will take you to Scarborough?'

'It's a long way, do you think he would?'

'I know he would.'

Hannah stayed in the back room for a few more minutes until she felt able to see people again. Yes, she would speak to Doug, and when she saw James, she'd make her mind up what to say.

She owed that much to him.

And to herself.

CHAPTER 38

*P*hoebe sat eating her lunch in the back room. She couldn't help worrying about Hannah. She hated to see her friend hurting so much, especially when she felt so helpless. She and Hannah had always been there for each other. In fact, she couldn't think of a time when Hannah hadn't been in her life. Nor would she have wanted it any other way. She was the best friend anyone could wish for, and Phoebe was so lucky to be blessed with her daily presence. She brightened up her life beyond words.

Hannah had been there when she got married, when Tilly was born, and later Elliott. She'd helped her through her divorce from Travis and had been her rock for many more things. Yet when she needed help, Phoebe felt unable to offer enough in return.

She couldn't begin to understand how Hannah must be feeling; she was finding it hard to comprehend herself. Why would Martha not tell Hannah that she had a brother? It didn't make sense.

Phoebe had loved Martha as much as she had her own mum. Having Hannah as her friend she would see Martha often, watching over her on the odd occasion that Hannah had to go out. It was never a burden. Martha needed someone there to help her to get from the bathroom to her bed if necessary or make her a cup of tea.

Phoebe would sit with her and reminisce about Hope Street. It had always been fun to recall the goings on.

The royal street parties they'd set up for weddings.

The time when everyone was up in arms about the cobbles being removed. Martha had started a petition and in the end they'd been left as they were.

Then there was the year they thought they might lose the community centre. The council were going to knock it down and sell the land but the people of Somerley had caused a fuss. It would have been demolished if Robin hadn't stepped in to buy it. Now it was the hub of the village.

Phoebe wondered if Martha had felt as helpless as she did right now when it came to telling Hannah about James. Hannah had deserved better from both of them. She was always looking out for other people, and was a much better person than Phoebe. She knew she wouldn't have had the patience to do everything that Hannah did. And if that made her sound selfish, then that showed how selfless Hannah was.

Phoebe had often wished she were more like her friend, putting other people before herself. Listening instead of going in feet first to disagree with someone. But on the other hand, Hannah was a wonderful friend yet it could be her undoing at times as some people took advantage.

When Phoebe had first met Hannah, neither of them knew their friendship would last so long. Over the years, they'd grown closer and closer. When a house came up in Hope Street, Hannah had practically burst with excitement telling her all about it. Living on the street meant that Hannah knew of all the vacancies before anyone else. Within a week, Phoebe and Travis were living a few doors across from Hannah. And she'd loved it here ever since.

Even though she still had a soft spot for her ex, she could never go back to how it was with Travis. Sure, he melted her heart every time she saw him, but she hoped to meet someone special again one day. For now, it was her and the kids. And Hannah, her lovely surrogate sister. If James didn't want to know, then she most certainly did.

So what could she do to make Hannah smile again? She would send her some flowers, she decided, and think of something more personal to do for her too, cheer her up. And then she'd talk to a few people and see what they could come up with.

Of course, there had been the party but that seemed to have made things worse. Phoebe was forty herself next year and knew how she was looking forward to it and dreading it in equal measures.

Maybe it was like that for Hannah, feeling inadequate for not doing anything with her life, although Phoebe would dispute that entirely. Why did everyone strive to do better? Why couldn't people be satisfied with what they had, the here and now?

Hannah deserved to be happy though. She did so much for other people. Yes, it was time to do something for her. She'd put on her thinking cap.

$\approx$

*A*fter work, Hannah had a visit from Doug.

'I wanted to check how you're feeling today,' he said as he stood on the doorstep.

'I'm okay, thanks.' She smiled, grateful for his concern. 'It's not so bad now that it's sinking in, I suppose. Are you coming in? Would you like a coffee?'

'I'm just going to sort out some pipework for Emily and Sean.' He stepped inside anyway. 'Another time soon?'

She nodded, wishing she could have shared his company that evening. But it was nice that he was doing jobs for some of the neighbours.

'Have you thought what to do about James?' Doug asked. 'Are you going to see him?'

'I thought I might send a letter first. What do you think? I really can't make up my mind what's best.'

'Aren't you curious to see him?'

'Of course, but it's a long way to travel.'

'I could come with you,' he offered. 'Better still, I could drive you there.'

'Phoebe did say to see if you'd take me but it's quite a way.'

'I can have you there and back in no time.'

'Only if you let me pay for the petrol.'

'I'm not sure about that. Although I could think of a payment in kind I'd prefer at a later date.'

Hannah lowered her eyes shyly. They still hadn't slept together and she knew they wanted to, but there was too much in the way yet. They both knew it would happen soon, and she was so thankful he wasn't pushing her.

He tilted her chin up, waiting for her to look at him.

'I'd like to take you.'

She smiled. 'In that case, thank you.'

'Great. Although before I go, I need to do this.'

His lips found hers again. Hannah didn't want to let him go and she almost melted into him. It was a kiss that said "hang on, there's more to come but this isn't the right time for it. But I have to kiss you anyway."

She was fine with that.

'Wow, kissing in the doorway, Hannah Lockley.' Phoebe shouted across to them as she walked home on the opposite side of the road. She tutted in mock disgust. 'Do you have any idea how many people will know about this by the morning?'

'Do I look like I care?' Hannah shouted back, grinning at Doug when she heard Phoebe's laughter.

~

*N*ext door, Thelma ducked behind her curtain as Phoebe walked past. She didn't want anyone to know she was trying to hear what Doug was saying to Hannah. She couldn't see them from where she was standing, but her window was open and she was trying to catch any conversation that might come her way. Hannah deserved to be happy after going through so much in her life.

She clapped her hands with glee when she heard Hannah and Doug were kissing. It reminded Thelma of long kisses with Harold, all those years ago. He had been the only man she'd ever loved, given her heart and soul to. And yet, that had been all over after the affair.

She was always thinking about him, wondering where he was, getting out precious photos of the two of them. Many a time she'd thought of looking him up, seeing if she could find out where he was. He said he'd never forget her, but that had been so long ago. She didn't dare in case she found he was no longer alive.

No, she preferred to think he was miserable without her. Better than finding out the truth. She wasn't entirely happy though, although she got on with life, very much like Hannah. She too loved living on Hope Street.

Thelma habitually looked out, people waving to her as they passed. Everyone seemed content with their lot, yet she often wondered what was going on behind closed doors. It was such a happy place to live and yet who knew what really went on when everyone was getting on with their own lives in private.

She could tell you so much about the people in the Street. Take Sean and Emily's house. Before they'd moved in last summer, there had been two sets of residents living at number seven that she could remember. First there had been Mr and Mrs Winters who had both died long ago now, bless their souls. Then there was William and George Reynolds, elderly twin brothers who had hardly left the property at all.

William had died first, George three months later. The house had been in a terrible state of disrepair and it had taken Sean and Emily an age to put right after the basics had been replaced. But they'd made it into a loving home, full of warmth and colour. Little Marco coming along had been a joy. There hadn't been a baby on Hope Street for a few years.

At one end of the street was Annie Merritt. Thelma cast her mind back, trying to think how long she'd been there. When she'd moved in twenty years ago, Annie had shown her around and told her who was who.

At the other end was Alf Stonier. His wife had died when he was thirty-eight and he had never remarried, choosing to stay loyal. Thelma would join him sometimes in the Hope and Anchor, but not for long. Just the odd sherry tipple.

She glanced the other way, her eyes landing on number thirty-nine. Ethan had lived there for about eight years now, with his dog, Jimmy. More recently he'd moved his girlfriend in. Riley was the manager of Chandler's shoe shop in the high street.

Next to them were Phoebe and her children. Phoebe was doing such a good job of raising her two as a single parent. Elliott was a little darling, and Thelma always had time for talented Tilly. She was a lovely child to chat to.

And then there was Hannah next door. Thelma hoped she got to see her brother after finding out the way she had. It would be terrible if he didn't want to see her. Mind, she didn't think anyone wouldn't warm to Hannah. She was the salt of the earth, through and through.

It was lovely to see the budding romance between her and Doug, although Thelma was slightly worried that he might leave. It wasn't a definite in her opinion, not if you watched his eyes light up every time he saw Hannah. She hoped they could work things out, follow each other either one way or another. Selfishly, she would hate to see Hannah leave the street but equally she didn't want her to end up as lonely as she had, because her family had disowned her.

CHAPTER 39

*H*annah hauled her handbag and carrier bag into the back seat of Doug's truck and then settled into the passenger seat. According to Google Maps, it was eighty-two miles to Scarborough and would take just over two hours if they didn't hit any traffic hold-ups.

She'd been trying to keep her nerves at bay all morning but now they were about to leave, she felt all antsy again. Phoebe had sent her some beautiful flowers yesterday and she'd burst into tears at her thoughtfulness. Awash with emotions, she hadn't felt so sensitive in her life ever.

'Thank you for agreeing to take me,' she told Doug as she fastened her seatbelt. 'I really appreciate it.'

'Not at all. What do you have in the bag?'

'Provisions.'

'Provisions?' he parroted.

'A flask of hot water, two mugs, tea bags, coffee. A small carton of milk – semi-skimmed, hope that's okay? A few chocolate biscuits, two bananas. I only had one apple left, so you can have that. There's a bag of toffees too. I also have ham and cheese on brown bread.' She glanced at him.

Doug laughed. 'Ever heard of service stations? There are plenty on the way.'

'Full of overpriced food. I thought this might go some way towards the petrol that you won't let me pay for.'

'Did you pack the shovel in case it snows?'

She punched him playfully on the arm as he started the engine.

They were on the motorway within half an hour. Traffic was moving steadily in each lane and Radio Two was on air. Hannah had just won Doug on that morning's pop quiz. She was glad she had something to listen to, to slow her mind and ensure she didn't go into panic mode again.

'Oh, I love this song,' Hannah cried out as the sounds of Culture Club invaded the cab. 'It reminds me of when I was a little girl. Me and my sister used to dance around the bedroom with our hairbrushes.'

Doug laughed. 'Tell me some of your favourite bands.'

'Well, there's Take That of course.'

'They weren't a band,' he protested.

'You have no taste. I managed to see them before they split up and again when they re-formed. They were incredible both times.'

'You're going to tell me you had Robbie Williams's posters all around your bedroom, aren't you?'

'How rude.' She shook her head. 'It was Gary Barlow for me, and no one else. He gets better with age too. Very distinguished.'

'Okay, okay,' Doug said. 'Moving on... did you ever enjoy anything soulful?'

'Now, you're talking. Like the Backstreet Boys?'

'What? No.'

'I'm joking.' Hannah giggled. 'Yes, I like a lot of the R&B groups, but I also enjoy listening to Northern Soul and some of the Motown classics.'

'Now we *are* talking.' Doug nodded. 'I used to go to all-nighters back in the day. And I had a Lambretta scooter.'

'Really?'

'You sound surprised.'

'I wouldn't have had you down for a Mod.'

'I'll have you know I still have my parka. I don't think I'll ever get rid of that.'

Hannah smiled, then looked out of the window at the passing fields, the odd group of cows and sheep in the distance. Her stomach lurched every time she thought of seeing her brother. She didn't want to think about what would happen if he wasn't there. It had taken enough courage to visit as it was.

'Music you like?' Doug broke into her thoughts.

Hannah smiled, realising he sensed she was getting apprehensive once more.

'I enjoyed a lot of it when I was younger. Before any of this business with Mum and Dad, I had a really good childhood. Lots of happy memories. But they get forgotten because of the accident. It changed my life as well as my mum's.'

'What can you remember about your dad?' Doug asked.

A warm smile crossed her face. 'He was kind and funny. When me and Olivia were younger, he smoked a pipe. I used to love the smell, but not the smoke in the room. Then one day he just gave up. Great willpower.'

'You take after him.'

Her smile turned into a grin. 'He was a stickler for punctuality, as well.'

'Mine was too.'

'I guess because I was always wanting to stay out later, I was invariably at least ten minutes late. I tried to push him all the time. My sister got away with a lot more.'

'My brother did as well. Part of growing up. My kids did

that too, but they were usually in around nine and were playing at friends in the cul-de-sac we lived in. I'm thinking of going to see them soon.'

'Oh?'

'You made me realise that family is important. I let mine down and—'

'No, you didn't.'

'I did, and I'm not sure I'll ever be able to make up for that. But I'm thinking of flying out there next month.'

The tension crackled in the cab, the melancholy mood returning for a moment. Hannah sensed the unsaid words. *After I leave Hope Street.* She didn't want him to go to Australia because she knew he'd return to Manchester.

'Great.' Hannah made out she was genuinely pleased when it couldn't be further than the truth. 'I hope it works out for you.' She pointed to a sign. 'Junction 9. We have to turn off here.'

'Yes, boss.'

As Doug manoeuvred into the right lane, Hannah's stomach lurched again. Parker Motors was seven miles from the motorway which meant they would be there before she knew it.

'I wonder if your dad had any idea about James?' Doug indicated and moved onto the slip road.

'Well, my sister found out. But that doesn't excuse them not telling me.'

'I guess. I'm just thinking aloud. Trying not to let you get too nervous.'

'Believe me, there is nothing you can do to stop that happening.' She held out a shaking hand. 'Look.'

'You'll be fine.' He patted her thigh.

Twenty minutes later, they pulled into the car park of Parker Motors. Set back from the busy main road, it was on a large plot. Row after row of cars were for sale, bunting around the entrance flapping slightly in the breeze. A single-storey building housed the reception and sales room, more cars in the main part.

Hannah removed her seatbelt and sat for a moment.

'Are you ready?' Doug queried.

Would she ever be ready for this?

At last she nodded. She got out of the truck and made her way round to him. Doug took her hand in his own and she smiled at him, liking the feeling it gave her. Safe, protected, not alone.

'Let's have a walk around as if we're punters,' he said. 'Knowing sales people, someone will be out to us soon.'

But Hannah had frozen.

Doug stepped forward and then turned back to her. 'What's wrong?'

'It's him,' she whispered.

'Who?'

'James – who else?'

'Oh! Where?'

'He's walking towards us.'

'Are you sure it's him?'

'Yes.'

'Stay calm,' he whispered back. 'I'll do the talking.'

'Hi, there.' The man held out his hand as he reached them. 'Welcome to Parker Motors, the finest family-run establishment in Scarborough, even though I do say so myself. I'm James Parker. What can I help you with today?'

CHAPTER 40

*H*annah couldn't speak as she shook hands with her half-brother. Closer to, it was even more noticeable that they were related. He had the same hair colouring, although peppered with grey, the same crinkles around his eyes as he smiled. He was ageing well, his physique one of someone who took care of themselves. She wondered what he did to stay so trim.

Her eyes brimmed with tears and she looked away to compose herself. How she wished she'd known him when she was growing up. Things could have been so different. After all, look how he'd turned out.

Everything I have known up until now has been a lie.

All that went through her mind in a second. Then, remembering her manners, she shook his outstretched hand.

'We're looking for a runaround for my wife,' Doug said, squeezing Hannah's hand.

'Right.' James gnawed at his bottom lip. 'Not to stereotype you, but is it for carrying people or shopping?'

'Sorry?' Hannah didn't understand.

'Would you like a large vehicle or a small runaround?'

'Oh. Small all the way for me.'

She didn't know what else to say. She hadn't expected to bump into James immediately on getting there: she thought she'd have time to study him first. As a family-owned firm, she'd expected him to be in the background, inside the offices while he had younger staff, or maybe his children, working on the forecourt.

Hannah kept glancing at him surreptitiously. He was showing Doug a shiny blue hatchback when all of a sudden, his demeanour changed.

'It's you, isn't it?'

Hannah turned round so quickly she caught her arm on the wing mirror and cursed under her breath.

'Hannah. Hannah Lockley.'

She gasped. 'How do you know my name?'

'Well, you obviously know mine. Why didn't you say who you were when you arrived?'

'I – I wanted to see you first. Do you know who I am?'

He nodded. 'Yes, you're my sister.'

Hannah frowned. How did he know that?

And then it sank in. If he knew her name, it meant that someone had told him about her.

It meant that he could have visited Hope Street.

It meant that he could have met her mum and she hadn't told her.

It meant that he knew about her but didn't want to find her.

Still, she couldn't be heartless. She had to tell him what had happened.

'Mum died,' she said quietly, a pull of emotion in her voice.

'Oh, no. When was this?'

'In February.'

'I'm really sorry to hear that.' He ran a hand through his hair. 'Is that what brought you here?'

Hannah nodded. 'She left me some letters, telling me about you. It seemed as if she wanted me to find you. I thought you might not know you had a sister, two actually. And I was worried about telling you in case you didn't know you were adopted.'

'I've always known that.'

'Have you always known about me?'

'Not until these past few years.'

Hannah's heart sank. 'How many?'

'About five.'

'And yet you never wanted to meet me?' She turned and walked away, unable to take in any more disappointment.

~

'*Y*ou could have been a bit more diplomatic,' Doug snapped after he'd shouted Hannah back but she'd kept on walking.

'How was I to know she'd turn up unannounced?' James insisted. 'And why now, after all this time?'

'Unlike you, *she* didn't know anything about you until last week.'

'Oh, I thought—'

'You thought she was as heartless as you and had known about your existence for a while.'

'You know nothing about me.'

'I sure don't but I know a lot about Hannah. She gave up her life to care for *your* mum after her accident left her in need of twenty-four-hour help. She looked after her sister too, before she walked away, leaving Hannah to do everything. She is incredibly smart but never had the opportunity to use her talents. She didn't have time to meet many people, go to university, or have the chance to start a family of her own. She gave *everything* she had to look after her mother. Pretty special, huh?'

'Don't you dare judge me. I—'

'Whereas you, even though you were adopted, went to a family where you've been given the chance to grow and be wealthy. Hannah has had to watch every penny she's had. But I tell you one thing. She's worth ten of you.'

'I had no idea.' James had the decency to hang his head for a moment.

Doug took a few deep breaths. He needed to calm down, anger bubbling inside after he'd spoken so passionately about Hannah. He pushed it away, as well as the mounting dread that he had been dishonest with her too. He should have come clean when they'd first had something to eat together.

Was he as much in the wrong as James?

A man in a suit, his red tie flapping behind was on his way over. James held up a hand and shook his head until he retreated.

Doug drew out his wallet and searched out a business card. He wrote down the number of his spare phone and passed it to him.

'In case you want to contact her, do it through me, please.'

James took it from him. 'I'm sorry I upset your wife.'

Doug marched back to his vehicle. He wasn't going to explain they weren't married.

Rage tore through him but it wasn't all to do with James. It was because what James had said back there could relate to him too. Until now, Doug had never looked after anyone but himself. Of course, he had played the "I-provide-well-for-my-family" card but that was *why* he'd lost his family, his wife. Because of his workaholic, obsessive, and selfish ways.

He knew he was being judgmental, but James had reminded him of an earlier version of himself. It had been like looking into a mirror. And he'd wanted to smash it to smithereens with his fist.

He needed to protect Hannah from the pain she would be feeling right now. She deserved better.

She deserved his honesty too.

When he got into the truck, Hannah didn't look at him. Doug couldn't even begin to imagine what she was going through, how she felt about what had happened. No one should do that to her.

'Come on,' he said starting the engine and leaving her alone. 'Let's get you home.'

CHAPTER 41

*I*t was late when they arrived back at Hope Street. Her heart aching, Hannah tried not to look at Doug. He wouldn't want to see her snivelling again.

'Would you like me to come in with you?' he asked.

Hannah shook her head, unable to speak. Even though she knew it was ignorant she didn't thank him for taking her. She'd do that tomorrow.

After letting herself into the house, she went through to the kitchen. She poured a glass of water and popped out two painkillers. Her head was banging as she flung herself down on the settee.

How had it gone so wrong? She had been so full of hope when she'd left the house that morning. Of course she'd known it might not work out, but she hadn't actually expected it not to. In her mind, she'd seen her reunion with James as something totally different. She had told him who she was, he had enveloped her in his arms, cried with her as they hugged. Smiled with her afterwards as she went on to meet his family and spend the evening getting to know them, introducing them to Doug. There would have been lots of photographs and memories to share. Now, all that was gone.

She recalled the look on James's face when he realised who she was. Oh, maybe there had been an ounce of shock but the rest was pure panic. It was all to do with the money: it had to be. Perhaps he thought she was after some of it. Even before the accident, the Lockleys were only an average family. But Hannah hadn't known any different. She'd never felt as if there was anything she couldn't have.

She pressed her face into the cushion and pummelled her fists either side as she screamed into it. Why wasn't she good enough for him and his family? Was it because she came from nothing?

But then again, did *he* know that? James certainly knew who she was, but how and what exactly did he know? Did he know about the accident? Did he know he had two half-sisters? Did he know how drab her life had been?

She tried to work it all out but her head hurt even more.

'Mum, I hate you right now, do you hear me?' she cried.

The doorbell rang a few minutes later. She was about to ignore it when the letter box rattled.

'Hannah, it's Phoebe.'

She dragged herself to the door and let her friend in.

'Doug came to see me. He told me what happened and suggested you might need company from someone who knows you well. He said he was worried about you.'

'James doesn't want to know.'

Phoebe drew her into her arms. 'Oh, Hannah, I'm so sorry.'

'What's wrong with me?'

'It's him who's a thoughtless prick. He should have known better than to take it out on you. It isn't your fault, none of this.'

Hannah buckled, tears pouring down her face again. 'I'm not good enough, am I?'

'Enough of this nonsense.' Phoebe wasn't having any of it. 'If he can't see what a sweet, awesome, intelligent, caring, loving sister he has, then he doesn't deserve to know you.'

Hannah couldn't help but smile as Phoebe went on.

'I wish I'd been with you. I would've punched him between the eyes for hurting you. But let me tell you straight, this is a blip in your journey, a fork in the road. Your mum dying changed the dynamics of your life almost overnight. You're starting off on another path now. So if James can't see how amazing it would be to have you in his life, then tough. We all appreciate you.'

Hannah knew Phoebe was trying to make her feel better, even though she was going over the top. She was about to speak when Phoebe continued.

'We're your family, Han. We all love you and Hope Street wouldn't be the same without you. And if I'm honest, I didn't want you to go to Scarborough, fall in love with another family and move away. I'd be lost without you in my life every day – even though I cringe when I realise how selfish that sounds.'

'It doesn't. It sounds nice.'

'Why don't you stay at home tomorrow?' Phoebe brushed hair away from Hannah's face.

'Oh, but—'

'Really, Han. Actually, take a few days. You haven't had any time off since your mum died. We can manage.'

Hannah smiled through her tears. That was the best thing about Hope Street. Sometimes it felt claustrophobic. Sometimes it was annoying that everyone knew your business. But other times, when best friends came to cheer you up like this, it was the only place to be.

≈

*D*oug paced the living room. How dare James act as if he didn't want to know Hannah? He would have been distraught if Alex had behaved in that manner.

But then again he remembered the look on James's face when he'd figured out who Hannah was. He had been terrified, not disappointed. It seemed as if Hannah showing up would get him into trouble. What was all that about?

As soon as Hannah had closed her front door, Doug had gone to see Phoebe. He hoped Hannah didn't think he was meddling by telling Phoebe what had happened. Hannah needed someone to get her through this. It would be better to be comforted by her best friend, someone she'd known all her life rather than for a few weeks.

Even though his heart was calling out to comfort her, take her in his arms, it wasn't his place. Maybe after she'd got over the shock, he could be there for her.

So he wasn't expecting a knock on the door that evening, and to find Hannah on his doorstep. The sight of her near on broke his heart. She was a mess, her make-up non-existent except for black smudges underneath red swollen eyes and her hair all over the place.

'I can't bear to be alone in my house tonight,' she said quietly. 'Could I – could I stay with you? I just need someone to hold me.'

They chatted for the rest of the evening, drinking a bottle of wine between them. When it came to where to sleep, Hannah surprised him by asking to share his bed.

'We're both old enough not be embarrassed about things going any further until the timing is right, okay?'

He nodded. 'I can take the settee, though, if you prefer. You can have my bed.'

'No, I want to sleep next to you. I want someone's arms

around me, reassuring me that everything will be okay. Actually, I don't want someone.' She gazed at him, resting her hand on the side of his face. 'I want it to be you.'

Getting into bed a few minutes later, Doug spooned around her, hoping his body wouldn't embarrass him too much as he pulled Hannah in close. It was enough for now to feel her in his arms, comfort her when she cried. Because he knew he was as bad as James when it came to deceiving her.

The guilt was weighing him down now, with every second that passed. Hannah meant the world to him. To see her hurt pained him too. He couldn't be a source of that. And he would be if he wasn't honest with her. It would be worse too because Hannah knew him, trusted him.

He held on to her tightly, knowing that it may very well be the first and the last time they shared a bed.

CHAPTER 42

*a*fter their night together, Doug decided he should speak to Hannah and tell her the truth. But he had to tread carefully. Hannah had not only found out she had a brother, but it seemed as if she'd lost one too.

It hadn't seemed appropriate that morning so he'd made a special journey back with Dylan on the premise of wanting to speak to Robin. He spotted Hannah inside the community centre and waved for her attention.

'Hey.' She came outside to him. 'We have spotted dick for pudding. Want some?'

Doug roared with laughter, feeling his cheeks reddening. When he looked at Hannah, hers were the same.

'Spotted dick sounds great to me,' he replied. 'How about you?'

She laughed and turned to walk away but he reached for her hand.

'How are you feeling?'

'I'm okay.'

'That's good to hear. It must have been quite a shock for you.'

'I guess, but what did I expect really? I should have contacted him first.'

'Hindsight, and all that.'

Hannah nodded.

He took a deep breath. 'What are you doing on Sunday?'

'Apart from having 'someone' round for lunch?' She smiled. 'Not much. Why?'

'I'd like to take you somewhere, show you something actually.'

'Ooh, sounds sinister.'

He tried to laugh a little but his nerves got the better of him. 'How about I pick you up?'

'From across the street?'

'Yes.'

'But you're already there.'

'I will *actually* pick you up and carry you to my truck if you're not careful.' He grinned. 'Be ready for 10 a.m.?'

'Where are we going?'

'Wait and see.'

'Do I need to bring a bag of provisions... at the least a shovel?'

'Just bring yourself, that's more than enough.'

$\sim$

On Sunday morning, Hannah was on the phone to Phoebe while she waited for Doug to indicate he was ready to go.

'Has he said where he's taking you?' Phoebe wanted to know.

'No, not even a hint. Which doesn't give me any clues as to what to wear either.'

'What have you chosen?'

'I've gone with a dress. As long as the weather stays as hot as planned, it's a catch-all, really.'

'Are you nervous?'

'Of course I am. Wouldn't you be?'

'Me? I'm never nervous.'

Hannah wanted to say that Phoebe was when she was around Robin but knew she would deny it.

She heard a horn and her heart gave a flip. 'I have to go. Doug's ready. Speak soon.'

'You'd better let me know as soon as.'

'How are you feeling now?' Doug asked once they were on the way.

'I've heard nothing from James.' Hannah shook her head. 'It's a shame, but it is what it is. I can't change it.'

'Sorry.'

'Oh, I don't mind you talking about it. I just don't want to tell anyone else. As far as I'm concerned the handful of people who know is enough. At least it didn't get out all over the street. I wouldn't have liked that. Where are we going?' She changed the subject.

'Not far now.'

Hannah gave up guessing, although her eyes widened when she spotted the signs for Manchester Airport. Surely he couldn't be taking her anywhere without any luggage? She shook her head in mirth; she didn't even have a passport. Was she that desperate to spend a night with him?

Yes.

After an hour's drive, Doug turned off the motorway and busy roads changed into winding country lanes.

'You're not going to introduce me to anyone, are you? Because I'm extremely sweaty and certainly not in my best bib and tucker.'

Doug laughed. 'You look gorgeous. And no, I'm not going to introduce you to anyone.'

'Then where are we going? I don't like surprises.'

'Oh dear.'

'What?'

'Nothing.'

Her nerves building up, she clasped her hands together over and over. Then she moved to tapping them along the side of the door. Then they were back in her lap.

'Relax, I'm not going to bite you,' Doug joked.

'Oh, I'm just thinking about James and what if.' Sadness tinged her voice.

'That's understandable. Why don't you email him in a week or so? Just a few lines and ask to keep in touch?'

'I couldn't bear the disappointment twice over.'

'He might be more receptive now that he's got over the shock.'

'He could ignore the email too, and that would hurt just as much.' She shook her head. 'I'd rather not know.'

They dropped into companionable silence again. Finally, he pulled up outside a property surrounded by a high brick wall. Wrought-iron gates stood between them and a sweeping drive, gardens in colour either side.

Hannah turned to him with a look of confusion as Doug pulled out a bunch of keys and pressed a fob. The gates opened, and he drove in. She glanced over her shoulder to see the gates closing behind them.

'Are we having lunch somewhere nice?'

'No, it's just you and me.'

Doug continued forward. He parked up in front of a large farmhouse and killed the engine.

Set back, the property was over two floors, a newer build on one side and what looked to be the original part built in stone on the other. Vast gardens were spread out all around it. There was a garage to the right that would fit at least three cars inside and a room above it, two windows popping out of the roof like eyes. At the centre of the farmhouse was a glass porch, double wooden doors giving access to it.

Doug got out of the car and Hannah quickly followed behind him. He unlocked the porch, and then the front door. She heard beeping as they stepped inside, watching as he disarmed a burglar alarm. Then he put down the keys and took her hands in his own.

'Hannah. I haven't been entirely truthful with you. I – I've wanted to ever since I've met you but I didn't want to blow my cover and—'

'Wait a minute.' Hannah pulled her hands away from his. 'I don't understand.'

'This is my home.'

'This?'

She scanned the hallway taking in the large marble tiles on the floor, the Art Deco on walls painted a delicate shade of blue. There were three sets of doors, leading off to other rooms she presumed, and a thick-pile woollen circular rug that ordinarily she would have loved to swish between her bare toes.

She followed the line of the stairs with her eyes, finding a galleried landing up above. A sky light was set in between oak beams. The room was bigger than her two downstairs rooms that had been knocked into one.

Doug dropped his keys onto a table that stood next to a hat and umbrella stand, a hedgehog boot cleaner at its feet. The large mirror on the wall showed her shocked reflection, making her realise she was staring wide-eyed.

'You said you were a builder, and that you live from contract to contract?' Her brow furrowed.

Doug reached for Hannah's hand again and, before she could pull away, took her through into the biggest kitchen she'd ever seen. A set of folding glass doors gave her a view over fields and trees for as far as her eyes could see.

The garden area was like something out of a stately home. Shaped bushes and large lawns amid a riot of colour led to a wooded area. It had obviously been maintained while he'd been away.

'I'll make coffee and then I can explain.' Doug pointed to a chair. 'Please, sit down.'

Hannah couldn't tell him to get stuffed if she wanted to. Dumbstruck, she gazed around in awe. It was like something you would see in *House and Home* country magazine, and it was obvious that someone fetched in shopping for him. At the very least he had a cleaner and help with the garden.

Her head was full to burst with questions. Who was he? He wasn't just the man across the street.

A few minutes later, Doug brought over drinks and a fruitcake. He placed them down on a glass coffee table in front of them and then sat down beside her. Taking her hands in his again, she watched his Adam's apple move up and down as he swallowed.

'Okay, you must promise to hear me out,' he began. 'Because ever since this business with James, I've been feeling terrible about not being honest with you.'

'You're going to tell me that your name isn't Doug, aren't you?'

'No, but my surname isn't Barnett. It's Peterson. I did have a heart attack. My doctor told me to change my lifestyle or I was in severe danger of having another one.'

'What exactly do you do to... live here?'

'I run a property development firm with my brother. It's a family-run business. We've had full control of it since our father died.' Doug got up and fetched a photo in a frame, brought it back to her. 'This is Alex.'

Hannah saw two men, almost identical in looks. They were smiling, arms wrapped around each other's necks. She could see the love they shared, the closeness. All of a sudden, it reminded her of Olivia. They had been that close for a long time too.

'We've now grown a small business into an empire because of our foresight to buy run-down properties at low prices,' Doug continued. 'We developed the better ones and then waited for the market to see the others favourable again, hence making a hefty profit as we went along.

'But it's been stressful too. I was taken ill while I was in the office. Alex was with me so he called for an ambulance. Honestly, I thought my life was over and it changed my outlook almost overnight. It was such a scary experience, but it made me realise how precious life is.' He looked away momentarily. 'I lost my wife and children because I worked too much. I put the business before them. That's why I needed to take time out, because I couldn't let that continue. I decided to stay away and get my health back.'

'So when you came to Hope Street?' Hannah's voice was barely audible.

'I wanted to be a nobody, someone who was there for a few months before moving on. Alex has been dealing with the business. But I hadn't planned on enjoying myself when I was away from it all. And I *certainly* hadn't planned on meeting anyone like you.'

Hannah freed one of her hands and clutched it to her chest. How she'd longed to hear him say something like that but everything had changed now. He wasn't who he said he was. Doug had lied to her. She shook her head to rid it of its confusion. But it stayed with her.

'I'm really sorry that I tricked everyone, especially you,' Doug went on. 'But I had to fit in. If anyone had known who I was, people would have treated me differently. Having a lot of money isn't always a good thing. It makes you wonder who you can trust. Who is out to fleece you of it. Who is really a true friend or a lagger-on.'

'You have that much money?'

Doug nodded. 'Alex and I are millionaires.'

Hannah pulled her other hand free and stood up. Doug followed suit.

'It's only money. It doesn't mean anything.'

'It means a lot to me,' she cried. 'I've lived my life on the breadline. Why wouldn't you tell me?'

'Would it have made a difference?'

She didn't answer. Maybe she'd have thought differently to begin with. She might not have got to know him, thinking she wasn't good enough. Yet if she'd got past that to the real Doug, she wouldn't have been bothered. It was him she had feelings for.

She walked over to the kitchen while she willed her tears not to fall. How could he locate into Hope Street, even for a few months?

It was then she realised how sincere he was. He was prepared to leave all this behind for his health. He meant well, even if he had been economical with the truth.

But that didn't mean she could forgive him, did it?

CHAPTER 43

*H*annah ran a hand over the granite worktop on the kitchen island that was as big as her bathroom, listening to Doug prattle on as he told her about the tap that had constant boiling water and then would change to ice-cold with the touch of a button. Was he nervous and filling in the silence? Or had he missed these things? She knew she would. How on earth he'd settled in Hope Street at all without the luxury she'd never know.

'I can guess what you're thinking.' He came to join her. 'But honestly, I rattled around in this place on my own. It feels more welcoming in Hope Street, even though there are *a lot* of things that could be done to make the property better.'

'Tell me about the business.' She didn't want to show an interest but she needed to know all the same.

'My dad started working for himself in 1970. He did the building work, hiring sub-contractors to help him out, and my mum took care of the paperwork and admin to keep it going. From there, he ended up having over fifty men working for him. When Alex and I were old enough to work, we had jobs for life. We've always enjoyed working together, but we felt we could do more.

'When Dad got sick, we were respectful of his wishes to let the business continue as it was. When he died, we expanded and bought run-down properties and did them up.'

Hannah froze. She put up a hand.

'Are you trying to telling me that you own Regency Property Management?'

There was a slight pause. 'No, but Alex and do I own most of the houses in Hope Street. I'm the landlord that everyone despises.'

Hannah sat back down again with a bump. This was too much to take in.

'We hired Regency to look after everything for us. You might not believe it but we pay a hefty monthly fee for the properties to be maintained. There should be a caretaker on stand-by at all times if anything went wrong. But, as you know, there isn't, and we'd had a few complaints.

'Despite going to see them several times, they profusely denied any wrong-doings. But it was still worrying us that things were going on that were out of our control. So when I had my heart attack, I suggested to Alex that I go undercover, and be our own tenant for three months. That way I could see how everything was – or wasn't – working. It was a perfect ruse as long as no one found out my real identity. Not until I'd had the chance to come clean after my findings.'

'And what have the findings revealed?'

'That the company *are* ripping us off – ripping us all off. Like that first one hundred pounds to pay before they do any work. That isn't a legality: they were pocketing it. I doubt we'll get that back from Regency but we're going to refund every penny to the tenants, anyway.'

Hannah sat quiet for a moment, unable to take everything in.

'I'm sorry,' Doug went on. 'I—'

'I'm tired of everyone lying to me.' She shook her head in dismay.

'It wasn't a lie. And I couldn't tell anyone about Regency until I knew if I was right or not.'

'You see, you don't trust me.'

'Oh I do. If you hear me out, what I plan to do in the future would very much include you, if you were up for it.'

'I don't want to know.' She sat in silence, fuming. 'You've lied about… everything!'

'I didn't lie. Regency were billing us for work we thought had been done, and we happily paid. Then we got a double bill for number 17 to have a new boiler. They'd only had one six months previous, so it pinged up on our records. It turns out they were charging us for lots of extra things.'

'You should have trusted me about who you were, though.'

'I wanted to, believe me. But the plan was always to stay for three months, sort out the letting company and then come back. What I hadn't *planned* on was falling in love with you.'

It was a good job he couldn't read Hannah's expression as she stepped further away. It was a cheap trick to show his feelings. She couldn't work out if she was mad at him for that or shocked at his final admission.

He was waiting for her to speak but after a long few seconds it was clear she wasn't going to.

'I'm sorry I hurt you. I never intended to do that,' he said. 'These last few weeks with you have been the best I've had in years. I've found my zest for life again. I no longer think of work twenty-four-seven. I have a new purpose—'

'And what were you planning on doing after the three months were up?'

'That would very much depend on you.'

She shook her head. 'I can't leave Hope Street. And this is your life here, your lifestyle. I don't belong in it.'

'You think I don't know that? I've thought of nothing else for the past week. I want to be with you, but I can't run the business from Somerley.'

'So what did you expect me to do?'

'I don't know.'

She went quiet again, unable to take in everything he had said. She could see Doug was about to break into the silence so she decided to beat him to it.

'You can't buy love. You of all people should know that.'

CHAPTER 44

*H*annah was sorry she'd said the words as soon as they were out of her mouth. She knew Doug's intentions were good, but did he really think she would up-sticks, leave all her friends, her life in Hope Street to start again with him? They'd only known each other a few weeks. It wasn't long enough to make such a huge decision.

Although hadn't she said to Doug only last week that she wanted to live dangerously? Part of her wanted to go for it, try something new, break out of the mould. She'd been held back for so long. This would be like starting over. But she pushed the thought away from her. She belonged in Hope Street.

Wait. He'd just said he'd fallen in love with her. Isn't that what she'd wanted to hear for the past few days since realising she felt the same? Yet how could she have a relationship with someone who'd been so dishonest? Doug hadn't been truthful about owning the properties in Hope Street. He hadn't lied as such – he'd just avoided the truth.

She was all out of words as her head was full of muddled thoughts.

Doug, however, wasn't.

'That's a cruel thing to say,' he cracked, his voice holding a slight tremor of irritation. 'I may never have to worry about anything financially, but I keep my feet firmly on the ground. I thought you would have known that by now.'

'I didn't know *this* about you yesterday,' she said in her defence. 'I thought you were an honest person. And now all these lies.'

'I just didn't tell you the truth until I needed to. A bit like when Colin proposed to you.'

Hannah's mouth dropped open. 'That's not the same at all.'

'Isn't it?' He shook his head, disappointment clear to see. 'Why didn't you want to tell me?'

'Because I didn't want to…'

'Hurt me?' He finished. 'Well, likewise.'

They stood in silence.

'Does anyone else know?' Hannah asked eventually. 'In Hope Street?'

'No. Only Robin knows my true identity.'

'He knew too?' That hurt her almost as much as being betrayed by Doug. 'I've known and trusted Robin for years.'

'He's a friend of my brother. Alex introduced us.'

'He still should have told me.'

'I'm to blame for that. I insisted he kept it to himself. You know how quickly news travels. I didn't want anyone thinking I was some posh bloke.'

'But you *are* some posh bloke.' Hannah was so confused. 'How long have you lived here?'

'Nearly fifteen years. We moved in when it was a wreck and we did it up as and when.'

Hannah was surprised how the word "we" stung.

'The kids loved it. It comes with seven acres. There's a small woodland I can show you, if you like?'

She turned to look at it for something to do. What could she see, though? Her future living here with Doug? Is that why he brought her here? Because she wasn't sure she'd ever leave Hope Street. Not even for a life of luxury. It wasn't her.

Although, how would she know?

Or did he bring her here to confess? Did he feel better now he had been truthful with her? She did appreciate his honesty – well, finally coming clean at least.

Maybe it was because of her proposal from Colin?

So what she really needed to figure out was exactly what she felt about Doug. But right now she couldn't be in the same room as him.

'I – I think I'd like to go home now,' she said.

'Just hear me out before—'

'I don't want to.'

He stopped pacing long enough to look her in the eye. 'Look, we've said some things in the heat of the moment. Let's talk about this when we've calmed down.'

'I'm not sure there's anything else left to say.'

The ride back to Somerley was torturous. There was the odd bit of polite conversation but mostly they sat in stony silence. In the end, Doug switched on the radio.

Hannah was thrown out of sync at the enormity of what he'd told her. Why was life always letting her down? The best thing that had happened to her in a long time had gone sour. All she'd ever done was help people. Now it was her turn, surely she deserved a bit of happiness?

Or maybe she was destined to live her life alone.

Back at home, she rang Phoebe. As soon as she answered, she let it all out.

'Doug and his brother own the houses in Hope Street. They're the landlords who don't care about their tenants enough to give them a decent standard of living. Regency Property Management are paid by them to look after everything. Not that they've ever done a good job, but that's beside the point.'

'What? Slow down – I don't understand.'

She told Phoebe some of what Doug had told her. She didn't need to tell her everything. Just enough to make her realise what had been going on.

'I just can't believe it. He didn't seem that ruthless.' Phoebe paused. 'Holy shit, wait a minute. Are you saying that our homes belong to Doug?'

'Yes.'

'And he knew all along?'

'Yes.'

'The conning… I've a good mind to have words with him.'

'There's no need. I think I gave him enough of my own to do irreparable damage.'

'Oh, Han. Are you okay?'

'Not really, but you know me. I'll brush it aside and just get on with life.'

'Don't be bitter. It doesn't suit you.'

'Yeah, because everyone only knows nice, sweet Hannah who will do anything for anyone. Well, I'm not nice, or sweet. Right now I feel cheated, and disappointed in myself for being made a fool of. But most of all, I feel broken-hearted.'

'You have every right to be upset. Your life has been in a turmoil these past few weeks. I don't know how you've coped. A proposal from Colin, then the chance of a good time with Doug going wrong and finding a brother you never knew you had. A lesser woman would have been in pieces long before now. Do you know, Hannah Lockley, you are one strong cookie to get through it all.'

But Hannah couldn't see that at the moment. She was all out of hope.

CHAPTER 45

*A*fter work the next day, Hannah sat at the dining room table, putting together the jigsaw that she'd foolishly broken apart. But her mind wouldn't rest enough to join any of the pieces.

She couldn't believe how much had changed again in a matter of days. First James and now Doug. The two men who might have come to mean something to her had turned out to be disasters in their own rights. And now here she was, all alone. Phoebe had invited her for tea with the kids but she'd declined. Who would want to look at her miserable face as she moped around?

She moved to the front window, looking out over the street. She couldn't help but wonder what Doug was doing. There was no one in his window that she could see, but his truck was parked out front. She fiddled with the curtains, when all she longed to do was run across, bang on his door, and throw herself in his arms when he answered it. Everything could be sorted out with a kiss, surely?

But then reality hit her. It wasn't that easy to forgive him. After he'd lied about his identity, how could she trust him again? And he was going to leave soon, anyway. It was best not to get any more attached. The closer they became, the worse it would be when he moved back to Manchester. Because he couldn't live here and be happy, could he?

If only he hadn't come into her life and made such an impact so quickly. She would still be lonely but she wouldn't be heartbroken with a head full of possibilities.

What must it be like to be as successful as Doug, or even James? To have made so much money that they could retire right now if they wanted and still be rich for the rest of their days. They were both the same age, fiftieth birthdays coming up next year. How had they done so well and she hadn't?

She imagined being a child growing up at Doug's house, like his two children had. Wanting for nothing, most probably having the best of everything bought for them. She couldn't begin to understand how that would be. She was so used to living from week to week.

Of course she could remember happier times with her parents, and with Olivia. They'd always had to share a room in Hope Street, so she'd had to suffice with bunkbeds and then single beds squashed together.

What would she do if she could do anything, if money wasn't a problem? When she was younger, she'd always wanted to open a bakery. She enjoyed working in the hairdressers, and wouldn't want to have a high-flying career. But she would love to be able to put her money into something that she could build and feel passionate about, like Robin had with Marriott Training. It wouldn't be about making money for her. It would be more about fulfilment, making others happy. She was good at that, she smirked. Putting other people first.

She picked up her phone, her hand hovered over the keypad. Maybe she should send a message to Doug.

No, he'd be leaving soon. Like it or not, no matter how

hard it was going to be, Hannah needed to move on too, without him.

She couldn't wait for everything to stop hurting. One thing was certain, she would be fine on her own once it did. It would be easier once he was gone.

Or would it?

'What should I do?' she asked the empty room. She hadn't spoken to her mum since she'd found out about James, but now it seemed as natural as a comfort blanket.

'I need him but I don't think I'm good enough for him.' She ran a hand through her hair. 'Thing is, I love him. I'm not sure I can give him up.'

*A*cross the street, Doug stood behind the nets in the upstairs window. He'd disliked them when he'd moved in, hadn't seen anything like them in years. However, they had served their purposes.

In Manchester, his farmhouse wasn't overlooked so it had been a shock at first to think he would be visible here. He'd often walk around in his boxer shorts at home, but here the neighbours across the street would have been able to see straight into this room. At least Hannah or Thelma hadn't had to suffer him streaking to the bathroom downstairs in the hot weather.

But best of all, it meant that he could stand here and watch the street without anyone seeing him.

He never thought he'd do that either.

Downstairs, Hannah's curtains were open as normal and he could see into the empty front room. He knew she was home. He'd watched her go in about an hour ago, seen her in the window a few times. He'd stopped himself from marching across there three times already. It wasn't his place to go to her. She needed time away from him. He'd hurt her unintentionally.

Thinking what to do next was like playing a game of tug of war. Could he leave everything in Manchester behind and move to Hope Street? He'd have to make things better first, although he wasn't sure he knew how.

Why had this happened now? All he'd needed was another two weeks and he would have been ready to tell her, anyway. He just hadn't got all his plans in place yet.

He moved to the settee and sat down, unsure what to do with himself. When the doorbell rang ten minutes later, his poor heart practically leaped into his mouth. It had to be Hannah, come to talk to him. He would do whatever he had to do to win her back. He would grovel, he would plead, he would...

'Phoebe.' His shoulders drooped.

'You have some bloody nerve.' Phoebe flew forward and slapped him across the face. Before he had time to react, she pushed past him, his shoulder hitting the wall with a thump.

Closing the door, he followed her into the living room. She stood with her arms folded, the look of fury in her eyes obviously for his benefit.

'How could you do that to Hannah?' she demanded.

'I didn't mean to hurt her.'

She stabbed the air with her finger. 'What I can't understand is why you weren't upfront with her – all of us – from the start.'

'Did she tell you everything?'

'I doubt that. She's loyal, unlike *some* people. But she did tell me about Regency Property Management and that you have a little more than spare change in your pocket.'

'I needed to work undercover to get to the bottom of some things,' Doug tried to explain. 'If they'd got wind of who I was, it would have been even harder to prove and sort out. I do have the welfare of the tenants at heart, you know. I'm not an ogre.'

'Oh, really?' Phoebe's laugh was cruel.

'Yes, really. But I hadn't planned on meeting Hannah. I just thought I'd be here for three months and then going home.'

'And now?'

'Now I have no idea.'

A stony silence stretched in front of them until Phoebe broke into it.

'I really want to punch your lights out. Hannah is so precious to me.'

'I would never hurt her intentionally.' He raised his hands in surrender. 'She means the world to me, too.'

'I don't care how much pain *you're* in. I only care about Hannah.'

'We both do.'

'I've known her most of my life, and you for a few weeks.' She shook her head. 'Yet even then I thought you were a decent guy. It was me who was pushing her to go out with you. I feel sick about that now. I thought you would be good for each other.'

'I thought so too,' Doug admitted.

'Well, you've ruined it.' Phoebe folded her arms and pouted. 'And *I* have a problem with my bath. There's a damp patch on the kitchen ceiling beneath it so it must be leaking. Perhaps you can sort that out now? You *are* the landlord after all.'

Once Phoebe had left, he sat down with his head in his hands. His face still stung a little where she'd sliced her hand across it. The dig at him was what he deserved. He couldn't blame Phoebe for feeling protective of Hannah. Right now he was feeling the same too.

He didn't know what to do. He could stay, try to mend

their relationship, tell her his plans for the future. Or he could go, leaving his heart here with Hannah.

In the end, he took his smartphone out of the drawer and switched it on. There were so many unanswered emails but he wasn't interested in them. He needed the one he'd asked his brother to send to him.

CHAPTER 46

*H*annah was about to make her third cup of coffee when there was a knock on the front door. She almost broke a foot as she hurried to answer it.

This had to be Doug. Maybe they could work things out now, after a stern chat. She hadn't overplayed it too much but she wouldn't be a pushover either. She would tell him how upset he'd made her feel, but that…

'James?' Her voice was low, as if she couldn't believe he was here.

'Hi.' James cleared his throat of its wave of nerves. 'I – can I talk to you?'

Hannah led him through to the living room, ashamed by its shabby look. Before she'd fallen out with Doug, she'd been fine with what she had. Now, after seeing his home, and also realising that James too must be rich beyond her wildest dreams, it only added to her embarrassment.

How dare you put yourself down like that, Hannah Lockley? Money isn't everything.

She righted herself. Neither of them was any better than her.

They stood in the middle of the room.

'Nice place you have.' His eyes skimmed everything quickly.

'How did you find me?' she asked.

'Your husband gave me a business card before you left.'

'My husband?' For a moment, she was confused. Then she remembered their ruse. 'We're not married. We thought we'd pose as a couple to have a look around your garage before I decided whether I dared speak to you or not.'

'Yes, Doug told me.' A flicker of a smile played with his lips.

Hannah cursed inwardly. How could she blame Doug for telling white lies when she was using them too?

'Sorry about that. I wanted to see you first in case, well, what happened would happen. But then I blurted out who I was, anyway.'

James sat down at her suggestion. 'I want to say how sorry I was for how I acted when we met. Overreacted would be a better word. I had no right to be so rude. I'd often thought what it would be like to meet you, and Olivia.'

Hannah tried not to flinch at the mention of her sister.

'I panicked,' he went on. 'I hadn't expected ever to see you. And to find out that Martha had died, it was just too much. I felt that I'd let her down by not being in her life, and *then* I felt that I'd let you down as well. So I reacted in the only way I could – by making you feel as if it was your fault. It was only to cover my embarrassment.'

'I guess it was a surprise to see me,' Hannah concurred.

'You could say that. Although I did visit once.'

'Did you?' She tried not to gasp. 'When?'

'Your mum wanted to see me and I was curious. We talked about what had happened. Thought it would be better left in the past now that she'd made her peace. Then we both felt it would upset you too much to tell you.'

'That should have been my choice,' Hannah retorted.

'It was your mum who insisted we didn't meet. She did what she thought best at the time. I'm sorry. I should have put myself in your position when you told me she'd died. Being adopted you always have a sense of not belonging anywhere fully. I never thought you might feel the same.'

'I didn't, because I never knew about you.'

'Maybe that's why she didn't tell you.'

'Maybe.' Hannah gnawed her bottom lip before continuing. 'You said your family didn't know about me?'

He shook his head, shamefaced. 'My wife knows, my children too. I always hoped one day you would turn up. And when you did, I made a dick of myself. I'm sorry for the pain I caused you. They'd like to meet you.' He chuckled. 'You can bring your husband along too.'

Hannah half-smiled at his joke, even though that wouldn't be happening any time soon now. She turned away from eyes that looked so much like her own to register the rest of his words. James had caused her a lot of pain. She had lost sight of who she was – and become someone so small that she'd felt insignificant.

Had *she* overreacted when she'd found out about Doug? He had clearly been working behind the scenes to get James to visit.

'Does Olivia live local to you?' James broke into her thoughts.

'I have no idea.' She shrugged. 'She left when she was eighteen and hasn't been back since.'

'Do you think she found out?'

'Yes, she knew.'

'Perhaps it was too hard to handle.'

Hannah thought about it. Then she shook her head. 'Olivia was hot-headed but she would have said something to me.'

'She probably didn't want to upset you. It's not every day you find out you have a brother.'

'Maybe it was because she was ashamed Mum had a baby with another man.'

'Another man?' It was James's time to frown now. 'Don't you know? We share the same mother *and* father.'

CHAPTER 47

*H*annah frowned, flabbergasted by the revelation. She had never even thought of that as a possibility, and yet it made perfect sense.

'He was just seventeen when it happened. Your mum – our mum – was barely fifteen. They both knew he might get into trouble so they left his name out of everything. Your grandparents thought he wasn't good enough for her, anyway.'

'Why?'

'Something to do with him being a labourer. But he was a hard worker and he provided well for his family. So she never told your grandparents who the father was. Of course they guessed but she kept on saying it wasn't him. For a whole year, they met in secret and when she was sixteen, she started seeing him again in public.'

'Something else I never knew.'

'Things were different back then, I suppose. Yet they stayed together, proved everyone wrong. I think they always regretted what they did, about putting me up for adoption, but I can see they had no choice. They were young, and I guess if you're told to do something at that age in the care of your parents, most of us would have no choice.'

Hannah nodded her reply. It was then she noticed he had the look of her father. She'd focussed on her mum's features but now, it was like seeing a younger version of her dad.

He was her brother, not her half-sibling. It felt good to hear.

'Wow,' she said at last. 'I wish I could tell Olivia.'

'Maybe we need to give the detective skills a whirl?'

'She did send me a birthday card but there was no return address on it. I don't think she wants to be found. Oh, I have something for you.' She held up her index finger. 'Wait there.'

Hannah went upstairs and fetched the letter that her mum had written for James. Coming back downstairs, she gave it to him.

'Mum left this for you,' she said.

'I'll read it later, if you don't mind.' James popped it into his pocket. 'I don't want to blubber in front of my sister.'

A warm glow flowed through Hannah at his words.

'I meant what I said.' James handed her a business card. 'I'd love to introduce you to my family.'

Hannah nodded. 'I'd like that.'

While he had his wallet out, he showed her a photo. 'My wife, Rosie, and two boys, Sam and Taylor.'

Hannah saw an image of a family. The four of them were sitting around a table, out having a meal. What looked to be the younger of the two boys had taken a selfie. Rosie looked as happy as Hannah did when she was with Doug.

'I can't wait to meet them,' was all she managed to say as feelings began to overwhelm her again.

When he was ready to leave, at the doorstep James leant forwards and kissed her on the cheek.

'Thanks for the warm welcome after I was so nasty.'

She pulled him close and gave him a hug. 'We all say

things in the heat of the moment,' she acknowledged, meaning herself as well as him.

She waved him off. Left on the pavement, she glanced over the road. Doug's truck was there but she still couldn't bring herself to go across to him, make the first move. Wanting to be alone, she went out to get some fresh air.

She walked along the high street, casting her mind back to remember the shops of yesteryear, and was glad to see that some had survived hard times. The chemist was next to the bank that stood empty having closed several years ago. The haberdashery-shop-that-sells-everything stood where Frank's Newsagents had been. Somerley Stores had been a fruit shop before turning into the minimart it was today.

Time never stood still, she mused. One minute something was here; the next gone, and everyone was meant to continue as before. It wasn't fair, but it happened all the time.

She walked further on, the noise from passing traffic at a minimum now. A group of teenagers hanging around outside the chip shop reminded her of how she'd done the same with Phoebe at their age. Carmichael's Fish 'n' Chips had stood there for four decades now, being passed down the family. Actually, some things had stood the test of time.

Around the corner was the small park where Olivia had fallen from the slide and broken her ankle when she was twelve. There was the church hall where she and Phoebe had been members of the youth club one winter, only because it meant they could shelter from the cold.

Next to it was the church where Hannah had seen several members of the street be hatched, matched, and dispatched. She'd said goodbye to her parents in there too before they were buried in the cemetery.

She walked through the square and on to where Phoebe used to live. Past the row of garages where she and Phoebe had made their first den at the back of them. Through the small playground and the school's playing field. Along the old railway line that hadn't been in operation for over thirty years.

Then she was back in Hope Street, the place she'd always called home. All at once, she had the feeling it was holding her back. Would she want to spend the rest of her life here now, with or without Doug?

It was getting dark but it wasn't this that made it seem alien. For the first time, home didn't seem as welcoming.

Had she moved on?

Should she make plans to leave?

She couldn't stay in Hope Street now. There was no way she was paying rent to Doug.

No, she, Hannah Lockley, would surprise everyone and go out into the world alone.

She snorted under her breath. Of course she would.

*A*fter another restless night, Hannah answered the phone the next morning to Phoebe.

'How are you feeling?'

'I'm doing okay, thanks.' Her voice was more buoyant than she felt.

'He's a prick. How dare he do that to you? I hope you don't mind but I went to see him and gave him a stern telling off.'

'You didn't.' Hannah's eyes widened in horror.

'I might have slapped him too.'

Hannah sighed dramatically. That was all she needed. But she couldn't help nodding to herself.

'You're right,' she said. 'He is a prick.'

'What are you going to do about him?'

'I don't know. My head is telling me to leave well alone, but my heart is telling me to work things out.'

'He did seem really sorry when I spoke to him, though.'

'You've changed your mind quickly.'

'I didn't know he was rich then.'

She was trying to make Hannah smile. And it was working. Phoebe always had that effect on her.

'I'm just saying that maybe you should give him another chance,' Phoebe went on. 'He can buy me a pair of Jimmy Choos to say sorry then.'

Hannah giggled. 'If he's buying shoes for anyone, it will be me.'

CHAPTER 48

*A*fter a couple of days without contact from Hannah, Doug had made his mind up about what to do. It was depressing packing his belongings away. How different things were since he'd first arrived. He would do anything to go back to the day he'd met Hannah and start again. He'd never meant to hurt her.

He recalled the first time he'd seen her, that morning in the community centre. How his heart had skipped a beat when she'd turned her head. How her smile had lit up her beautiful face. Her raucous laughter when she'd mentioned her boiler needed fixing. He had been smitten from that moment.

He looked through the upstairs window one last time, remembering the last glimpse of her. He'd watched her leaving for work that morning, the way she'd almost dragged her feet along the pavement. He'd even caught the tiny glance across to look in his direction.

It had taken all of his willpower not to go thundering down the stairs to her. But even if they did make up, he wasn't right for her. Because he couldn't figure out a way to make her see that she meant everything to him.

At least she had James now, and a family she'd known nothing about. James had sent an email to say everything had gone well with their meeting. Maybe Hannah would move to Scarborough to be close to them. Then he shook his head. She would never leave Hope Street.

Once he was ready to go, he jogged across the cobbles to post the letter he'd written through Hannah's letterbox. He couldn't be that close to her and not be *with* her. It had to be all or nothing. Sadly, he hadn't planned on it being nothing.

He started his truck and drove down Hope Street. Before pulling out onto the high street, he paused for a moment and looked through the window of the hairdressers. He could just about see Hannah's head above the etched glass. She was holding up a small mirror, showing a woman what she'd done to her hair.

Man, he loved her. His heart wouldn't let him give in – maybe they could work this out. For a long time, he'd never been as happy as he had over these past few weeks.

One thing was certain. Doug had left Manchester to mend his heart, but he would be leaving Somerley with it in an even more fragile state.

~

*H*annah left work with Phoebe that evening after working extra hours to do a stock-take. As Phoebe locked up, Hannah glanced down the street.

'The truck isn't there again.' She sighed. 'I blew it by not talking to him, didn't I?'

'I don't know, Han.' Phoebe pulled down the shutter, locking that too. 'But I hate to see you looking so sad. Want tea with us? I can offer you oven chips and maybe a fish finger or two if Elliott doesn't finish them off.'

'I'm good, thanks.'

'You said that last night when I offered.'

'Tomorrow, I promise.'

Hannah said goodbye to Phoebe when she drew level with her house and crossed the road. She missed seeing the truck as much as she missed seeing Doug. She smirked a little unneighbourly, knowing that Mr Wendover would be pleased that he could park easier outside his home now.

Her feet dragged across the cobbles at the thought of another night alone. She could have taken Phoebe up on her offer but she wanted to wallow in her misery, and that wasn't good for anyone to see. She was going to eat all the sweet stuff in the house, sink some wine, and slob out on the settee. That was the only thing that could possibly make her feel a teeny bit better for now.

Inside, she picked up the post. There was an envelope with her name handwritten on it. Was it from Olivia? Had she come back to Somerley?

She sat down. With a bit of intrigue and a lot of apprehension, she opened out the letter to read:

Dear Hannah,

It's been a while since I've handwritten anything so forgive the scrawl. But I couldn't leave without saying a few things, even though you probably don't want to hear from me.

I've longed to walk across the cobbles, bang on your front door, and take you in my arms as soon as you've opened it.

I've longed to tell you just how I feel. But in the end, I thought it best if I just left. By the time you read this, I'll be on my way to Australia. I'll be there for a month. I can't wait to catch up with my children. Without you saying I'd regret staying away, I don't think I ever would have gone.

I know I'm repeating myself, sorry, but I needed a break from everything. I did de-stress – and then I met you. In such a short time, my life changed completely. I'm good at hiding my feelings, you see. It's how I tackle life. Not like you. You tackle everything head on.

Stuff it. I need to tell you how much I love you. I love every-thing about you. I love your ambition, your zest for life. The way you always want to help everyone and always put yourself last. I love the way you do that little snore (yes, you snore too) the way you smile, the way you tilt your head when you're confused. I don't love the way you dragged the duvet off me that precious night we slept together.

I love that we share a delight for gooey garlic bread. I could stare at you all night as you put the jigsaw together. One day the skyline of New York will be complete.

I could go on and on. I love everything about you and yet I messed up.

I wish we'd had the chance to show each other what true love could be. I want to be with you all the time. But I know I misled you and I'm sorry.

I'm not sure what will happen when I get back, except that I probably won't be returning to Somerley. I couldn't stay at number thirty-five knowing that you are across the street. It would hurt too much to see you and not be able to be with you.

Rest assured there will be someone new to look after the houses. They will be well maintained from now on, I promise. We will employ a reputable company that we can keep an eye on. No more dodgy boilers and flaky ceilings. Everyone deserves a decent home.

I'll miss you, Hannah. I think we could have been good together. But it was my fault it went so wrong. I hope one day you can forgive me.

All my love

Doug x

Hannah almost laughed through her tears as she read the letter. If this was a novel or a film, she'd have had time to race to the airport and stop Doug from boarding his flight. First, she'd have got stuck in traffic, then fallen over a suitcase in the departure lounge, and arrived at the last possible minute looking sweaty and bedraggled. *And* she would have her man. But this was real life, even with all its bumps and hurdles along the way.

Doug was being dramatic. She adored him for it but really, he didn't have to go so over the top. Of course it wasn't his fault it all went wrong. What he'd kept from her wasn't enough for their foundling relationship to finish.

The reason things were over between them was because she wouldn't be able to bear it if he began to despise her for trapping him in something below his standard.

She felt sad that Doug had gone, especially without speaking to her first. Had she pushed him to go? It was hard to see, but at least she knew for certain that the relationship was over. Not that it had actually started in some ways.

Would she move to be with Doug? She didn't know. And now she never would. She was glad of two things, though. At least he'd listened to her, taken her advice, and gone to see his children. And he had opened her mind to the possibility of a better future.

Although she was lost again. With no purpose in life. Back to square one.

What the hell was she supposed to do now?

CHAPTER 49

*H*annah didn't want company, nor did she want to stay in alone so she decided to sit under the oak tree in the square. Despite not thinking she'd be able to do that without her mum, it was almost as if Martha was there with her. She felt a breeze pass over her as she sat down on the bench.

A couple walked past hand in hand talking animatedly. Hannah wondered where they were going, found envy ripping through her when she imagined what they might do next. She regretted that she and Doug had never got together now. If she'd known he was going to leave beforehand, she'd at least have had a bit of loving first.

Sex with someone special must be amazing. She couldn't remember ever having that experience. Of course she'd been in lust a few times in her teens, but not really in love. After her parent's accident, there hadn't been as many opportunities to meet anyone.

'Are you here, Mum?' she whispered into the evening air. 'I need someone to talk to. Everything is such a mess.' Then she looked around to see if anyone had heard her. It was one thing to talk aloud at the cemetery but it would look weird if someone caught her out here.

Was it strange that her life at the moment seemed to be a bundle of correspondence? There were the letters from her mum about James. Then there was the birthday card from her sister. And now she had Doug's letter.

She was aching to see him, to tell him how she felt. Because she knew she loved him too.

So engrossed in her thoughts, she hadn't noticed someone walk across the square.

'Hey.' Robin stopped in front of her, making her jump slightly.

'Hey.'

'Mind if I join you?'

She shrugged, knowing it was childish but she was still stinging from his betrayal. They'd had words after she'd found out he knew about Doug and things had been icy between them.

'I was driving past, saw you sitting here,' Robin said. 'Are you okay?'

'Never been better.'

They sat in silence for a moment, uncomfortable for two such good friends. Robin broke into it first.

'I miss him being around,' he said.

'He's not dead,' she snapped, then horrified at her petulance, she sat wide-eyed. 'I'm sorry, that was rude and uncalled for.'

'I agree.'

She glared at him until she saw the corners of his mouth twitching. She gave a weak smile.

'I miss him too,' she admitted. 'But he lied to me. He should have come clean from the start.'

'Don't you think he wanted to?'

'Even so, we're not right for each other, Rob.'

'Why not?'

'We move in different circles.'

'Because he has more money than you?'

'Of course.'

Robin huffed. 'That's shallow.'

'Sadly, it's true.'

'No, it isn't. And especially not in Doug's case. I've never seen a man looking so forlorn after such a short time in Hope Street.'

'What do you mean?'

'You broke his heart. That's why he went to Australia.'

'He said he went to see his children.'

'He was going to take you with him.'

'What?' Hannah's shoulders drooped at the revelation. She couldn't believe he would do that.

Actually, she could.

But it still didn't alter anything. Even if she had gone with him, they would have had to part ways, eventually.

'I can't hold him back.' She shook her head. 'It wouldn't be fair. Have you seen his house, where he lives in Manchester? It's a mansion compared to Hope Street.'

'Wouldn't you like to live in it?'

'Of course, but I don't belong there. I belong here.'

'That's good because he told me the house in Manchester means nothing without you being part of his life.'

Hannah turned to him. 'When did he say that?'

'Before he went to Australia.'

'But he would have left soon anyway, once his contract was over.'

Robin started to laugh.

'What's so funny?' She folded her arms.

'That was a cover story too. Doug was working with me but he was never paid. He volunteered. He could leave – or stay for as long as he wanted.'

'But I thought—'

'So he didn't tell you of his plans?'

'He did mention something.' Hannah looked sheepish. 'But I didn't give him the opportunity to finish.'

'Doug's heart attack made him re-evaluate his life. He intended to come here to chill out and then go back to Manchester refreshed. But while he was down here, he found he enjoyed working with the lads. Once he had enough evidence to figure out what was wrong with Regency Property Management, he needed to find another firm to handle Hope Street. He asked me for advice on setting up something similar to me – training teenagers to do property maintenance, working for him while he runs the company.'

'He was going to leave Manchester and set up here?'

He nodded.

'But what about his business, and his brother?'

'The business practically runs itself now. And Alex said he loved the change in Doug. He wanted to meet you. And Doug wanted you to meet everyone too.'

'Oh, gawd.' Hannah cringed. 'Tell me I haven't messed up.'

'He was willing to put all that on the line for you.'

'But what happens if he did all that and then found out he hated it here, hated me for keeping him here? And he lied to me, remember?'

'For good reason. Surely you can't blame him for that?'

Hannah had, but she didn't know how she felt now.

'Why not flip it around? What happens if he loves it here, and being here with you?' Robin added.

'I doubt that.'

'You don't always have to focus on the dark side, Han.' He put an arm around her and drew her in close.

'That's easy for you to say.' She snuggled into him.

'Why? Because I have money too?'

She couldn't speak, the conversation beyond cringeworthy now. She had ruined what chance she had of being with Doug because she'd become too sensitive. He had never said she wasn't good enough. She'd just thought it.

'It's too late though isn't it?' she said.

'Not all of us need to live with regret.'

She frowned: he seemed to be talking about himself. Was he referring to the break-up of his marriage or Phoebe? She wasn't going to ask, didn't want to interfere. He might tell her in his own time, though, now they were friends again.

It's never too late, she contemplated. How she wanted to believe Robin but found she didn't dare. Hannah had thrown away her best shot at a better life. Nothing to do with monetary value but she'd lost the love of a good man. And there wasn't anything she could do about it now.

Or was there?

CHAPTER 50

*H*annah sat on her bed, pen in hand. Talking to Robin had been an eye-opener and a lot of things he'd said made sense now. There were some things she needed to think more about, like the fact that Doug had been a volunteer. No wonder he hadn't wanted to take money from anyone. That had been kind of him, especially knowing how people might feel if they found out his background.

And what Robin had said about Doug being forlorn made her hopeful. Maybe on his return they could at least stay friends. Doug must have to come back to Hope Street one more time before leaving, surely? She hoped he hadn't taken everything.

Actually, she could tell him he had taken her heart with him. And she wanted that back.

But first there was something she needed to do. She began to write:

Dear Olivia,

I really don't know where to start with this letter, but I thought I'd take a leaf from Mum's book and just do it. She's quite good at writing letters, most of them containing devastating secrets. Maybe it's easier to do it in the written word, rather than tell someone face to face.

So as I don't know where you are and I can't ask to meet for a coffee, I thought I'd write something down, in case you never come back. It's more of a therapy for me, I think. Anyway, here goes.

When you left, for a long time I blamed you for how my life turned out. I was envious that you could go into the world and do what I wanted to do. I was upset that you left everything to me. I was jealous too.

I tried to track you down on Facebook but unless you're not using your real name, then you're not there. I want to know if you're happy, Olivia. I want to know what kind of job you got when you finished university. I want to know if you are married, have children – I could even be an auntie.

Finding out about James was hard for me. To think that I not only have a sister I haven't seen for years but a brother I'd never met too. Yet it was also one of the best things that has ever happened to me. I still have family. Meeting James has made me realise that I would love to know what happened with you. Why you left so suddenly and why you never came back.

I don't blame you at all for being angry. It was a shock to me at first. And I do hope that you know everything and not half the story. I hope you didn't hold it against Mum, because it was Dad who was James's father. We are all from the same pod.

I cherish all the cards you sent. I still have every one of them. It's like a little part of you will always be with me. I wish you were around though. Anyway, I've hit a low point in my life and I'm going to climb out of it. Once I have, I'm going to try to find you. Because we are sisters, blood relatives, and I think we've left it too long.

Of course, if you don't want to know me once I do find you, then that's fine. I won't be angry. I'll just let you get on with your life wherever you are and I'll return home to mine.

Above all, I want to know if you are okay. Because if you are, that's all that really matters, isn't it?

Love Hannah x

After putting her pen down, Hannah folded the paper in two and popped it into an envelope. Then she put it inside the box that her mum had used. She would keep it on top of the wardrobe for if ever she found Olivia.

She curled up on her side, her hands tucked underneath her chin, remembering the times she'd done that while her sister had been in the opposite bed and they'd chatted. Mum and Dad used to shout up the stairs at them to get to sleep nearly every night. Why had she never come back? Leaving was fine, returning wasn't.

Yet writing her own letter had made Hannah realise how hard it must have been for her mum not to tell her about James. She'd wanted to be angry with Olivia for leaving but found she couldn't. All she wanted to do was see her, hold her again. Even if she was never part of the family.

She sat up and reached for the pen again.

Dear Doug

I miss you so much.

In a huff, she ripped the paper from the pad, screwed it up, and threw it to the floor. Then she tried again.

Dear Doug,

Thank you for your letter. It meant such a lot that you would write to me before you left. I hope you're enjoying yourself in Australia. It's strange not to see you across the street.

She groaned, ripped the paper off, screwed it up, and threw it to the floor. There was no way she could put her feelings for Doug into words and then store them away in the box as well.

CHAPTER 51

*E*llen Savage had known Hannah since she was in her teens, when she and Gray had bought Somerley Stores. Back then, the shop had been half the size it was today.

She could still remember that feeling of overwhelm and dread they'd both had when they first moved in and wondered what the hell they'd let themselves in for. The previous owners had fiddled with the profit margin and they'd been left with a huge cash flow problem. But they'd rallied through it and now look at them.

Ellen had been coming to Hope Street Hair since the first day it had opened. At first, she used to go to Phoebe but as Hannah started to progress with her training, and Ellen got used to her hair in a short sharp bob, she'd never wanted anyone else to do it for her. Which is why she knew so much about Hannah. No one at the hairdressers got away with keeping anything to themselves. It was like that programme a few years ago, she mused. *Cutting It,* that was it.

Most people in Somerley knew everything about each other anyway. Take Hannah, for instance. Ellen had watched her turn from a scrawny teenager into a young woman. Beautiful at that. She had also seen her change since the accident that killed her father and injured her mother, and again when Olivia left.

Ellen couldn't begin to understand how she was feeling, her own mum alive and kicking very well for the past seventy-two years. Hannah had been a stalwart for her mum. Ellen could just about remember her sister too. No one ever really mentioned Olivia any more. Occasionally she was brought up in conversation at the pub when everyone was reminiscing but no one asked Hannah about her. It was as if she'd vanished in a puff of smoke. Ellen hoped one day she would find it in her heart to come back. Especially now Hannah seemed so lonely.

Hannah had always been a warm, kind-hearted person, willing to lend a hand on every occasion, there to be relied on without a doubt. There weren't many people in the world like her. Ellen hoped Hannah would be truly happy one day. She really did deserve it.

Which is why she didn't like to see her so upset today. She had popped in on an impromptu visit and bagged the last appointment.

'Hannah, what is wrong with your pretty face?' she questioned. 'You're usually the one who cheers everyone else up. Are you okay?'

'Oh, I'm fine.' Hannah brushed away her comment. 'I think it's because my birthday has come and gone and I'm feeling really old and boring, with nothing to look forward to.'

'Ah, the dreaded four-oh.' Ellen nodded. 'I remember mine well, even though I'll be fifty soon. It's almost as if I changed overnight. And all those hormones and the menopause to look forward to.'

'Are you trying to make me feel better or worse?' Hannah forced out laughter.

'Sorry, sorry.' She patted Hannah on the arm. 'Just remember, you have plenty of years ahead of you. Lots of time to make the most of life.'

'Indeed.' Hannah sighed. 'And all the years I've lost.'

'Pardon?' Ellen frowned, trying to catch what she'd said.

'I said it would be good to take a holiday soon.'

'With a handsome chap who's moved into Hope Street?' Ellen whispered conspiratorially as Phoebe moved past Hannah for a pair of hair straighteners. 'He's such a lovely man, and so right for you. Although, come to think of it, I haven't seen him in a while. He's still here, isn't he?'

'He was but he left to go on a trip to Australia.'

'Ooh, how fabulous,' Ellen replied. 'Had he already got it planned? I'm certain he'll be missing you until his return. The man was besotted with you. It was lovely to see.' She sighed. 'I wish I could have my time again. Me and Gray have gone so stale. I love him to bits, but I wish I could add a bit more sparkle back into our lives. We always seem to be working.'

'You do.'

'Was it planned?'

'Yes, it was pre-booked, I think.'

'Ah, so he hasn't left you at home intentionally. I bet you can't wait for him to return.'

'Something like that.' Hannah smiled.

'Good, because it was about time you dumped that stupid Colin.'

~

*H*annah thought on Ellen's words long after she'd gone. It looked as if she'd got away with a few more white lies. She wasn't going to be the one who told everyone the truth about Doug and who he was.

She was glad of her part-time job at the moment, which gave her time rather than having to work every hour of the night and day. Ellen had said her life was all work and no play. That could make anyone dull.

Was that how Doug had felt too in the end? Exhausted, but unsure what to do about it? It had been two weeks since he'd left Hope Street. Yet, even though she was unhappy, Hannah still felt warm and fuzzy inside whenever she thought of him. She missed the camaraderie, the banter, the double entendres even. And she certainly missed the anticipation of what was to come.

No one knew about her brother yet either. For some reason she didn't want to share the news about James until she had to. People were bound to find out sooner or later when he visited Hope Street but for now she wanted him to be a secret for a little longer.

The salon had just closed. She and Phoebe were going to the Hope and Anchor later that evening.

'You do realise it will be all around Somerley by the time we get to the pub tonight?' Phoebe broke into her thoughts.

'About what?'

'Doug buggering off to Australia.'

'It's old news now.' Hannah shrugged. 'I'm not missing him one bit, really.'

Phoebe's eyes widened and although Hannah was sad, she couldn't help but find it funny.

'You could go to him,' Phoebe remarked as she cleared the till of cash.

'To Australia? It's a little far, don't you think?' Hannah joked.

'I *mean* you could visit him in Manchester once he's home. Give him a week to settle back in and then turn up on his doorstep.' She held a finger up. 'Hey, how about wearing high heels and a long coat with nothing underneath it? Reveal yourself to him slowly.'

'It's the first of July. I'd stick out like a sore thumb.'

'That's not the only thing that might stick out when Doug sees you.'

They both laughed. But then Hannah shook her head. 'I wish it were that easy. Even if we do make up, I can't leave Hope Street.'

'He doesn't want you to. And there are other streets in Somerley, you know. Nicer homes you can share.'

Hannah felt her skin reddening, embarrassed when she remembered what she'd said to Doug about him trying to buy her love. Even so, she'd thought about it a lot. The opportunity to move out, leave the memories behind, and start again sounded tempting.

'I can't move in with him. I don't have anything to offer.'

'He wants you. Nothing else.'

'But this is where I belong.'

'No.' Phoebe shook her head. 'Home is where the heart is. And yours is somewhere in Australia now.'

'You said you couldn't live without me if I moved away.'

'Oh, that was then. I was trying to cheer you up about James.'

'Charming.'

'You know what I mean.'

'I do.' Hannah smiled. 'You're the best friend a woman could ever wish for. I'd be lost without you.'

Phoebe raised her eyebrows. 'I can't mend a boiler or fix a broken heart.' She retrieved her phone from her pocket and began to scroll through it. Then she pulled a reluctant Hannah to her feet and passed her a hairbrush.

'Let's have a dance before we go.' She picked up a comb. 'No one can see us. It's just us besties.'

As the music started they pranced around as if they were sixteen again. To a track by Little Mix, they marched up and down saluting until they were laughing hard.

When the song finished, they hugged each other.

'I'm so sick of crying, Phoebs,' Hannah said. 'I think that's enough for now.'

'It's going to be okay, kiddo,' Phoebe replied. 'I have your back, and I always will. Now let's go and have some fun. Life begins at forty, so someone told me.'

'You'll be there soon.'

'I have exactly ten months and two weeks before I can join that club. But until then, I'm going to live my life. I've decided I need to get out more, join a dating app or something. Find myself a man. I'm thinking of taking Elliott to some football matches. Robin says he'll come too.'

Hannah couldn't think of anything worse. Nor could she ever get her head around the offside rule. But she did know what her best friend was up to.

'Football matches with Robin? I knew there was unfinished business between you.'

'Oh, that was years ago.'

'But you still would, wouldn't you? Stick the sausage in the roll, or whatever it is you say.'

'I sure would. He's matured nicely for his age.' Phoebe grinned. 'Now, come on. We have to be out in less than an hour.'

Hannah smiled back. As long as she had good friends, and the residents of Hope Street, she would be fine. What else did she need?

CHAPTER 52

*J*ust over an hour later, Hannah got a text message letting her know that Phoebe was ready. Tilly and Elliott had gone to spend the weekend with Travis, who had stuck to his word and collected them on time for once.

They met each other on the street and walked along the pavement to the Hope and Anchor, chatting all the way.

'It still feels as if we're sixteen, Han.' Phoebe linked her arm through her friend's. 'Except we're not off to the school disco wondering who we might snog before the night is out.'

'Speak for yourself.'

'Little did we know that the path to true love would be extremely bumpy.' Phoebe sighed. 'I rather wish I was sixteen again.'

'I don't. All the expectation and angst.'

'Do you remember when we set up that double date with Peter Miner?' She laughed. 'He thought he was being clever by wanting to see us both. I still think of him. Do you?'

'Not really. He didn't break my heart.'

'He didn't break mine either.'

'He did.'

'He never.'

At the door to the pub, Hannah felt the urge to give Phoebe a hug. There was no need for words. She was going to be fine. Then she pushed her friend inside before those tears she'd refused to let fall had their way.

Half an hour later, Hannah had her back to the doors as she chatted with Phoebe and Robin. Already she was feeling like a gooseberry as the two of them moved closer and closer. Why was it that everyone else could see what they couldn't? Robin couldn't take his eyes from Phoebe and Phoebe was lapping up his every word. But when she said anything to either of them, they flatly denied there was anything but friendship there.

Her eyes scanned the crowd to see if there was anyone she could slip off and have a chat to. For once she'd love to find out some gossip before her best friend. But then she noticed the two of them staring at her. Phoebe raised her eyebrows; Robin broke out into a grin.

'What?' Hannah looked down at her top. 'I haven't spilled lager down my front, have I?'

'If you have, please let me wipe it off for you.'

Hannah gasped. It sounded like Doug but that couldn't be right.

'Is it?' She looked at Phoebe for confirmation.

Phoebe nodded vehemently.

Hannah turned round quickly. 'Doug! You're back – early.'

Although the music was playing in the background, it seemed as if the whole of the pub had stopped what they were doing and were waiting for his answer.

'I couldn't stay away from… Hope Street,' Doug replied. 'I've fallen in love with the place.'

In his right hand, he had a pilot's hat. He put it on, stepped forward, and picked Hannah up.

'No one puts Hannah in the corner,' he said.

'Even though technically you're standing in the middle of the bar,' Robin added. He groaned when Phoebe elbowed him in the ribs.

Hannah swiped the cap and placed it on her head. Amid cheers, Doug carried her through the crowd towards the door.

'Way to go, Hannah,' Phoebe squealed.

Hannah waved over her shoulder as Doug manoeuvred her through the doorway.

'My back is killing me.' He stumbled as a joke, before putting her down on the pavement.

'Cheeky sod.'

'Let's go and sit at the top of the street. At least we might get a bit of peace and quiet there.' He took her hand, walked a few metres, and then stopped. He pushed her up against the wall and kissed her.

Hannah drowned in the scent of him, the "Dougness" that she'd missed so much. The feelings he gave her of hope, security, and warmth. Something she didn't want to let go of.

'You came back,' she stated the obvious when they stopped for breath.

'I wasn't sure if I'd locked the front door.'

They grinned at each other.

'How was Australia?'

'Amazing. It was wonderful to see everyone. And not awkward at all. I'm going again next year.'

Hannah smiled, pleased for him. They carried on down the street, her hand tucked into his. Alf was sitting outside his house, the front door wide open.

'Evening. Nice hat.' He doffed an imaginary cap.

'Hi, Alf,' Hannah beamed, praying he didn't want to chat.

As if he sensed that, Alf let them pass.

They sat down on a bench, looking back along Hope Street.

'So, you're back.' Hannah couldn't help repeating.

Doug stretched his legs out in front. 'Thing is, when I was in Melbourne, I couldn't stop thinking of you. Even my ex told me to stop moping.'

'Awkward,' Hannah chuckled.

'She turned to me and said "Doug, who is she?" I said "who" and she said, "the woman you're in love with." She knew.'

'Even more awkward.'

'Not really, because I knew too. I had a good chat to her about you.'

'Oh?'

He nodded. 'It was her who said I should cut short my trip and come back home.'

'She wanted rid of you, really.'

'She *said*,' Doug continued, 'I should see if I could make it work this time. She told me not to mess up. So I got on the next flight back. And here I am.'

'Here you are.'

There was so much she wanted to say, to hear, to find out that she didn't know where to begin. Alf's radio was the only thing they could hear. There was some guy talking about football, the odd cheer and excited raised voices now and then.

'She also said any woman would be lucky to have me,' Doug added.

Hannah gave a mock yawn behind her hand.

'It's true, don't you think?' He nudged her playfully.

They sat for a moment, content listening to the sounds of the street. Hannah could feel the tension between them, the anticipation, the nervousness, the electricity. Perhaps waiting for fulfilment had heightened her senses but she wasn't complaining.

They both watched as Alf got off his stool and took it indoors with him. Then Hannah spotted Phoebe's head around the door of the pub. It disappeared a few seconds later.

Hannah wasn't going anywhere yet. She wanted to ask Doug something.

'What's your proudest moment? Apart from your children, obviously.'

Doug pulled his face deep in concentration and then went with the flow.

'Can you remember the TV programme, *Secret Millionaire?*'

'Oh, very funny.' She sat forwards. 'You don't have hidden cameras, do you? Not after you've just kissed me up against a wall.'

'I'm being serious.'

'I remember me and my mum crying after watching most of the episodes. It was so moving.'

Doug nodded. 'It always reminded me and Alex of how far we'd come. So I guess one of my finest moments was when we donated fifty thousand pounds to revamp the local playground. The old one was a riot of mud and run-down equipment. When my nephew fell over and almost took his eye out on a broken piece of a climbing frame, we decided that instead of complaining to the council we would offer to do it up. We worked with the planning department and then we got our team on it for free.'

'Like *DIY SOS*.'

He smiled. 'So what about you?'

'Well, it's hardly as glamorous as yours. I was going to say that my proudest moment is realising that I don't need to change to enjoy life. I was talking to Tilly a while back about spreading her wings when she leaves school and do you know what? She said she wanted to stay in Somerley. I got so hellbent on thinking I missed out on so much that I hadn't realised how good it is to live here.'

'It's often a case that the grass isn't always greener,' Doug said.

She blushed at the intensity of his stare, but she hadn't finished yet.

'You're right. We should be proud of what we achieve, no matter how big or small. We all move forward in life one way or another. It's taken me a while to realise it, but I'm okay as I am. I'm doing fine. I'm happy, I have a roof over my head, great friends and neighbours, and enough to eat and drink. I think that's sufficient for me.'

She looked at Doug and saw tears in his eyes. She thumped him on the arm.

'Don't go all mushy on me now.'

'I don't know anyone quite like you.' He reached for her hand again. 'You're amazing, do you know that?'

'Of course.' It was her turn to smile. 'Robin told me of your plans.' She prayed she wasn't too late to be a part of them.

'I've had a lot of time to think about them in more detail. I really enjoyed working with Robin and the lads here. As you know, most of them are either just out of school or have been excluded, troublemakers. But as we also know, given half a chance they'll go on to do better things. And it's a perfect way to give back to a community. Plus, Robin says I can poach Dylan to work for me.'

'It sounds great.' Hannah's heart was beating erratically as she sat close to him. Was he saying what she thought he was? Because if so, she needed him to be a lot clearer.

'Oh, I have something for you.' He pulled out an envelope from his jacket pocket.

'What is it?' Inside were two plane tickets. Her eyes widened.

'New York.' She squealed.

'Well, you did accuse me of buying love so I thought I might as well treat you.'

'Yeah, sorry about that. Someone had turned my world upside down with his revelation.'

Doug pulled her close, forehead to forehead. 'Peterson Property Maintenance. I still think I could make it work. But that would depend on you, of course.'

'I'm happy to help out, if you like?' Hannah offered, hoping that wasn't all he meant. 'I love what Robin has done.'

'I don't think I'd want to do it without you.'

'Well, that's that then. Welcome back to Hope Street.'

'Yes, home is where the heart is.'

That reassurance was all she needed. When Hannah spotted Phoebe's head for the fifth time, she sat upright.

'We'd best be getting back to the pub, or else Phoebe will be along to us soon.'

Hand in hand, they walked down Hope Street together. At number thirty-five, Doug stopped and kissed her again.

'Now that the formalities are out of the way, I was thinking that you might want to spend the night at my gaff?' Hannah said, rather bravely she thought. 'Obviously you won't have any... milk or anything at yours.'

'As long as I can avoid Harry this time.'

'Are you two coming back or NOT?' Phoebe shouted to them. 'I can't keep popping my head out all night.'

Doug took her hand in his again. 'I was told that this pub was the best place for a grope.'

'Yeah? Who told you that then?'

'Oh, just some crazy bird I met.'

CHAPTER 53

$\mathcal{H}$annah and Doug spent a very frustrating time in the Hope and Anchor before calling it a night. Doug hadn't let go of Hannah's hand except whenever necessary, and she had felt a warm glow as his fingers wrapped arounds hers. His thumb rubbing back and forth across her index finger was almost orgasmic, and she'd tried not to think of what would be happening later. Tonight *had* to be the night.

Finally, they said goodbye. The sounds of music, laughter and chatter were left behind with the close of a door and they stepped onto the pavement. Hannah wondered where Doug would end up living but found she didn't care as long as she could be near him.

See him every day.

Fall more in love with him by the minute.

Inside number thirty-four, as soon as he had closed the door, Doug pulled her into his arms, kissing her with the passion that she had missed. His hands roamed her body, her breath leaving it when his fingers caressed the places they had yet to explore. She pulled out his shirt, loving the gasp that escaped him as she connected with his skin.

His lips moved to her neck, his hands to the bottom of her top. He lifted it in one go and removed it, doing the same with his shirt afterwards.

They stood facing each other shyly.

'So how about it, Han?' Doug nodded his head in the direction of the door to the stairs.

'How about what, Doug?' Hannah's hands moved across his chest, feeling tiny hairs between her fingers.

'You're going to waste what's precious if we don't hurry.' His eyes moved lower for a second before finding hers again.

Hannah laughed. 'Best get a move on, then.'

He reached for her hand and led her to the door. At the bottom of the stairs, Hannah turned to where her mum used to sit when she'd been alive. It was such a shame she never got to meet Doug, but Hannah knew she would have loved him.

Tomorrow morning, she would go to the cemetery. She had to make her peace. She needed to tell Martha that she had seen James again. She also wanted to say that she knew she'd had her reasons, but that she still loved her all the same.

Hannah meant that with all her heart, still missing Martha every day. Soon, she was going to stay with James and she was going to tell him all about her. Doug would go too and she couldn't wait. On the way back, perhaps they'd call in to meet Alex and his family. It would be an emotional but happy trip this time, to both places.

She felt light-headed as they walked upstairs.

'Turn right,' she told him as they hit the top step.

In her room, she closed the curtains and turned to Doug, almost shy again.

He reached for her hand and pulled her into his arms.

'Now, where were we?'

~

*H*annah loved how warm weather could make you feel optimistic. They'd had almost three months of continuous sunshine that summer. She'd been told the summer of '76 had been hot but obviously she hadn't been around then. But Doug had been telling her tales of when he went to school in shorts and T-shirt rather than uniform for what seemed like ages.

She wished summer was like this every year but knew they'd be moaning about it come next year when everything was back to normal. The British people would be lost without something to talk about. Still, at least they had time for a few evenings sitting outside before autumn arrived.

Although it was early morning, the day ahead already seemed full of promise. The sun was shining through a clear blue sky. Phoebe had invited her and Doug to lunch the next day, the kids would be home by then and, knowing her friend, it would probably turn into an outside gathering for a barbecue. Hannah made a mental note to nip to Somerley Stores after work for some ice cream to take across with her.

A huge grin spread across her face when she remembered what had happened the night before. She stretched out; she really could get used to this.

'Hey, you.' Doug came into the room with a towel around his waist and another he was using to dry his hair. 'Sleep well?'

'Like a baby.' Hannah stretched again, almost purring with delight. She laughed out loud.

'What's the matter?' Doug turned to her.

'I don't know.' She laughed some more, and he came to lie down next to her on the bed. 'I guess I'm just happy.'

He pulled her towards him and kissed her on the nose. 'That's good to hear. Do you want to shower while I make something to eat? Or shall I wash your back?'

'Do your back in more like,' she teased. 'If only I didn't have to go to work.'

'Hey, less of the wisecracks, or else I'll take you over my knee and…'

She slapped him on the thigh and then he went all serious on her.

'What is it?' she asked, wondering if he was worrying about something after their conversation the night before. They'd talked long into the night, about possibilities and plans and above all, the future.

'Are you okay with this?'

'With you being a millionaire, or the fact that you'd been lying to me?'

'Well, I hadn't actually lied. I just went easy on the truth.'

'It's the same thing.'

'I know.' He covered his face with his hands for a moment. 'Am I forgiven?'

She nodded. 'But what about you? Are you all mended now?'

'I don't have any problems with my heart unless you're standing close to me. Then it starts to beat a tad erratic, and very loudly. I know that means I love you.'

'That's good because I love you too.' She grinned like a loon.

Doug was gone in a flash, his laughter trailing behind him. Hannah almost kicked back the duvet and jumped up and down childishly on the bed. Had the corner turned for her? Was this her destiny?

And at least she had something to brighten up her days at the moment. She was optimistic after last night.

She reached for her phone on the bedside table and sent a message to Phoebe.

I am SO happy.

She kept the phone in her hand and waited. A few seconds later, it began to ring.

'Tell me more,' Phoebe demanded.

'I can't right now.'

'Oh, you are such a tease.'

'Sorry. I've been a bit busy…'

A squeal and Hannah realised her friend had clicked.

'You haven't done it?'

'We have.'

'Hannah Lockley, at-bloody-last!'

A LETTER FROM MARCIE

First of all, I want to say a huge thank you for choosing to read The Man Across The Street. I hope you enjoyed the first book set in Hope Street, found in the fictional market town of Somerley, and getting to know Hannah, Doug and all the residents Dan as much as I did.

If you did enjoy The Man Across The Street, I would be forever grateful if you'd write a review. I'd love to hear what you think, and it can also help other readers discover one of my books for the first time. Or maybe you can recommend it to your friends and family.

Many thanks to anyone who has emailed me, messaged me, chatted to me on Facebook or Twitter and told me how much they have enjoyed reading my books. I've been genuinely blown away with all kinds of niceness and support from you all. A writer's job is often a lonely one but I feel I truly have friends everywhere.

Why not sign up to receive an email whenever I have a

new book out, and download Coffee with Marcie too - five coffee break length short stories?

Keep in touch,

Marcie x

ALSO BY MARCIE STEELE

The Somerley Series

Stirred with Love (Book 1)
Secrets, Lies and Love (Book 2)
Second Chances at Love (Book 3)

ABOUT THE AUTHOR

My real name is Mel Sherratt and ever since I can remember, I've been a meddler of words. Born and raised in Stoke-on-Trent, Staffordshire, I used the city as a backdrop for my first novel, Taunting the Dead, and it went on to be a Kindle number one bestseller and the overall number eight UK Kindle bestselling book of 2012.

Since then, my writing has come under a few different headings – grit-lit, sexy crime, whydunnit, police procedural, emotional thriller to name a few. I like writing about fear and emotion – the cause and effect of crime – what makes a character do something. Working as a housing officer for eight years also gave me the background to create a fictional estate full of good and bad characters (think *Shameless* meets *Coronation Street*.)

But I'm a romantic at heart and have always wanted to write about characters that are not necessarily involved in the darker side of life. Coffee, cakes and friends are three of my favourite things, hence writing under the name of Marcie Steele too. I can often be found sitting in a coffee shop, sipping a cappuccino and eating a chocolate chip cookie, either catching up with friends or writing on my laptop.

Marcie x

Copyright © Marcie Steele 2019

All rights reserved.

The right of Marcie Steele to be identified as the author of this work has been asserted in accordance with the Copyright, Designs and Patents Act 1988. All rights reserved in all media.

No part of this publication may be reproduced, stored in or transmitted into any retrieval system, in any form, or by any means (electronic, mechanical, photocopying, recording or otherwise) without the prior written permission of the publisher. Any person who does any unauthorised act in relation to this publication may be liable to criminal prosecution and civil claims for damages.

This is a work of fiction. Names, characters, businesses, places, events and incidents are either the products of the author's imagination or used in a fictitious manner. Any resemblance to actual persons, living or dead, or actual events is purely coincidental.

Cover design copyright © Marcie Steele

Image - Shutterstock 550777774

Printed in Great Britain
by Amazon

39091419R00160